Also by RM Johnson

Do You Take This Woman?
The Million Dollar Divorce
Dating Games
Love Frustration
The Harris Family
Father Found
The Harris Men
Stacie & Cole

The Million Dollar Deception

RM Johnson

Simon & Schuster
New York   London   Toronto   Sydney

Simon & Schuster
1230 Avenue of the Americas
New York, NY 10020

First Simon & Schuster hardcover edition September 2008

SIMON & SCHUSTER and colophon are registered trademarks
of Simon & Schuster, Inc.

For information about special discounts for bulk purchases, please contact
Simon & Schuster Special Sales at 1-800-456-6798 or business@simonandschuster.com.

Designed by Davina Mock-Maniscalco

Manufactured in the United States of America

3   5   7   9   10   8   6   4   2

Library of Congress Cataloging-in-Publication Data
Johnson, R. M. (Rodney Marcus).
The million dollar deception : a novel / RM Johnson.
New York : Simon & Schuster, 2008.
p. cm.
Sequel to: The million dollar divorce.
1. African Americans—Fiction. 2. Divorced women—Fiction.
3. Triangles (Interpersonal relations)—Fiction. I. Title

PS3560.O3834M54   2008
813'.54—dc22   15153084

ISBN-13: 978-1-4165-4040-3
ISBN-10:   1-4165-4040-7

To my mother—for your undying love and support
I cherish you

The
Million Dollar
Deception

1

Lewis lay in the darkened bedroom, under the blankets, trying to control his nervous breathing. He stared at Monica. She was beautiful—her light brown skin, big black eyes, and full pink lips. But she lay next to him, silent.

He was waiting on her decision.

Lewis tried to stop telling himself that it still was too soon, but this week he had bought the ring anyway and, moments ago, presented it to her.

She had been asleep only five minutes when Lewis pulled the ring out from under his pillow, slipped it on her finger, then kissed her.

Monica stirred. Lewis kissed her again till she had woken.

"Are you okay?" Monica asked, her voice groggy.

"Will you?" Lewis said, smiling.

"What? Will I what?"

"Will you marry me, baby?"

There was no answer. That had been like a minute ago, and still no answer came.

Lewis rolled over in bed, turned on his bedside lamp.

When he turned back, he saw Monica, her black hair falling into her eyes, staring down at the ring with a pained expression.

"What's the matter?" Lewis said. "It's a simple question. Yes or no."

"You know it's more complicated than that."

"No I don't," Lewis said, throwing the blankets off and climbing out of bed. "Just answer it."

"I haven't even been divorced a year yet. I'm not trying to jump back into a marriage this minute."

"Or you aren't trying to jump back into marriage with me?"

"Lewis," Monica said, turning, glancing at the alarm clock. "I'm not having this conversation. It's almost two in the morning."

"Fine," Lewis said, moving his tall brown frame to the dresser and sliding open a drawer. He pulled out a pair of jeans, put them on.

"What are you doing?" Monica said, sitting up.

"I asked you to be with me. You said you don't want to, so I'm leaving." He pulled a T-shirt over his muscled torso.

Monica hurried out of bed, around to him. "I didn't say that. I said I wasn't ready to get married *yet*."

"It's the same thing."

Lewis had on shoes now. He moved quickly through the room, grabbing a bag, stuffing it full of the first clothes he yanked from the closet.

"Where are you going?" Monica asked after Lewis opened the bedroom door.

"I don't know. We'll find a place."

Monica halted there in her nightgown. "What do you mean, we?"

"I'm not leaving my daughter here with you. You don't want me, you don't want her either," he said, staring right in her eyes, as if expecting this to change Monica's decision.

Lewis turned, walked down the hall toward the three-year-old's room.

Monica followed behind him, whispering, "Why are you doing this?"

Lewis carefully opened his daughter's bedroom door. Inside, a night-light burned, painting the entire room a dim gold color.

He bent over her small bed, slid his arms under her, and scooped Layla up in her blankets.

Monica pulled on his arm.

"Don't. Don't do this now. At least wait till the morning."

"So you can say no then." Lewis turned to her, the child in his arms. "You know what'll make me stay. Just say yes."

Monica loved the man and his daughter. She didn't want them to leave. But she could not let herself be manipulated into agreeing to marry him. She dropped her head. "I can't do that right now."

Lewis held out his palm.

Monica glanced down at it. "What?"

"The ring, please."

2

Five A.M. Tori Billups lay in the center of her king bed, staring through the darkness toward the ceiling, her eyes filled with tears.

She clutched one of her pillows tight to her breast as though it were her husband, who had been missing now for seven days.

He would call, she told herself, the cordless phone just to her left on the nightstand. But until now, he had not.

One morning a week ago, after she had made Glenn breakfast, had handed him his briefcase and kissed him on the lips, he walked out the front door to take a business flight to Detroit. He did not return.

"He'll be back," Tori's girlfriend told her after he had been gone for two days. She held Tori's head in her lap, smoothed her hand over Tori's sandy brown hair, trying to comfort her. "Maybe his plane got rerouted and he lost his cell phone. He'll be back, girl."

But as Tori lay there, wetting Sarah's skirt with her tears, she didn't believe the words her friend said to her.

The next day, Tori went to the police to file a missing persons report.

"The moment we hear anything, we'll call you . . . Mrs. Billups," a square-jawed, graying detective named Reynolds said, having to glance down at the paperwork to remember Tori's name.

She returned home, sat in a kitchen chair for hours, staring at the phone, crying.

"Why are you doing this to me?!" she screamed, grabbing the glass pepper shaker from the table and slinging it across the room, where it shattered against the far kitchen wall.

When she first met Glenn, Tori had only been in the small California city of Torrance for two months. She had fled Chicago with more money than she thought she'd ever see in her life, and she wanted to make a new beginning for herself.

She bought a house and settled in.

The first month had been bearable. She allowed her thoughts to be consumed with what color to paint the walls, the style of living room furniture, and whether the blinds she hung should be vertical or horizontal.

The following month, loneliness had found her. Most often it was at night, while she lay in bed alone, after spending the entire day by herself.

She wanted love again but was afraid.

One night she suffered from a terrible migraine. She walked into the bathroom in her slippers and robe to take some medication. Standing in front of the open medicine cabinet, she eyed the bottle of Tylenol. She pulled out the bottle of prescription sleeping pills instead, thinking, Maybe if I just slept.

Tori shook one into her palm, then two. She paused, looking up into the mirror, thinking about her lonely nights. They were becoming insufferable. If she wanted, she would never have to deal with them again.

Tori tilted the bottle, letting the remainder of the pills fall into her hand.

She grabbed the glass of water from the edge of the sink. It would take just two quick motions—pills, water. Down her throat they'd go, she'd fall off to sleep, and she'd never be lonely again.

That night, Tori stopped herself and was glad she did. For if she hadn't, she wouldn't have known Glenn.

She met him in the cookie aisle at the grocery store.

"Which are better? Chips Ahoy or Oreos?" he said, holding a bag of each.

It was a come-on line, but Tori was lonely, and the man was strangely cute, with squinty eyes and a deep dimple in his right cheek.

She stopped her empty cart, leaned on its handle, allowed herself to play the game.

"Why ask me? You're the one that has to eat 'em," Tori said.

"You're right. Then I guess there's only one way to find out." He opened the bags, pulled a cookie from each, and took bites from both.

Tori could not help but laugh.

"Have one?" he said.

"I think I will."

Two weeks later, Tori lay in her bed, receiving a good-night kiss from Glenn after the first time they made love.

Four months after that, as they walked hand in hand at dusk down a wooded bike trail, Glenn stopped, pulled a ring from his pocket, lowered himself to one knee, and proposed.

"Yes," Tori said, a lump in her throat so big, she thought she would choke.

She had fallen in love with this man, even after Chicago, even after she had endured the hateful things Nate Kenny, the last man she loved, had done to her. Now Tori was in love again and getting married.

Two months after their wedding, Glenn told his wife, "I'm going to start my own consulting firm. Why do for them what I can do for myself?"

She held her husband's hand tight from across the kitchen table, smiled, proud of him. He was brilliant and already a success, could have run the financial consulting firm he worked for by himself.

"I just have to find some investors. This is gonna cost," Glenn said.

"Don't you worry about the cost or the investors," Tori said, taking both his hands in hers. The money Tori had left Chicago with amounted to well over a million dollars. She had wondered how she would invest it. Now she knew.

"What are you talking about?" Glenn said.

"I have a little something in the bank that I've been waiting to do something with."

"Are you sure?" he said.

"Positive," Tori said, smiling.

Glenn threw his arms around his wife.

His hands on her shoulders, he said, "Then we're partners. Okay, honey. You and me!"

Tori now turned her head away from the clock: 5:08 A.M.

It had been almost eight days and no word from her husband. An image of his face, covered with blood, flashed in her mind. His body was twisted, clothes torn. He lay in a Dumpster, shot in the chest.

The phone rang.

Tori gasped, rolled in bed, lunged for the receiver, pressed it to her face. "Glenn!"

"Mrs. Billups?" a firm voice said.

Tori was hesitant, frightened. "Yes."

"This is Detective Reynolds. You need to come to the city morgue. We found a man matching your husband's description."

Then it was all true, Tori thought two hours later as she was being led down a narrow tiled hallway, under bright fluorescent lights. Someone had killed Glenn, robbed him, taken everything from him, and left his body in the trash.

That's where the detective said the unidentified body had been found, and it explained why Tori's credit card had been declined yesterday when she had tried to buy groceries.

She had reached into her purse, tried the other three she had.

"I'm sorry, ma'am," the cashier said to her. "They've all been declined."

"All of my money has been stolen," Tori had told Sarah later that day, pacing frantically in front of her.

"I'm sorry," Sarah had said, stepping to Tori, her arms open. "It's not your fault you trusted him with your money."

"Who are you talking about?"

"Your husband. Isn't that why he hasn't—"

"No! You don't know him. He wouldn't do that!"

The detective stopped Tori and stood with her before a thick glass window, shielded from the inside by a white rubber curtain. If nothing else, Glenn's death proved that Sarah had been wrong about him.

Of course it was no consolation that the man she loved, planned to spend her life with, was lying dead just beyond the glass before her. She tried to stop her sobbing, but could not, and just pressed the tissues the detective had given her hard against her eyes.

"Are you ready, Mrs. Billups?"

Tori prepared herself as best she could. "Yes," she sniffled, not looking up.

Detective Reynolds rapped twice on the glass with his knuckle.

Tori listened as the metal rings of the curtain slid back across the metal rod.

"Take your time," Detective Reynolds instructed.

Tori looked up. The body on the table was sheathed in a white bag. It was unzipped from the top to expose the head, face, and shoulders. Tori saw the gunshot wound that penetrated his left lung and started crying harder at the sight. She dropped her face into her hands and sobbed loudly. The detective placed an arm around her.

"So is that him, Mrs. Billups? Is that your husband?"

"No," Tori said through her tears.

At her front door, Tori wiped a hand across her cheek, smoothed the last tear away, then slid the key into the lock. When she turned it, the tumbler inside did not move. She twisted the knob. It opened. The door was not locked.

She quickly recounted her movements before leaving and knew she had locked the door. That meant only one thing to her. Tori quickly pushed through the door, hurried into the living room, and stopped. She stood silent, feeling a presence in the house.

"Glenn? Is that you?" Tori called, feeling her heart pounding in her chest.

"Up here," she heard him call, his voice muffled by distance and walls.

Tori took the stairs quickly, pulling herself up them two at a time.

Across from the bedroom, Glenn's home office door was

slightly ajar. Tori stopped just in front of it, took a deep breath, and tried to suppress the huge smile on her face, telling herself she needed to be mad.

She pushed the door open, saw the man sitting in there. Tori gasped, staggered, and almost fell.

3

Nate Kenny, now forty-one years old, sat in Glenn's office in a tailored beige suit that contrasted sharply with his maple brown skin. He relished this moment.

Tori had stumbled backward, and if it wasn't for the wall behind her, she would've fallen at the shock of seeing him there.

It had been a year since Nate had seen her. The last time was at the divorce hearing.

Nate had sat confidently beside his high-priced attorney, knowing he was just going through the formalities. His soon-to-be ex-wife, Monica, had no leg to stand on. She had cheated on Nate, he had proof, and per their prenuptial agreement, he had the right to divorce her without having to give her any financial compensation.

Nate looked over at his wife. She did not return his stare, but continued looking down at her hands. He did not want a divorce, but regardless of how many times before the trial he had tried to reason with her, Monica still wanted to go ahead with it.

So be it, Nate thought. I'll keep my sixty million dollars, and she'll have nothing.

That was until Mr. Spiven, his wife's aging, white-haired attorney sat up in his chair and said to the judge, "We have a piece of evidence that I believe will alter the outcome of these proceedings." He held up a videotape. "May I?"

The judge glanced at Nate and his longtime attorney, Jeremy Talbert, then said, "Be my guest."

Mr. Talbert turned to his client. "What is this, Nate?" he whispered into Nate's ear.

"I don't have the slightest idea."

Mr. Spiven slipped the tape into the VCR, punched a couple of buttons. The screen went black. Then an image of Nate, stark naked in a hotel room, screwing his secretary, Tori Thomas, blinked onto the screen. She was on her back, her light brown hair fanned out over the pillow, golden tan legs spread open, hooked over Nate's shoulders. Nate was on his hands and knees, thrusting himself into her. Spiven quickly fumbled with the volume, turning it down as the loud groans and grunts of Nate and Tori filled the conference room.

Monica turned away in disgust.

"Note the date and time displayed on the video, Your Honor. This occurred before my client filed for divorce, meaning that Mr. Kenny also violated the terms of the prenuptial agreement."

"Nate, is that you in that video?" Mr. Talbert said in Nate's ear, his hand pressed down hard on Nate's arm. "Is that the real thing?"

Nate sat there, seething, knowing the tape could have only come from one person—Tori Thomas.

She had been his secretary for five years. He had dated her, knowing it was wrong because she was under his employ, and for that reason, he knew it could not last.

When he met Monica, Nate ended things with Tori. Not long after, Nate married Monica. But three years after that, he had discovered some shocking news that Nate knew he could never deal with, and this was what ultimately motivated his need to start divorce proceedings. Only then did Nate realize that Tori would've been a better candidate for marriage than Monica had been. So he restarted his affair with Tori, telling her, "Once my divorce with Monica is final, I'll marry you and you'll have my children."

Tori was reluctant at first, said she did not want to get hurt again by him, but Nate wore her down. She warmed to the idea of being Mrs. Kenny, then fell in love with it, as she had fallen back in love with Nate.

But Nate changed his mind and decided he wanted to stay with his wife. Then Nate not only dumped Tori, he also fired her.

To Tori, the turn came from nowhere. One moment she was to marry a millionaire and have his children; the next, she was manless and jobless.

Not a week later, scorned and determined, she had phoned Nate.

"Meet me or your wife will know every sordid detail of this affair, down to the brand of wine we drink before sex."

He had no choice. Nate met Tori at the hotel she designated, discovered that his desire for her had never waned. She said she wanted him. He told her it would be the last time. She smiled as she disrobed. "I understand."

What happened that night was what Nate and everyone else in the conference room was looking at right now.

"Turn it off!" Nate's attorney said, rising from his chair.

The tape was as damaging as Tori knew it would be.

Monica's offense, her infidelity, was negated by Nate's, so the proceedings now carried on as though it was a normal divorce, entitling Monica to everything she normally would've had right to—half of all Nate's assets.

Nate knew Tori, and as he sat there, seething, learning of all the money he would lose because of the new "evidence" that had been introduced, he knew Tori wouldn't have just given that to Monica free of charge. Tori had sold that tape to his wife, and that was only possible because she had planned the entire event.

Nate had been tricked, double crossed, and that day he vowed that whatever happened, he would get his revenge on Ms. Tori Thomas.

Now, as Nate sat in Tori's house, in the office that she had made for her husband, he smiled and told himself the day had finally come.

His hands were folded in his lap. He appeared calm, tranquil, the smooth brown skin of his face without worry, his dark, normally fiery eyes smoldering. Nate's right leg was crossed casually over his left knee. The expensive Italian shoe on his right foot bobbed up and down as if he were grooving to a song he liked.

"Hello, Tori," he said, as though they had just spoken yesterday.

"What are you doing here? Where is my husband?" Tori said, as though she knew Nate was involved.

She had never been more right.

"You thought I wouldn't find you?" Nate said. "Do you know the money I lost because of you? How much did you make out of the sweet deal you brokered?"

"Where is my husband?" Tori said again, frenzy in her voice.

"You could've come to me. I would've given you as much. More. But you had to be conniving. You stole from me. You thought I would not find out?"

"Where is my husband? Have you hurt him? Where is Glenn?"

Nate chuckled. "You haven't gotten this yet, have you? He's not your husband, and his name is not Glenn. He's an employee of mine, paid to come to California, find you, marry you, and get my money back."

"No," Tori said, her back against the wall, her face dropping into her hands. "He loves me."

"He doesn't love you."

"He does! You're wrong. Bring him back."

"Tori, he doesn't—" Nate said, standing.

But Tori staggered across the room, threw herself at Nate, grabbing him by his lapels. "I don't care about the money. Keep it. But that man loves me, and I love him. You promised you'd marry me, and you left me, fired me. I just wanted money for a new life. Didn't I deserve at least that?"

Nate did not want to admit it as he looked at Tori, her face wet with tears, but she might have been right.

"I move away, find a man I love, and you come and take that away from me. No!" Tori said, beating at his chest now. "Bring him back! Please!"

Nate grabbed her by the wrists, tried to steady her. When he knew she would not fall, Nate let her go. He pulled a hand-kerchief from his back pocket, extended it to her. "Pull yourself together."

Tori took the cloth, dabbed at her eyes and nose. Her uncontrollable shaking lessened to a tremble.

"I know you don't believe me, but he loves me, Nate. Please bring him back to me."

"I can believe you, because I loved you before. The fact of the matter is he has no feelings for you. You were a job, an assignment, nothing more. I came because I wanted to see your face when you found out that what you stole from me, I've now gotten back," Nate said, beginning to feel sorry for the woman. "If you know what's best, you'll get over him. Understand?"

Tori dabbed at her eyes again with the handkerchief, then gave it back. "Yes, I understand," Tori said, her voice a whisper. "I'll be right back."

Nate watched her step out of the room. He shook his head, turning his back, leaning his hands on the edge of the desk.

Surprisingly, Nate wasn't as satisfied as he thought he would have been after pulling off this caper. Oh well, the money had been retrieved and was resting securely back in his account. That counted for something.

Behind him, he heard Tori step back into the room.

"Nate."

He turned and was mildly surprised to see her pointing a gun at him. His heart did not thump in his chest, nor did his palms coat with sweat, because he knew Tori. He knew she could not kill a man, or even shoot a man for that matter, especially not him. And even if she did have it in her, he was confident in his ability to convince her to lower the gun without incident.

"You're not going to do that, Tori. So put it down."

"You are a hateful man." The gun trembled in her hand.

"Tori, put it down." He took a step forward.

"I thought I loved you then, but I realize I never could have. Not you."

"Just put it down." Another step. "Killing me would solve nothing. You'd still have to live with your pain."

By the look in her eyes, Nate could see something click in Tori's head.

"You're right," she said, quickly turning the gun, pressing the tip of the barrel to her temple.

Nate threw himself over the few short steps between them, lunged at her. He was too late.

Nate heard the deafening blast. Saw the flash of orange fire spurt from the gun's barrel, and saw the fine red mist of blood spray from the side of Tori's head. She went limp, the gun dropped from her hand, and Nate caught her in his arms before her body fell to the floor.

4

Monica sat on her best friend Tabatha's sofa, wearing house shoes and a trench coat over her nightgown. Her eyes were bloodshot, her nose pink from crying.

Tabatha, who was tall and thin and never regarded as much more than cute by men, walked in from the kitchen, her brown hair pulled back into a ponytail, carrying two cups of tea. She set one down in front of her friend, beside the box of Kleenex she had gotten Monica a moment ago.

"There's a little something in there to help you calm down," Tabatha said, sitting right next to her. "Now what happened?"

"He proposed like I told you he was going to."

"And you told him no, right?"

"I told him I'm not ready, which I'm not."

"And . . ."

"And then he started grabbing shit out of the closet and just left."

"Aww, baby," Tabatha said, giving Monica a hug. "Where is the little girl?"

"He took her with him."

"You're better off."

"I don't feel that way."

"You know it was never supposed to go this far anyway."

Monica knew that. She remembered the night her divorce from her husband had been finalized.

She had shed tears, cried painfully at the thought of never being with Nate again.

Tabatha had come over to comfort her. She had held Monica in her arms. "It's okay. Everything's going to be all right," Tabatha said that night.

"I should never have gone through with it," Monica cried. "I should have stayed with him."

"As messed up as it sounds, he didn't want you anymore, Monica."

"But I loved him," Monica said, smearing tears across her cheeks with the back of her hand. "I still do. I always will. I need to call him." She tried to pull away from Tabatha.

Tabatha held tight to Monica's arm. "No. After what he did, you needed to go. You run back to him, he'll know he can treat you any old way he wants. If you two are meant to be together again, he'll come to you."

"And what if he doesn't? I don't want to be alone. After almost four years I don't know how to be alone," Monica cried, lowering her head onto Tabatha's chest.

Tabatha smoothed her hand over Monica's hair. "You'll find someone else."

"There is nobody else."

"Then stay with Lewis, the man your husband hired to seduce you."

Monica lifted her head, leaning away from Tabatha, giving her a questioning stare.

"I know he isn't the man he said he was, but you said you

liked him. I know it's not right. But it'll be something to do, someone to be with until Nate finally comes to his senses."

Monica sniffed, her crying finally stopping. "Do you think that I should?"

"At least you won't be alone."

"It wasn't supposed to last, and it didn't," Tabatha said now, bringing Monica out of her thoughts. "At least now you won't have to be the one who breaks it off."

"I don't know if I still want to break it off."

"The man has nothing. He's twenty-seven years old, he works part-time. He has no money, no common sense, and no education. The only reason he's trying to get one now is because you're paying for it."

"Alright, Tabatha."

"I'm just saying," Tabatha said, springing from the sofa. "The nerve of his ass, trying to demand that you marry him when he ain't got shit!"

Monica dried the last of her tears with a Kleenex. "This is the third time he asked. Maybe I should just . . . I'm raising his child . . . he bought me a ring."

"Was it real?"

"It looked real."

"Then he bought it with that bank card I told you not to give his ass. Monica, there are plenty of other men out there. Men who are worth a damn. Hell, if you don't want any of them, there's always your ex-husband."

"I've gotten over that fantasy. It's been a year, and I haven't heard a thing from him."

"Yeah, well a year ago you were saying how you would never stop loving him."

"Like I said, I've gotten over that."

"And if he were to contact you, would you—"

"Lewis is the man in my life now. I don't know how many times I have to tell you that before you accept it," Monica said with the slightest bit of attitude. "All he's done is treat me with respect and love me unconditionally. I know the plan wasn't to stay with him, but maybe I should change the plan."

"That would be the biggest mistake you could ever make. He is not the man for you."

"Thanks for your opinion, but I think that's my decision to make."

5

In the pitch-black basement, Freddy's eyes were open wide.

He listened intently.

His girlfriend Kia stirred beside him.

"What are you—," she tried to say.

He spun, covered her mouth with one hand, showed her the gun he was holding in the other.

"Somebody's upstairs," he whispered. "Stay here."

Freddy eased out of bed and cautiously climbed the stairs from his basement apartment.

At the door leading to the first floor, he held the gun high beside his head, listening. It could've been his mother moving about, but those weren't her familiar, slow sounds. As he pressed his ear to the door, he knew there were at least two people shuffling about. Then he heard men's voices whispering.

Freddy's heart pounded in his chest. His hands coated over with sweat. He grabbed tightly to the gun, slowly twisted the door's knob with the other hand. He swallowed hard, then swung the door open. He saw shadows, heard a glass break, a chair skid across the kitchen floor. He saw the silhouette of a man dart through the room. Freddy leveled his gun on the figure, pulled the trigger, squeezed off three shots. Fire blew from the gun.

"Motherfucker!" someone yelled.

A shot was sent back at Freddy. He heard something whiz past his head. The wood of the door frame splintered beside him as a bullet tore through it.

A kitchen window shattered as the man dived out of it.

Freddy ran through the dark hallway, the gun pointed in front of him, into the living room, where he heard another man.

He saw a form speed past him, cloaked in shadows.

Freddy fired a single shot. The man cried out, turned, fired back at Freddy.

Freddy dived behind the living room sofa.

He heard the front door swing open, the intruder scurrying through it.

Freddy raised his head, fired two more rounds through the door. The room went silent, and Freddy stood slowly, his face covered with sweat. He hurried to the door, looked out. A dark-colored older Chevrolet roared to life, then raced away.

Freddy heard a noise behind him. He whirled around, leveled the gun again.

"Freddy, no!"

He pulled the trigger. The gun clicked on an empty chamber. Freddy gasped. He'd almost shot the girl standing there in the doorway.

"Are you okay?" his girlfriend said, shaking, crying. She stumbled toward him.

"Go back downstairs!" Freddy ordered her.

"But—," Kia said.

"Go back downstairs. I got to check on Moms," he said, running to the stairs, taking them two at a time, the empty gun still in his fist.

If something had happened to his mother, he thought, he would not be able to forgive himself. Never. Freddy ran down the hall to the last room, stopped at the door. Pressing the side of his face to the door, he said softly, "Moms?"

"Fred?"

Freddy forced open the door, prepared to give his life. The door slammed against the back wall. He rushed in, the gun raised, but did not see his mother in her bed.

"Moms!" Freddy yelled.

"Down here."

Freddy followed the faint voice, saw his mother cowering on the floor beside her bed.

He set the gun on her dresser, rushed around the bed, helped his heavy, sixty-five-year-old mother from the floor. He hugged her tight, thankful she had not been hurt. Fearful tears ran down her sagging, copper-colored cheeks. "Was it another break-in?"

"Yeah," Freddy said, desperately trying to control the rage he felt filling his body. "It was another break-in."

6

Nate was meeting with Aaron Hunter, a.k.a. Glenn Billups, in the California office of one of his associates. Aaron was six feet tall, broad shouldered, and neatly groomed. He was ex-military and carried that demeanor about even after working for Nate for the last two years.

As Nate sat up in the executive chair behind the desk, Aaron Hunter stood straight, arms stiffly at his sides.

"Let me ask you again, Aaron," Nate said. "Did you have feelings for Ms. Thomas?"

Aaron looked straight ahead at the space a foot above Nate's head.

"You gave me the assignment, Mr. Kenny, and I did it. I believe that was all that was required of me."

"That's correct, but—"

"You said I was successful. I was, wasn't I?"

"Yes, but—"

"Then with all due respect, sir, why must I be questioned about my emotional position regarding—"

Nate quickly stood from his chair. "Because I want to know." His voice was not loud, but it was firm. There was silence in the room. Nate took his seat again.

"She said you loved her. Is she telling the truth?"

Aaron Hunter continued staring ahead, making no comment.

"Well, she loved you. As you probably would have assumed, she was pretty distraught at what happened. She pulled a gun on me, threatened to kill me."

"I see she was not successful," Aaron said, glancing at Nate, then looking away.

"No, she wasn't. But then she turned the gun on herself."

Aaron turned to Nate again, fear on his face. "Is she all right?"

"Tell me what I want to know. There will be no repercussions. Just—"

Aaron quickly stepped to Nate's desk, threw his hands on it, leaned over. "The woman is still my wife."

"And you are still my employee. Now tell me. Tell me, and I'll take you to her."

Aaron looked up, resentment on his face. "Yes, I love her, Mr. Kenny. And I didn't want to leave her, but I kept my agreement with you."

The man who stood before Nate and Aaron wore pale blue hospital scrubs and a white lab coat. His name was Dr. Frist.

"This is Mrs. Billups's husband, Aaron," Nate said, as the three men stood just outside the door of Tori's hospital room.

"Well," the balding doctor said, pushing his glasses up his nose. "She missed. The bullet did tear into her skull, chipping some of the occipital region away, but the wound was largely superficial."

"Will she be okay?" Aaron asked.

"She'll be fine," Dr. Frist said, smiling a little. "She's recovering from surgery, but she should be awake by now. You can talk to her if you like, but only for a moment."

"Thank you," Aaron said.

"Thanks again," Nate said, shaking the doctor's hand, then following behind Aaron toward Tori's hospital room door.

Aaron stood at the door's entrance, staring in.

Tori lay under white sheets, bandages wrapped countless times around her head. Her eyes were closed, tubes seeming to run from every part of her body to bedside machines that beeped, blinked, and charted her vital signs.

"What can I say that will make her forgive me?" Aaron said, his eyes still on his wife.

"She'll forgive you. Just tell her the truth."

"And what if she doesn't accept that?"

"Then you'll have work to do," Nate said. "I never meant for it to go this way."

"But it did," Aaron said. "I should talk to my wife alone now."

"Wait." Nate pulled a brown envelope padded with cash from his breast pocket and handed it to Aaron. "You take some time and let me know when you're ready to come back to work, okay?"

7

Lewis stood over his daughter while she slept in the big hotel room bed.

He felt awful for taking Layla away from what had been the girl's home for the past eight months. It had been a good home. But Lewis had always felt that it was temporary. He had tried to make it permanent.

Layla coughed a little in her sleep. Lewis pulled the blankets up over her shoulders.

Layla had always been sickly, always had respiratory problems. As an infant, she would catch a cold or come down with a fever if the wind changed. It had been that way since her birth.

It was because of Selena, Layla's dead mother, a drug addict.

She had quit her old habit when she found out that Lewis had gotten her pregnant, but Lewis still feared the lasting effects of the poison had taken their toll on his child.

When Layla was an infant, Lewis and Selena often had to sacrifice paying a utility bill or buying food to afford the pink stuff prescribed to Layla by the overworked doctor at the free clinic.

The medicine would work fairly quickly, but when they couldn't afford the drug, they would have to nurse Layla back to health themselves, allowing her weak immune system to slowly fight off the illness. It was torture to watch his child suffer like that.

Lewis always tried but never managed entirely to avoid laying blame on Selena. But it was his fault as well. If Lewis had had a decent job, he would have been able to take his child away from there. He could have put Selena in a real drug addiction program, and maybe she would never have done the heroin that killed her.

He remembered the last time he went to visit Selena, pushed open the unlocked door of her project apartment to find the woman dead on her sofa. A needle was hanging from the vein in her arm. Worst of all, their child, Layla, was on her mother's chest, bawling her eyes out, screaming. The child had witnessed it all, seen her own mother die.

Lewis told himself he would never subject his daughter to a life like that again, no matter what he had to do.

So now here he was, Lewis thought as he lowered himself to the bed, sitting beside his daughter, wondering if he had made the biggest mistake of his life.

The truck that brought Lewis and his daughter to the hotel was the Land Rover Monica had bought him.

The ring he had bought Monica was paid for with the card she had given him. It had his name on it and everything. And it was to her bank account, with over a million dollars in it. The woman had trusted him that much. And he had up and left her. What the fuck was wrong with him?

Great going, Lewis, he thought to himself, standing and peering out of the hotel curtain.

But he prayed it would work out.

He had been put out of Selena's place when she was tired of him, when he wasn't making much money, and Selena didn't have a damn pot to piss in.

For the eight months that Lewis had been living with Monica, he had always felt he was just a moment away from being asked to leave.

He wasn't supposed to be with a woman like her.

She had everything, and he had nothing. But he loved her, and even if she did not love him the same, he told himself, he would make it work. Not just for his sake, but for the sake of his daughter. He wanted her to have a good home, have a mother who cared about her and loved her.

Monica was that woman. But Lewis always felt there would come a day when she realized he wasn't enough.

That was the reason for the proposal tonight—for the last two proposals. Yes, she had taken care of the both of them, gave Lewis money whenever he needed it, loved him, gave him exhausting, passionate sex to prove it. But there was never a guarantee it would last.

He felt she didn't think much of him, and he knew that was the reason why she pushed and pushed for him to go back to school. He figured she wouldn't want to admit to her friends and colleagues that not only was she dating a man who didn't have much of a job, but one that had no education as well.

This was her way of shaping him, trying to improve him.

Lewis told himself he would play along as long as she guaranteed they would be together, but now she had made her decision, and he had foolishly run out without a plan.

He pulled his wallet from his pocket, parted the billfold to count the forty-six dollars he had there in small bills.

He would have to do something. He just didn't know what.

8

Hours later, Freddy was pacing the living room, the reloaded gun still in his fist.

He looked out the window again, turned to his girlfriend.

"This shit," he said, waving the gun. "It's been almost four hours since we called the police, and they still ain't come."

"Would you please put that gun down?" Kia said, sitting on the sofa. Her short, straight black hair was undone, and the nightgown she still wore flowed over her thin, model-like body, protruding only slightly around her belly.

Freddy walked over, opened a cabinet on the living room chest, set the gun inside, and closed the door again.

"I'm so sick of this," Freddy said angrily.

"Just try to calm down," Kia said, rubbing her belly, which had grown rounder with her two-month pregnancy.

"I can't calm down. Those fools had guns. What if they shot Moms or, God forbid, you? What if they killed our child?"

"Don't say that."

Freddy walked over to Kia, knelt in front of her, took her hand. "You're not staying here anymore. You grabbing your things and you got to go."

"Where? Where am I going to live? You know my father won't take me back."

"You can get your place in the dorms back. You just got a year left in law school. You can deal with it for that long."

"I'm not going back there carrying this child."

"I'm taking a chance on you getting hurt, living in this house. I won't let that happen."

"And what about you and your mother?" Kia said. "If you two can live here, then I'm staying."

Freddy stood up, looked toward the door. There was still no sign of the police. "Then we all should leave. Find somewhere else to live."

Just then, Freddy's mother stepped into the living room. She wore a new, cheaply made polyester skirt suit. It fit snug around her shoulders and arms and hips. Her graying hair had been set in curlers, and she wore her better pair of "seeing glasses," the ones that weren't all scratched up. "I have to leave. I can't be late for this interview."

"You ain't going to the interview," Freddy said, standing, walking over to his mother. "Those fools could still be out there."

"And that's supposed to do what, Fred? I need to get this job, and I'm not going to let some thugs stop me from getting it." She stepped around Freddy, walked over to Kia, placing a hand on her belly. "Good-bye, child. And wish me luck, Kia."

"Good luck, Mrs. Ford."

"Moms," Freddy said.

His mother walked past him to the closet, taking out her jacket. "I'll be home no later than six."

"Moms, I said you shouldn't go," Freddy advised again.

"Freddy, just let her do what she has to do," Kia urged him, standing beside Freddy now, softly taking his hand.

Freddy's mother opened the front door, still ignoring her son. "I'll cook dinner when I get home."

"Moms!" Freddy yelled angrily. "I said you ain't going no-where!"

His mother froze at the door. Freddy's voice seemed to echo through the old house, then disappeared, leaving a deafening silence.

The old woman turned from the door, leveling narrowed eyes onto her son. "What did you say to me?"

Freddy swallowed hard. "It's dangerous out there, and I got a job. You don't need to be—"

"You got a job, that's right, Freddy," his mother said, closing the door and taking two steps toward him. "And you don't make enough money to support us. We are a partial payment away from getting every utility in this house cut off, and can barely afford to put food on the table every day. I want this job, but more importantly, I need this job."

"But Moms—"

"No, baby," his mother said, standing just in front of him now. "I live here, too, so I should contribute. I know you still thinking because of what happened that you should fill your father's shoes, take on all of his responsibilities. But that comes in time. Till then we gonna make the best of this old house in this awful neighborhood, 'cause it's all we got. Okay?"

Freddy lowered his head. His mother reached out, placed her fingers under his chin, lifted his face. "Okay, son?"

"Yeah," Freddy said.

"Good. But let me tell you one more thing. You ever raise your voice like that to me again . . ."

"I know, Moms. I'm sorry."

Freddy's mother smiled, leaned in, kissed his cheek, then walked back to the front door.

"I hope you get the job, Moms. But you won't have to keep it for long, 'cause I'm gonna get us out of here," Freddy said.

His mother looked back at her son and his pregnant girl-friend and smiled. "I know, Fred. I know."

9

In the parking lot at Chicago O'Hare Airport, Nate placed his garment bag into the trunk of his black 2007 Mercedes S600. After paying the parking attendant and driving out of the lot, he assessed the results of his operation with Tori Thomas.

He had not expected the bloodshed, but he had gotten back what he had set out to get, and that was all that mattered to him.

After his ride home, Nate pulled into the driveway of the six-bedroom brick mansion where he had now been living for a year. After his divorce from Monica, he couldn't take walking through the rooms of the penthouse they had shared for the four years of their marriage. Too many memories, too many reminders of what could have been.

It had to go.

Every now and then, Nate missed that place, as he still missed his wife on occasion.

He told himself to squelch those feelings, replace them with hateful ones. Nate had loved his wife, knew he wanted to be with her from the first day he met her in the clothing store where she worked. He asked her out that day. Six months later, they married.

It was all based on the assumption that she would give him children. A family was what Nate had wanted all his life.

But she made him wait three years, telling him she wanted to build a firmer foundation. Against his will, he waited for her okay for them to conceive, always trying to convince her to get pregnant sooner.

After the three years, she had allowed them to start trying. But it was too late. At the age of thirty-one years old, his wife had gone through early menopause. She would no longer be able to conceive children.

Nate thought that maybe it was something that he could have accepted, just as if she had come down with cancer or some other disease that would have stopped her from giving him a family.

But when he learned from her doctor that this ran in her family, that her mother and her sister had gone through the same thing, and Monica knew it could happen to her, Nate knew he could not just let that pass.

The doctor confirmed for Nate that if his wife just would have allowed them to get pregnant when they first got married, Nate would have had a child or two by the time she had gone through menopause.

After hearing those words, and knowing how much he wanted a family, Nate decided he had a decision to make. Stay with his wife and never have children, or divorce her, get with someone else, start over, and have the family he always wanted.

He decided to divorce his wife. But there was the slight issue of his sixty million dollars.

Divorcing her would entitle Monica to half. Nate told himself he would not pay that woman thirty million dollars for making him wait three years not to have a family.

He spoke with his attorney. Then Nate was reminded of the prenuptial agreement stating that if Monica was ever to commit adultery, she would be entitled to nothing. This was the out Nate needed. The only problem would be getting his wife to cheat on him.

Nate devised a plan and found a young, good-looking man named Lewis Waters, down on his luck, without a job, without money. He set this man up in one of the town houses Nate owned. He gave the man a five-thousand-dollar clothing allowance and five thousand dollars a week as compensation. Nate gave him a new identity as a young, successful real-estate developer. Gave the man a bank account, business cards, and most important, all the information he would need to get Nate's wife in bed.

The plan worked as Nate hoped it would, but afterwards Nate realized that he still loved his wife, that he had made a mistake in ever devising such a plan.

But it was too late. Monica had found out all about the scheme. And even after Nate begged her not to divorce him, she did anyway, and with Tori's help, she took him for fifteen million dollars of his money. Nate figured he should've felt lucky, considering she only took fifteen, when she was entitled to twice that.

Nate jumped out of his car, retrieved his bag from the trunk, and walked into his house. He stepped across shining hardwood floors, under the towering ceiling, and through rooms with antique furniture set against dark wood walls.

"Mrs. Weatherly," Nate called out to the woman he had hired a year ago to take care of the house and whatever else he required. Nate laid his garment bag over one of the ten chairs that sat around the formal dining-room table, then stepped into the kitchen, loosening his tie.

On the refrigerator door, there was a note.

Dear Mr. Kenny, Gone for groceries. Will be back soon.
Mrs. Weatherly.

A cold-cut sandwich, sliced carrots, and baked chips sat on a plate under Saran wrap on the kitchen counter. Nate took off his suit jacket and rested it on one of the kitchen chair backs. He grabbed the plate, unwrapped it, sat down, and took a bite of one of the halves.

He stared, glassy eyed, at the far kitchen wall as he chewed. After Tori had gone on the run, it had taken a year to find her, get close to her, win her trust, and finally get his money back. Since his ex-wife lived here in Chicago (and probably felt that he had forgotten all about her), Nate figured it wouldn't take half as long to deceive her in some similar fashion and take the money she had stolen from him back. All he had to do was decide how.

10

Monica sat at the dining room table, still in her pajamas, a blanket around her. It was the room she, Lewis, and Layla had spent the least amount of time in, the only room she felt she could tolerate at that moment.

Despite what Tabatha had told her, Monica had rung Lewis's cell phone half a dozen times. He did not answer, nor did he respond to her messages.

She thought back to the day her divorce papers had come in the mail. That was the day Tabatha had mentioned getting back together with Lewis. Monica had never thought of that possibility until then.

The next day while driving, she had thought about him. He wasn't the wealthy, educated real-estate developer that Nate had disguised him as, but Monica had enjoyed the time they had spent together. And the times they made love were mind-blowing.

Most important, Monica thought as she turned her car in the direction of his last known address, he was willing to accept her as she was, had even made her an offer.

On that day when Monica came to his house to end things with him, Lewis said, "You can't have children, and my daughter needs a mother," the little girl in his arms. "We could be a family."

Monica was insulted, asking herself how he could use his daughter just to get with her, insulted that he actually thought she would consider his offer just because she couldn't have children of her own. But it did stop her for a moment, did get her thinking of the possibilities. It was an opportunity for her to be the mother she had always wanted to be.

She had turned him down that day but had gone back to him not two weeks later, and as she had hoped, he was there, waiting for her.

Since then, Lewis had loved Monica the way she needed to be loved.

No, he wasn't the kind of man she was used to dating. There were conversations that Monica just could not have with him, because he did not care much about politics, art, or business. There were times, while lying beside Lewis in bed, or while out at the park, playing with Layla, when she became depressed, knowing one day their differences might cause them to separate. She would look at Lewis and tell herself this was not the man she should spend the rest of her life with.

She scolded herself for those thoughts. Was she being too hard on him? No, he was not perfect. He had no money, education, or drive to do much more than he was doing. But he was home when she came in at night. He kept her company, made her laugh, held her when she needed to be held, and made love to her whenever she even thought she needed it.

And now, at the dining room table, as she pushed the blanket off her shoulders, stood, and headed upstairs to shower, she knew she did not want to let that man get away.

11

Lewis pushed the last of his books into his bag while the other students, kids in their late teens, filed out of the classroom.

He hadn't wanted to come today, hadn't wanted to just drop Layla off at day care, considering what was going on, but he had already missed more classes than he should have. Another one, and the teacher could fail him.

It had been another boring hour and a half of nonsense about essay writing that he didn't understand, but it was over for the day, and that was all that Lewis cared about.

He shouldered his book bag and headed for the door, the last student to leave.

"Good-bye, Professor Jennings," Lewis said to the bearded, middle-aged teacher sitting behind the desk.

"Oh, Lewis. Can I have a moment with you, please," Professor Jennings said.

Lewis stopped, looked back. "Uh, yeah."

"You know that you aren't doing very well in this class, don't you."

"I got a D on the midterm progress report. You said that was passing."

"It is for the midterm report, but not for the class. If you don't get at least a C you'll have to take it all over again. You don't want that, do you?"

Lewis hated Professor Jennings at that moment. Here he was, twenty-seven years old, being talked to like a child. "No," Lewis answered. "I don't want that."

"Have you been going to the learning assistance center?"

"No."

"Why not?"

"Because I have a job, and I can learn this on my own."

"Your work says different," Professor Jennings said. "Maybe you should look into letting go of the job, or maybe scaling back on some of the hours."

Lewis couldn't help but chuckle.

"Was that suggestion funny, Lewis?"

"I'm a grown man just like you are, need money just like you do, Professor Jennings. I won't be cutting back on my work hours," Lewis said, turning and walking toward the door. "But I'll bring that grade up for you. I promise."

Outside the door, Lewis stopped and leaned against the wall. Kids almost ten years younger than he was walked past wearing iPod earphones, swatting one another, running around as if they were on a playground. He didn't belong here. The only reason he was taking these stupid courses was because Monica had forced him to.

He didn't want to do it. But Lewis knew it was one of the unspoken requirements for being with her. He figured she was used to being with men with all sorts of degrees. If he wanted to keep her, the least he could do was get his diploma.

But that was then, Lewis thought, walking toward the school's exit. He had another class, General Science, but he knew he was failing that too, and he didn't feel like going anyway. Besides, since Monica no longer wanted him, there was no reason to continue to go.

He stopped at the trash can at the corner, just before the door, and zipped down his book bag. Lewis pulled the two textbooks out, dropped them in the can, and walked out.

12

Freddy knelt on his hands and knees, trying to let the anger flow out of him as he scrubbed the grout between the bathroom tiles. The police had finally come four hours after he had called them. The two black officers, one male, the other a short female, stood over the bloodstain in the center of the worn living room carpet.

"At least you got him," the woman, Officer Jackson, said.

Officer David moved over to the front door, examined the broken glass. "You did a lot of shooting. Your gun registered?"

"Yeah," Freddy said.

"You sure?"

"We're not the criminals here. We're the victims. You going to find who broke in here, or you going to worry about me?"

Officer Jackson stepped in front of her partner. "We're sorry, Mr. Ford. We'll talk to some of your neighbors and see what we can do."

Freddy knew that was a joke.

After the police left, he went to Home Depot to buy supplies to fix the windows and check on prices for security bars and a security door. If his family was to remain safe, it would only be because of him. Afterward, he had gone to work, where he was now. Doing work in the small bathroom, Freddy wore jeans, a light blue collared work shirt with his name stenciled on the breast pocket, and work boots.

Heavy-duty rubber gloves covered his hands as he scrubbed the tiles with a bucket of soapy water.

This was a house Freddy's uncle Henry had bought cheap in an auction and had agreed to let Freddy rehab in exchange for a portion of the selling price.

This was Freddy's plan for getting his moms and his girl out of that hellhole they lived in. If the neighborhood was better, Freddy would have asked his uncle if they could have moved into this house. Freddy and his best friend, Lewis, had done just about all the work that was needed, but the area was just as bad as, if not worse than where Freddy lived already. Freddy was grateful to his uncle for accepting the investment idea Freddy had brought to him.

He didn't have to agree, nor, four years ago, did he have to give Freddy this job.

His uncle Henry did not like him. He thought Freddy wasn't right in the head. Maybe he wasn't, Freddy thought, as he scrubbed harder at the tiles, but that was Freddy's father's fault—Uncle Henry's brother. Even at eight years old, how long was Freddy expected to suffer, hearing his mother getting beaten behind that locked bedroom door? How many mornings was he supposed to see her with blackened eyes and busted lips, saying she bumped into a wall or tripped over a chair?

Even then, Freddy knew that was bullshit.

He remembered asking her one night when she tucked him in, "Why you let Daddy beat you like that?"

His mother started crying all of a sudden. Just broke down and couldn't stop. She threw herself onto Freddy, grabbed him tight. Freddy held her back, but she would not stop. No matter how much he begged her, how much he cried too, she would not stop.

She slept with him there in his twin bed that night, as she often did, while Freddy's father worked the third shift over at the pipe factory. All that night, Freddy lay awake in bed. The next day, he left school at lunchtime and let himself into the house with his key.

"What we doing here?" Lewis said, stepping in behind Freddy. "Your father gonna kill us."

"Shhh. He asleep. Just be quiet."

Freddy tiptoed into his bedroom, grabbed the baseball bat from behind the door, then stood in the kitchen, just outside his father's door.

"Just stay out here, okay?" Freddy whispered to Lewis.

"What you gonna do?"

"Just stay out here," Freddy said, carefully opening the door and sneaking into his father's bedroom.

The man lay sleeping on his back, still in his work pants and boots, his mouth open, snoring loudly. Freddy stood beside the bed, and with both hands, raised the bat high over his head.

He swung the bat down with all the might he had within his little body. When it connected, Freddy heard a loud crack. Later, he admitted to knowing that it was the first blow that killed him.

But Freddy continued swinging till blood covered his face, his shirt. He swung till he was out of breath, could barely stand, could not raise the bat again.

When he walked out of the bedroom, covered with his father's blood, Lewis screamed.

Freddy stood up from the bathroom floor now and grabbed the bucket. His father's death was the reason his mother could no longer sleep in that first floor bedroom and had to move upstairs. It was the reason Freddy and his mother had lived in damn near poverty ever since.

It was the reason she felt the need to go to some interview this morning, after being on disability for the past two years. Freddy's mother would never blame him for their hard times, but sometimes, in the things she'd say or the way she'd look at him, Freddy could sense the resentment she held about his father's death.

Freddy had been sent to a special school for the remainder of his grammar school years and was visited by social workers until he was fourteen years old. High school was rough for him, but he made it through. Jobs he could never seem to hang on to, but somehow, his mother had convinced her brother-in-law, Uncle Henry, into giving Freddy the job he had now. Since Freddy had been hired, he had come into work fifteen minutes to a half hour early every day. He paid close attention to every word his uncle said to him, trying to learn this trade as best he could. No one knew it, but Freddy even had been taking classes to qualify for his real-estate license. He had taken the test and was waiting for the results to come in the mail.

He vowed this would be the job that would turn him into a responsible man. He had no choice. Kia was pregnant, and his mother was in need. Despite how badly Freddy's father had beaten his mother, the man had been her husband, and it was wrong for Freddy to have taken him away from her. But Freddy would make everything better.

13

Nate had been preoccupied with all the time and effort it took to track Tori down, but now, sitting in the leather executive chair in his home office, he would be able to handle the task at hand.

"Thank you, Abbey," Nate said before hanging up on the private investigator he had hired to watch Monica over the last two weeks. She was the same dogged investigator who'd done the work on Tori Thomas.

The information that Abbey had given to Nate so far proved there was nothing going on in his ex-wife's life that Nate hadn't already known about.

Monica was living with that clown, Lewis Waters. She had used part of the money she had stolen from Nate to buy Aero, the three-store chain where she used to work. She had also bought a million-dollar home in the South Loop and was throwing away money caring for the baby of the fool she was allowing to live there with her.

The bastard child's name was Layla, Abbey told him. Nate

sifted through the file he had on Monica and pulled out a snapshot. Despite how much he did not want to admit it, the child was cute. She had long black hair and big brown eyes.

Nate assumed Monica was treating the child as though she were her own, considering she could not give birth herself.

It was probably the reason she had not yet grown tired of that worthless man.

Nate thought about the child he and his wife could have had together. Not biologically, but the child Monica wanted so desperately to adopt.

She had found him when they were having trouble, when their marriage seemed beyond salvation.

Monica had presented Nate with the boy's picture and the information she had gotten about him from the adoption agency.

"His name is Nathaniel, and he looks just like you, Nate. This could be our chance to have the family that you always wanted," Monica had said.

Nate was trying not to hear her. He wanted a child who was his own. He would not sacrifice that just because it was too late for Monica to have a child herself.

But after the divorce, after Nate realized he had made the biggest mistake of his life, he'd taken time off from work and sat at home for weeks by himself, brooding.

Many times, he would look to the front door, hoping his ex-wife would walk through it. Whenever the phone rang, he prayed it would be Monica on the other end. It never was.

After a while, he realized that in pursuit of what he believed was most important to him—a child—he had lost what was truly the best thing in his life—his wife. One day as Nate mourned the fact that he could not get her back, he found himself frantically rummaging through the drawers and cabinets of his house. He was searching for the packet of literature on the boy Monica had wanted to adopt. Finding it, Nate tore through the papers, searching out the number, punching it into his phone.

Nate was told by a woman at the agency that he could come in that day. He raced over, hoping the boy had not yet been adopted.

Nate didn't know why he was suddenly obsessed with the idea of having that child, this little Nathaniel, and no one else. Maybe because he felt it was the one thing that could bring him closer to his ex-wife, possibly even bring her back to him. Or maybe Nate was already thinking of how he could get revenge on Monica.

When Nate walked into the agency, a smiling woman wearing a flowered print dress greeted him.

"I don't know if you're the same lady, but some time ago my wife came here wanting to adopt a little boy named Nathaniel," Nate said, hopeful. He pulled the photo out of his briefcase. "This is him."

"Yes," Mrs. Wolcott said. "Mrs. Kenny, right? I do remember her. I wondered what happened."

"We were having some problems," Nate sadly admitted. "We ended up getting divorced. But if the boy is still available, I would very much like to inquire about adopting him myself."

"Well, let's punch Nathaniel's information into the old computer and see what we come up with," Mrs. Wolcott said, winking.

Nate's office door swung open, interrupting his thoughts. Little feet ran across the floor. Nate pushed back from his desk, opened his arms, and said, "Come over here, little fellow." Nate picked up his son, took him in a hug, and squeezed him tight.

"I missed you, Daddy," the three-year-old said.

"Well, I missed you too, Nathaniel."

"He couldn't wait to get back here so he could see his daddy. Daddy, daddy, daddy," Mrs. Weatherly said, walking into the room behind the child. "Good to have you back, Mr. Kenny. Was your trip to California productive?"

"Yes, very productive. Thank you, Mrs. Weatherly."

Mrs. Weatherly, who was thin, fair skinned, and always wore her salt and pepper hair in a bun, walked over to Nate's desk and grabbed his son's hand. "Come on, little one. Your father is busy working. You'll see him when he comes downstairs. It's peanut butter and jelly time for you."

"Peanut butter and jelly," the boy said, clapping. "Yay!"

Nate smiled, watching as Mrs. Weatherly carried his son out of the room and closed the door.

It could have worked for the three of them, him, Nathaniel, and Monica, but she didn't want to try. She turned Nate down and would not make the effort, would not even give it a chance. She preferred to leave Nate and start a life with another man. There were times when Nate tried to forget about Monica, raise his son, and go on with his life. But he simply could not. Something seemed to tell him that until she paid in some way for what she had put him through, he would never be able to move forward.

Nate reached out across his desk and grabbed the framed picture of the woman in his life now. The brown, dark-haired woman with the big soft eyes smiled back at Nate. This was wrong of him, Nate thought, devoting so much attention to Monica when there was a woman who loved him, truly wanted to be with him.

Daphanie was the third and last woman who Nate had tried to find something with after his divorce. He later realized he had intentionally sabotaged those first two attempts, but Daphanie would not allow any of that.

She fought to make them work, and they had.

Daphanie loved Nathaniel, and Nate's son was very fond of Daphanie. She was thirty-seven years old. There was still the possibility for children, which she said she definitely wanted to give Nate, but she realized if that were to happen, they would have to move quickly. Recently, they had even allowed themselves to go without protection. Nate always pulled out, but not with the urgency of a man decidedly against getting his woman pregnant. To him it felt that they silently agreed that if she wound up pregnant, then they'd have the baby.

Until now, nothing had happened, and Nate felt it was probably for the best. Because even though he was excited about the prospect of marriage and children with this woman, Nate knew none of that could happen until this business with Monica was settled.

14

After school, when Lewis went to pick his daughter up from day care, he noticed someone at the curb, staring at him from a car. The woman sitting in the big old Ford did not look away. Lewis squinted against the sun to get a better look at her and realized that he recognized her.

The car door opened and the woman stepped out and stood on the street side of the car, still staring at him from over the hood of her automobile. The woman was older, in her later fifties. Her graying brown hair looked like wire, held back with a rubber band. She was thin, almost gaunt, and wore a sweater despite the already warm afternoon weather.

"You promised us," the woman called out. "You can't say we can have her then just take her away."

Lewis looked over his shoulder, then quickly walked across the lawn, closing the distance between himself and the woman.

"It's over," Lewis said, his voice hushed, as if someone were listening in. "Do you hear me? I'm not going to tell you again. I've changed my mind."

"But you promised!"

Again, Lewis looked back toward the day care building, wary of anyone stepping out of the front door. He then started around the car toward the woman. She quickly pulled open the door, tried to sink back into the car, but Lewis caught the handle first.

"I told you, forget about that," he said, dipping his head into the cabin.

The woman sat, wide eyed, cowering behind the wheel.

"I've changed my mind, and it's over. Don't come around me no more. You hear me?"

The woman continued staring defiantly, saying nothing.

"You hear me?"

"Yes."

"Good. Now get out of here."

Lewis stepped back, watched the car drive off, and then walked back to the building to pick up his daughter.

Next, Lewis headed to his best friend Freddy's house. Since Lewis wasn't working that day, he wanted to ask how the rehabbing was going, see if there was anyone interested in buying the house.

Lewis hadn't expected to hear that Freddy's house had been broken into this morning and that Freddy had to damn near kill somebody.

As Layla sat playing in the next room, Freddy filled Lewis in on everything that had happened.

"And that's it? You ain't heard nothing back from the police yet?"

Freddy looked at Lewis like he was crazy, then flipped the grilled cheese sandwich he was frying. "And ain't gonna hear nothing back. You know how it goes around here. I'm going to put those bars up, buy some more bullets, and dare somebody else to come back up in here. That is until we sell that house, buy another, and do it again and again, until we're millionaires."

Those were the plans Lewis and Freddy had. Start buying

and flipping houses. They often sat around and dreamed of starting their own real-estate company, making the kind of money that would get Freddy out of the hood he was living in and earning Lewis the respect he felt he wasn't getting from Monica.

"You think that's ever going to happen?" Lewis said.

Freddy turned, the spatula in his hand. "I ain't got no choice. I been living like this all my life, and I'm not bringing my child into this nonsense. I'm getting my people out of here. And I don't care what I have to do to make that happen."

Freddy scooped the sandwich out of the pan, set it on a saucer, and halved it with a butter knife.

"You sure Layla ain't hungry? I can give her this one."

"Naw," Lewis said, his head down. "They fed her at day care."

"Then go on take half. I been doing these the same way since we was ten. Two pieces of cheese and a slice of bologna in the middle."

"I'm cool."

"What's up? My crib is the one that got broken into this morning, not the castle you live in."

"I ain't living there no more."

"What you do this time?"

"I proposed again last night."

"Why you keep doing that? I told you to stop doing that. She just got divorced. You ain't even been living there a year. She probably still asking herself if she made the right decision in leaving her husband, and you trying to force her to take a new one?"

"She ain't going to play me," Lewis said. "I'm living there, taking out the garbage, making her dinner, giving her the dick whenever she want it, telling her I love her. She got it made with me, but she don't want to commit."

"Don't even lie to yourself, Lewis. You two go at it like everybody else. You walk in late, not cleaning up after yourself, do the stupid shit that all men do, but she don't give you a hard way to go."

"She does," Lewis said. "She always complaining. Do this, don't do that. Just because she makes the money, half the time she thinks she can treat me like a child. Got me going to school when she know I can't stand that shit."

"That's because she trying to make you better," Freddy said, grabbing half of the sandwich and taking a bite. Then he grabbed the back of Lewis's chair and yanked on it. "You need to get out my house and patch things up with Monica before she comes to her senses."

Lewis stood. "I ain't going back there until she tell me we getting married."

"And if she don't, where the fuck you gonna go? You ain't got shit, Lewis."

"I got the job with you. We got the house we gonna sell, and the house after that, and the house after that, like you said."

Freddy just shook his head at his friend.

"I feel like I ain't got no say," Lewis said. "Ain't nothing stopping her from kicking me right out her crib, whenever she feel."

"Now she doesn't have to, because you walked out first."

"We get married, I know she making a promise to me. I know she's not seeing me as a child no more or just something to do no more, but a man she plans to be with her for the rest of her life. I know Layla gonna be taken care of. So if she can't do that for me," Lewis said, smirking a little bit, "I'm just going to have to wait till Waters and Ford Realty makes us enough money so I can buy my own castle."

Freddy smiled, gave Lewis some dap, and pulled him into a half hug. "Alright, man. You the one who's going through it, so I ain't gonna comment no more. I just hope you know what you doing."

"Yeah, me too."

15

As Monica wiped more tears from her eyes, she told herself she was tired of this.

She rolled over in bed, glanced at the alarm clock. It was 10:18 P.M. and still no word from Lewis.

She had been calling him all day. Monica had gone to pick up Layla at the normal time, only to be told that the child was not there.

"Yeah, her father came to get her about an hour ago," the young woman at day care told Monica.

She went by Lewis's job, only to find out that he was off today. Then as a last attempt, she called his best friend, Freddy, not half an hour ago.

"Do you know where he is?" Monica asked, trying to hide the sound of crying in her voice.

"I'm sorry, Monica, I haven't talked to him today."

She was quiet on the phone, not believing him, knowing the relationship the two men had had for most of their lives. "I respect that," she said, dabbing her cheek with a tissue. "But if you do talk to him, can you tell him I miss him and Layla and I want them to come back?"

"I'll tell them."

She had expected to get a call from Lewis not long after she had hung up with Freddy. It never came.

She tried to stop crying in the shower, but couldn't. Afterward, she went into Layla's bedroom down the hall to make sure the little girl's clothes were still in her drawers, her toys still in the closet.

Back in her own bedroom, after slipping on a nightgown, Monica sat on her bed and tried to imagine things really being over for her and Lewis.

As Tabatha told her, she had everything. The house she lived in had five bedrooms, four bathrooms, and three levels. She had all the money she could ever want, owned a business that she had brought back from mediocrity and had made to thrive, and she considered herself a decent woman.

Monica thought that should have been enough for Lewis. But she realized now she was wrong.

She pushed herself back into bed, starting to miss Lewis as though she was certain there would be no repairing the break between them. She began to think about the things she would miss most, and she could not deny that the little girl was one of them.

When Monica thought there was no hope for her ever being a mother, Layla had come into her life. The child was two and a half years old then, needing all of the attention Monica was so happy to give to her. She quickly fell in love with her, the toddler sleeping with her and Lewis for the first three months after they had moved in.

Layla had filled the void in Monica's life that she thought she would never be able to fill, and now there was the possibility Layla would be taken from her. And that's when the tears started to come again, and that's when she turned to see that at

10:18 P.M., Lewis obviously didn't care about all they could lose as much as Monica did.

But then the phone was ringing, and as Monica reached over in the dark room and snatched the cordless handset from its cradle, she realized she had been torturing herself for no reason. It would be Lewis on the other end, saying he was as sorry as she was, that things would be all better again.

"Hello," Monica said, sniffing once again, trying to mask the fact that she had been crying.

"Hello Monica," the voice said.

She didn't recognize the voice at first. "Who is this?"

"It's Nate."

16

Nate had not spoken to his ex-wife since the underhanded stunt she pulled at their divorce proceedings. The stunt that won her fifteen million dollars of his money, plus stocks.

Agreeing to hand over that type of money to his wife of four years didn't just sting, it scorched his ass, burned Nate to a crisp. But it was what it was, and all he could do was try to get on with his life.

But he failed.

A week after the divorce hearing, Nate found himself calling Abbey Kurt, a woman in his company who did investigative work for him. He gave her Tori's employment file and whatever other information he had on her.

"Dig up whatever you can on this woman. Then let me know when you find her," were Nate's instructions.

Crossing Tori off the list had given Nate a satisfying sense of closure. Last night, at eighteen minutes after ten o'clock, he had picked up the phone and called Monica.

She was crying.

"Is it okay that I called you?" Nate said, easing into the conversation. "I know our relationship hasn't been especially amicable, if you can even call it a relationship. If you want me to hang up and never call you again, I will understand."

It took Monica a moment to respond. "No," she finally said, as if still uncertain. "No."

But Nate could still hear that crying tone in her voice. When he asked what was wrong, Monica said it was nothing.

Nate sensed it had to do with that clown, Lewis, she was dating and thought maybe getting close to her would be easier than he had thought.

For the first five minutes their conversation was simply curt and civil, asking and answering how each of them was doing. After running out of conversation and a long silence, Nate said, "I'm calling because I know you've seen how your stock in Kenny Corporation has dropped."

"I have," Monica said. She had stopped crying, but her voice was still low.

"I noticed you haven't sold any of it."

"I have faith that you'll do whatever you have to do to bring back its value."

"The company was having trouble for a while. You know why that was, don't you?" Nate said, having to stop himself from sounding too accusatory.

"No. Why?"

Nate decided to change the subject, not admit to Monica just how distraught he had been after the divorce. "It was brought to my attention that you're now a business owner, and your stores are thriving."

"Really. Who brought that to your attention?"

"Monica," Nate said, avoiding her question. "I don't want this to be adversarial. I was calling because you know how much I value your opinion. I can't deny that part of the reason my business is a success was because of your input. I was just hoping that you could help me now."

The next morning, Nate stepped off the elevator and into the lobby where large silver letters, reading KENNY CORPORATION hung above the heads of two attractive dark-haired receptionists wearing phone headsets.

"Good morning, Mr. Kenny," the women said, almost in unison.

Nate nodded, walking farther onto the floor, past dozens of cubicles, along the east side, which was constructed of floor-to-ceiling windows, giving a spectacular view of Lake Michigan.

Nate took the long way to his office, through the break room, just to see if anyone was lounging on the clock.

The room was empty.

On the wall hung a fifty-two-inch plasma flat screen TV, airing twenty-four-hour business news and scrolling stock numbers. Nate's business had encountered some pretty serious problems, and although he had stopped himself from telling Monica, he could attribute them to her.

After his divorce, Nate had sat at home, depressed for a month, delegating his authority to his V.P., an older man named Eric Stancil.

Nate would receive daily phone calls from Stancil on situations needing Nate's attention.

Nate would simply order him to "handle it." Upon Nate's return, there was much catching up to do—clients that had gone neglected, deals that could have been brokered better if only Nate had been there.

It was something he wasn't concerned about at the time, and not until he had been back at work for three weeks did it finally start to hit him just how serious the situation was. The company had suffered losses greater than ever before, but since then, Nate had been diligent in working to return Kenny Corporation to its former status.

"Good morning, Mr. Kenny," Nate's secretary said when he reached his office. Sandra Browning was the woman who had finally replaced Tori. "Here are your messages, sir," the short, thirtysomething redhead said, standing from the desk chair to hand Nate the slips. Nate stepped into his huge, window-lined office and sat behind the massive oak desk.

Last night, after Nate's request for Monica's help, her end had gone silent. A moment later, he heard her chuckling a little.

"You serious?" she said.

"Very. Considering the number of Kenny Corp. shares you hold, I thought you might be open to the idea."

She accepted, and Nate told her they would need to meet.

"Where?" Monica asked.

Nate told her after being in his office every day, sometimes for twelve hours on end, he didn't want to have to stick around there a moment longer than he had to.

It had taken him almost a year to bring the Tori situation to a close, and Nate didn't want to spend that kind of time closing on Monica, so at the risk of being overly aggressive, Nate said, "I bought a new house. We can meet there. You can tell me what you think of it."

Again Monica was silent for a moment, making Nate think he might have blown a very important opportunity.

"Okay," Monica finally said, softly. "Give me the time and the address and I'll be there."

17

L ast night in his hotel room, Layla sleeping beside him, Lewis had gotten a call from Freddy.

"She's hating life without you, man. She's ready for you to come back."

"She said that?" Lewis said, pressing his cell phone tight to the side of his face.

"Yeah, said that she missed both of ya'll and wants you two to come home."

After the call, Lewis stretched back in bed, thumbed the volume on the TV back up two clicks, and thought about what his next move would be. He thought of calling Monica that second, telling her he was on his way home, but he didn't want to seem frantic. He knew Monica knew Freddy would call him, so he wanted her to think he got the message but was still deliberating as to whether or not he wanted to come back.

He tilted his head, saw the time on the alarm clock: 10:35 P.M. Lewis would make her wait, go home tomorrow sometime during the day and tell her he accepted her apology and hoped she had decided to go ahead and say yes to his proposal. Lewis smiled to himself, his arms folded behind his head, his feet crossed at the end of the bed.

He wished he had not taken the ring back earlier today, but he had spent more than eleven thousand dollars of Monica's money on it. He only did that because Lewis knew he would be able to pay it off once the house sold. Freddy's uncle Henry said together, the two of them should clear around thirty grand.

But still, Lewis didn't like using her card, didn't like taking her money like that. He felt it gave her one more thing to hold over his head. Everything would be all right though, he thought, as he allowed his eyes to close. But Lewis had only slept until a little past 2:00 A.M.

He was up, out of bed, scooping Layla up as he had the other night when he took her away from Monica.

Now he was taking her back.

All he could think about while in bed was how much he loved Monica, how relieved he was that she still wanted him. He had jerked out of his sleep, realizing what a fool he was to be playing with her like that. Half an hour later, Lewis was at home. He carefully climbed the stairs leading to the bedroom he had been sharing with Monica.

The door was slightly ajar. His daughter still in his arms, he turned around, shouldered the door open, and backed into the room.

It was dark, but Monica was there. She lay on her side but was not asleep. Lewis heard her sobbing quietly. He walked around the bed to her, lowered himself to his knees, placing Layla beside Monica.

Monica opened her arms, took the child, hugged her, and kissed her face.

"I'm sorry, baby," Lewis said, wrapping his arms around the two of them.

"No, I'm sorry."

"I shouldn't have walked out of here, but I need to know that you want to be with me. I know how bad you were treated when you were married. But I would never hurt you like that. I promise."

"I know, Lewis."

"I love you."

"I love you, too."

"I want you to marry me. I want you to be my wife."

Monica was looking down at his sleeping little girl. She wiped a tear from her own cheek. Monica stared at Lewis for a moment longer than he thought was necessary, and then finally said, "Okay."

Lewis took Layla to her room and put her to bed, then he and Monica made love. She cried some more, telling him she never wanted him to leave her again. He promised he wouldn't.

They went to sleep in each other's arms, and when Lewis woke up this morning, he had never felt more optimistic about their relationship. Then Monica walked out of the bathroom, half dressed for work, and said, "There's something I want to tell you."

Lewis smiled and sat up in bed, bare chested. "What's that, baby?"

"I spoke with my ex-husband, and I'm going to be seeing him tomorrow evening."

18

The first time Lewis saw Nate Kenny was more than a year before, when the man was staggering toward Lewis's car after he had plowed into the back of Kenny's priceless Bentley, totaling it.

Lewis had no insurance, no money to pay for the destruction he did. That bastard Mr. Kenny was going to call the police on him, was going to get him carted off to jail.

Mr. Kenny said Lewis's only way out was to seduce Monica, allowing Kenny to get proof of her infidelity so that he could divorce her.

"And that's what the fuck I did!" Lewis said to Freddy as they ate burgers and fries at a greasy fast food joint down the block from the management company. "Now he's trying to get back with her. I told Monica that's what he's doing."

"And what did she say?" Freddy said, sipping his Coke.

"She said it's some damn business meeting. That his company was doing bad, and he wants her advice to make some changes."

"And you don't believe her?"

"I believe her. I don't believe his ass, because he's talking about meeting at his house tomorrow night."

Freddy popped a fry into his mouth, then laughed. "Aw yeah, man. He's on some shit. No doubt. So what you gonna do?"

"I'm gonna let the fool know where to get off. I told Monica she ain't going over there alone. She said she was planning on me coming anyway. That's why she told me about it."

"I wish I could be there for that one. The rematch of Lewis versus Nate. Waters versus Kenny Two! If that was on pay-per-view, I'd go ahead and drop the fifty dollars."

"And it'd be worth it," Lewis said, drinking the last of his orange soda. "Because if that fool steps out of line in the least, I'm gonna knock his head off."

19

Monica walked into her third Aero store at 12:30 P.M. She had checked into her two other stores, the one up north and the other on the West Side, before walking into the Michigan Avenue flagship location. This was the one she liked the most and spent the most time in.

She had bought the stores nine months ago when the aging, overworked Italian owner said he was too old for the business and wanted to sell.

Monica had more than enough money after the divorce and wanted more to do with her time than just punch a clock and take orders, so she spent the money. She rearranged the stores, changed them from being just fine men's clothing stores to stores that also offered spa services from manicures and pedicures to massages, all given by beautiful women.

In the redesigning of the flagship store, she did not change much of anything. She kept the loft decor the same, the exposed brick walls and the cedar ceiling, the thick pillars running overhead. The hardwood floors stayed in place, along with all the distressed leather furniture. Monica had all black and gray fix-tures installed, either ceramic or marble, in the spa section. It contrasted sharply with the wood and brick, the warm reds and browns of the clothing area, which Monica liked immensely.

At half past noon, the store was already bustling, a little under a dozen customers browsed through the suit racks, while another two clients were being led back to the spa area by Lucy, a college student who worked there part-time.

"Miss Monica," Roland, the clothing receptionist, called in a sing-songy tone from his perch, raised two feet above floor level.

Monica climbed the four stairs up to Roland, who answered calls, greeted clients, and rang up the occasional customer when it got really busy.

She accepted the squeeze and kiss on both cheeks she always got from him. "How's everything today?" Monica asked, flipping through some papers at his work station.

"Floating like a swan on a placid river."

"Roland, you are a poet. When are you going to write a book?"

The man blushed, fanning his face with his hand as if to cool his warming cheeks. "Miss Monica, you say the sweetest things. But you know I'm a dancer. My life belongs to the stage."

"And rightfully so," Monica said, patting Roland on the hand. "Where's your boss?"

"Tabatha's in the back, eating lunch. For the past hour and sixteen minutes."

Monica smiled. "I'll tell her to come out and relieve you." She headed down the brick-walled hallway that led to her office.

Tabatha sat at her desk, her stockinged feet up, reading an *Esquire* magazine, fast food trash scattered around her. "Don't get your panties in a bunch, Roland," Tabatha said, not looking up from the magazine. "I'll be done with lunch in a minute."

Monica walked over, took the magazine out of Tabatha's hands, and tossed it on her own desk. "You're done now."

"Oh, what's up, boss? Good to see you back. How are you?"

"Wonderful," Monica said, walking to her desk, sitting down in her leather chair, and lifting the top of her computer.

"Really," Tabatha said, sounding skeptical.

"Really," Monica said, tapping on the keyboard.

Tabatha got up, walked over, and stood in front of Monica's desk, as if trying to find a lie in what she was saying. "What happened?"

"Lewis came back."

"Really. And that's it?"

"Yes."

"That's it?"

"Oh, yeah. And we've decided to get married."

Tabatha took a step back, turned in a circle, and then looked down at Monica again. "What does that man bring?"

"I don't know what you're talking about."

"What does he bring to the table, besides his needs, his mistakes, his regrets, his apologies, and oh, yeah, his daughter to feed and take care of?"

"Don't," Monica said, pointing at Tabatha. "I love that little girl like she was my own."

"I know. And maybe that's part of the plan."

Monica chuckled. "There is no plan, Tab. It's just this man and his daughter, trying to make it."

"That's right, and he's using you to do it. How much money did you give him today for lunch, or for some new tennis shoes, or maybe a new PlayStation Three game? I know how bad you wanted a kid, but I don't think he should be both your child and your man."

Monica stood up, stone faced, glaring at her best friend, finding none of what she said funny in the least. "Go home, Tabatha."

"What?"

"I think you had enough of work today, or to be more precise, I've had enough of you. Come back when you've learned that shit is supposed to come out your ass, not your mouth."

"Monica, I'm sorry. But I think I see what it is, and I don't want my girl getting taken advantage of. That's all, understand?" Tabatha said, stepping around the desk to Monica and opening her arms. "I care for you. If I don't have your back, who will?"

Monica stepped into Tabatha's arms and they embraced.

"And I'm not going anywhere," Tabatha said. "Even with Super Roland, it's too busy out there, and you know this store just ain't the same without me."

"Okay," Monica said. "But don't be talking about that man and his daughter like they're nobody. This is my situation now, and despite what you think, I love Lewis, and this is going to work. Alright?"

"You got it, boss," Tabatha said.

20

Nate cut out of work early in order to get back home to prepare for Monica's visit the following night. Still wearing his work slacks and a white shirt unbuttoned at the collar, he sat in the den with his son.

The phone had rung ten minutes ago in the middle of his playtime with Nathaniel. Nate hadn't bothered picking up the phone, for he knew Mrs. Weatherly would retrieve the call. A few seconds later, a knock came at the den door.

"Mr. Kenny, it's Ms. Coleman on the phone for you. Would you like to take it?"

"Yes, Mrs. Weatherly," Nate said. "I'll take it in here. Thank you."

Daphanie had only been away in London for three days on business for the pharmaceutical company she worked for. Nate found himself missing her more than he would have ever thought.

Maybe because even though they did not live together, over the course of their four-month relationship, more and more of

Daphanie's personal belongings had found their way over to Nate's house, and they had recently been spending the better part of the entire week together. Nate had even given her a key to the house. She was a good woman.

"No, I'm not doing anything I'm not supposed to," Nate said, smiling as he spoke into the phone. "And how about you? I know those Englishmen would love to get their hands on a fine American woman like you."

"They can't have what's not available," Daphanie said.

"Really?"

"Really."

She went silent for a long moment.

"You okay over there?" Nate asked.

"It's night, you know. And I'm in bed wearing nothing, my legs spread, and I can't do anything but think about you."

Nate felt a twinge in his pants, thought about the night before Daphanie left. An image of her underneath him, legs open, her breasts jumping each time he pushed himself into her.

"I want you so much right now," Daphanie said, her voice raspy.

Nate was almost lost in that voice, till he turned and saw his son staring right into his eyes. "Uh, Daphanie . . . yeah, we need to do this another time. Maybe when little ears aren't around."

"Oops. Sorry. Nathaniel's right there?"

"Yup."

"Let me talk to my sweetheart."

Nate held out the phone to his son. "Someone wants to speak to you."

Nathaniel placed the side of his face to the phone, listened, and then smiled brightly. "Hi, Ms. Daphanie . . . yes . . . yes. I'm fine. Okay . . . okay. I miss you, too. Bye-bye."

Nate took the phone back.

"I love that little boy," Daphanie said. "I'm going to let you two get back to business, cause I have some immediate business of my own I have to attend to in order to get to sleep."

"Don't have too much fun without me."

"Never, sweetheart. I love you, baby," Daphanie said, sincerely.

"I love you, too." Nate said, then hung up the phone.

He picked up one of the dozen or so photos he had of Monica that were spread out on the table before him. Some were of the both of them during vacations they had taken while they were still married, others were of her just posing, pretending to be a model. And the last few were shots Nate had taken of Monica in black and white.

Nate held one of the photos before his son, as he had done with the others before Daphanie called.

"Now who is this, again?" Nate asked Nathaniel.

The little boy looked at the photo, then at his father, and smiled silently.

"This is your mommy. Say it with me. 'Mommy,'" Nate said slowly. " 'Mommy'."

Still Nathaniel did not respond.

It would take a while, Nate told himself.

There was a knock on the door.

"Come in," Nate said.

The door opened, and in came Tim, Nate's younger brother by two years. They could have been twins, save for the three inches Nate had on Tim, and Tim's slightly broader nose and shorter hair.

Tim was a writer. He had only authored a handful of magazine articles and several drafts of a novel until he'd finally gotten a publisher to buy his first manuscript two months ago.

Nate and Tim had been very close until last year, when Tim went behind Nate's back and told Monica everything—the entire scam that Nate was running on her. At first Nate had thought that if it wasn't for his brother, Monica would never have found out about his scheme, and subsequently, Nate never would have lost those millions of dollars. He was planning on never forgiving Tim, on cutting him from his life. Then Nate found out that the fool Lewis had admitted everything to Monica anyway. It only lessened Nate's anger toward his brother a bit. But Nate decided to keep speaking to Tim, to consider the man his brother, even though Nate still harbored anger toward him for his betrayal.

"What you up to?" Tim said, looking down at the scattered photos of Monica after picking up his nephew and holding him in his arms.

"Rehearsing," Nate said, standing and gathering the pictures.

"For what?"

"I'm having a meeting with Monica tomorrow night, and when he sees her, I want Nathaniel to call her Mommy."

Tim was silent, his mouth falling slightly open.

Nate could look at his brother and know what was running through his self-righteous mind. He called for Mrs. Weatherly.

"Please don't tell me you're going to go through with what you were considering," Tim said.

"Yes, Mr. Kenny?" Mrs. Weatherly said, appearing at the door.

"Can you take Nathaniel, please?"

Mrs. Weatherly stepped in and eased Nathaniel from Tim's arms, then closed the door behind them.

"In answer to your question," Nate said, lowering himself into a leather armchair, "I have decided to go ahead with it."

"You shouldn't have gone after Tori. But you said that would be it."

"I changed my mind."

"What is wrong with you? You were the one who started all that nonsense with trying to get Monica to cheat. And now that she did, which made her divorce you, you're still pissed off because you have to give her the money she deserves."

"I didn't force her to divorce me," Nate said, his legs crossed, trying to remain calm. "I asked her to stay. Asked her to put aside everything that had happened, but she wouldn't. And I didn't start anything. It all started because she lied to me about being able to get pregnant. And I can't let her get away with that and collect fifteen million dollars from me."

"And what do you plan on doing? You can't get the money back."

"I can try. And if I can't, I'll do as much damage to her as possible."

Tim shook his head. "Please don't do this. You have a son now, and what about Daphanie? You have a woman who loves you. You have everything, but you're just angry because you got caught."

Nate practically leapt out of his chair, racing across the room into his brother's face, pointing a finger. "I didn't get caught. You told her! And because of that, I lose millions of dollars. You were supposed to be my fucking brother!"

"I was. I still am," Tim said, looking Nate directly in the eye.

They held each other's stare for a moment, Nate breathing hard through his nose, before he turned away.

"I appreciate your concern," Nate said, sitting again. "But I know what I'm doing. I got what I wanted from Tori, and I'll do the same with Monica."

"But you're using your son."

"He'll understand when he gets a little older. He'll be fine, and Daphanie will never know anything about this. It'll all be over before she gets back in the country."

"You sure?"

"Positive," Nate said.

21

Freddie woke up in his dark basement apartment.

It was only 7:30 P.M., but the foil he had taped to all the windows kept his space in a state of perpetual darkness, allowing him to sleep whenever he chose without dealing with the unwanted sunlight.

He had woken up angry.

Kia was beside him, still napping.

He wasn't mad at her but at what she had told him while they were lying naked together after making love.

Freddy had noticed that while he held her, kissed her, caressed her, there seemed something deep on her mind. Afterward, she lay off to his side, cradling herself.

"He said he won't continue to pay for my school if I keep seeing you," Kia finally told Freddy after he continued to pry.

"What the hell is wrong with your father? First he tries to get you to abort our baby, now he saying he doesn't want you seeing me anymore. Why?"

"You know what he keeps saying."

"What?"

"It's all bullshit anyway."

"What's he saying?" Freddy said.

"That you have nothing, come from nothing, and won't ever amount to anything."

Kia came from money. Freddy wasn't supposed to be with her.

They'd met at a club near the University of Illinois, where she went to school.

Kia was studying law there, wanted to go into public service. She was all about providing for the poor and underprivileged. Her father wanted her to come and work for his high-powered firm, doing corporate law. He held that over Kia's head, along with so many other things, trying to get her to be the exact daughter he wanted her to be.

Freddy knew she was probably only attracted to him because she was angry with her father, wanted to lash out at him, hurt him. She knew dating a so-called loser like Freddy would be the way.

Freddy didn't expect much from the relationship in the beginning, assuming she was using him. Freddy figured he was doing well just to be able to hit the fine piece this woman was, the type of woman he would never normally even come in contact with. But the more time Kia and Freddy spent together, the stronger their feelings became. Now two years later, here they were.

"I need to confront that motherfucking father of yours."

"No! All that'll do is make things worse."

"You don't trust that I'll be able to talk to him on his level?"

"I'm not saying that. It's just that the last time you two met, you almost got into a damn fistfight."

"I could've took him," Freddy said, softly. "Those things your father says about me, you don't believe them, do you?"

"No. Never."

" 'Cause I told you, I'm gonna make something of myself. I'm going to take care of my family."

"And I'm going to get through school."

"But how?"

"Loans. Financial aid. Everything is going to be fine. I promise." Kia slid closer to him, wrapped her arms around Freddy's neck, kissed him softly, and they fell asleep.

Now, Freddy woke up angry, thinking about all that had been said. But sitting up, he listened for movement. He heard nothing, which wasn't good.

Wherever his mother went, she was always back by six P.M., six-thirty at the latest, and Freddy knew this job interview would be no different. She was afraid to be out later than that, having to take public transportation at night.

It seemed almost every night on the news, there was some report about a senior citizen getting robbed somewhere in the area.

Freddy reached over, grabbed his cell phone off the nightstand. He hadn't heard it ring, but he scrolled through his log of missed calls just in case.

His mother had not phoned.

Freddy jumped out of bed, grabbed his clothes from the floor, and started putting them on.

Kia awakened and rolled over, groggy. "What's wrong, baby?"

"I ain't heard Moms come in yet, and she hasn't called me."

"Maybe you just didn't hear her walk in. Or maybe she just missed her bus or something."

"I'm gonna check," Freddy said, pushing his arms through a T-shirt and stretching the neck over his head.

"Just call her."

"Yeah. Okay, I will," Freddy said, leaning into the bed and giving Kia a quick kiss on the lips.

He ran up the stairs two at a time. "Moms," he called out. "You home?"

He quickly walked through the dilapidated old house, checking every room. He even ran up to the second floor, but she wasn't there. Freddy grabbed a jacket out of the front closet and stepped out onto the porch.

The sun was setting and the sky was darkening just the slightest bit. An old Impala with tinted windows sped by, the doors vibrating from the deafening bass that blared from the car's speakers.

Freddy took the stairs down, started walking. Across the street, a group of boys wearing saggy jeans and do-rags glared at him. Freddy stared back. They looked away.

People sat on their porches, wearing house shoes and wife-beater tees, staring out into the street like it was their job. Freddy hated his neighborhood, worried every time Kia or his mother had to be out in it.

He would get them away from there, he told himself again, stopping at the sight of red and blue flashing lights down the street.

Down there, a block or so away, he saw the gathering of people, two police cars, and an ambulance.

Freddy started quickly in that direction, pulling his cell from his pocket and punching the key for his mother's number. He hurried on, the phone pressed to his ear, seeing more of the group of people gathered around whatever had happened. Fifty feet away from the commotion, the phone stopped ringing and was picked up. There was silence on the other end. Freddy halted in his tracks, listened, then said, "Hello?"

"Hello," a male voice returned.

"Who is this?" Freddy said, frenzy in his voice.

"Who the hell is this?"

"Who is this? Where the fuck is my mother?"

The phone hung up.

Freddy ran to the crowd before him, pushed into the row of onlookers.

"What's happening? What's going on?" Freddy asked anybody who would listen.

"Some old lady got mugged," a voice called out.

It couldn't be, Freddy thought, forcing his way through the crowd. It just couldn't. But when he had surfaced, he saw the paramedics kneeling on the ground, their supplies laid out by their sides, leaning over a lady's body.

He couldn't see the woman's face, but looking down he saw her legs, her shoes. They were his mother's. Freddy immediately went wild, trying to rush over, but was stopped by two policemen.

"That's my mother over there! That's my mother!"

One of the officers looked toward one of the paramedics. The blond woman nodded her head. The cops let Freddy pass.

He dropped down to his knees at his mother's side. "Moms, you okay?"

Her hair was mussed, cuts criss-crossed her face, her jacket was torn near the shoulder, her knuckles scraped and bleeding. She wore an oxygen mask over her nose and mouth, and an IV had been poked into one of her veins.

"I . . . I . . . been robbed, Fred." She raised a hand, but one of the paramedics placed it back down.

"She's in shock."

Freddy felt rage burning inside him. He looked around, as if he could spot the one who'd done this to his mother, see the man turning a corner, her purse in his grasp. "She gonna be okay? She's gonna be fine, right?" Freddy asked.

"We're taking her in now," the paramedic said. "You can ride in the back."

22

That'll be twelve thousand six hundred ninety-eight dollars and twenty-four cents," the older, red-headed saleswoman said to Lewis and Monica. They were standing over the glass case of the Winston-Siegel jewelry store in the Water Tower Place mall. Monica had picked out the engagement ring she liked.

"How would you like to pay for that?" the woman asked.

"Credit card," Monica said.

"Your card, please."

Monica turned to Lewis, gave him a look as though she expected him to swing into action.

"Oh," he said, digging into his back pocket for his wallet, slipping out the Visa debit card that had his name on it but that was linked to Monica's account. He had tried to turn it down when she had presented him with the card a month ago.

It was after she had returned from a business trip. When she was gone, Lewis's truck had gotten stolen while he was out shopping with Layla.

It was late. It was raining, and Lewis only had sixteen dollars on him.

A week after Monica returned, the card came in the mail, and she gave it to Lewis. It would give him access to all the money she had in her savings and checking accounts.

"I can't take this. You don't know if I'll steal all your money and fly off to Mexico or something."

"I have money all over this house. You've been living here for months and nothing has come up missing yet. Besides, I wouldn't be with you if you were a thief. Take this card, boy."

"I can't do that," Lewis said, crossing his arms, shaking his head. "I don't want the responsibility. If a dollar comes up missing, I don't even want you to think about looking at me."

"You don't have the choice not to have the responsibility. Layla is with you, and there may be another time when I'm not around. You need to have this card. Now take it, before I have to make you."

"All right, all right," Lewis said, taking the card from Monica. "Don't hurt me."

The card was only supposed to be for emergencies. But lately, there were times when Lewis was out and Monica wanted him to pick up groceries or wanted him to fill up her car with gas. She'd simply say, "Use the card."

So now, when Lewis pulled out the card and gave it to the woman to make the charge, it almost seemed as though it was his card and his money he was using to purchase the ring again.

After the saleswoman finished the transaction, she asked, "Would you like this wrapped?"

"I don't think so," Monica said, holding out her left hand. "Give it to him."

The woman gave the ring to Lewis. He took Monica's hand, then gently slipped the ring on her finger. She looked down at the beautiful two-carat diamond solitaire on the platinum ring and smiled. "It's beautiful. Thank you, Lewis," Monica said, throwing her arms around him there in the store, squeezing him tight.

"But it was your money that—" Lewis tried to say, his face in her shoulder.

"Just go with it," Monica said.

Inside the mall, taking the escalator down, Monica stood in front of Lewis on the step below him, leaning back against him. Lewis leaned over her shoulder, whispered in her ear, "I'll pay you back every cent for that."

"I know you will," Monica said, seeming not to care as she held her hand at arm's length and admired the ring.

"You really like that, don't you."

"What's not to like? Tabatha is gonna flip when she sees it."

"So will your ex-husband."

"What did you say?" Monica said, turning, looking over her shoulder at Lewis.

"Nothing."

On the ground floor, Monica turned to face Lewis. "I said, what did you say?"

Lewis remained silent.

Monica angrily stepped away from the escalator. She walked over to a corner of the mall, away from the people milling about.

Lewis followed her, stood in front of her.

"Is that why you were so adamant about me calling the babysitter, about us coming out here before the store closed so we could get this ring, so I'd be wearing it for the meeting tomorrow?"

"I bought a ring the other day, remember? We're just replacing that one. This has nothing to do with your little meeting."

"I swear if you're lying to me, we can take this back right now."

"I told you I'm not," Lewis said, hoping she couldn't see the fact that he was lying. "I'm just happy that we're getting married and I wanted you to have the ring now."

Monica gave him a long, scrutinizing glance. "Lewis, there's nothing more to this meeting than I told you. Do you believe me?"

Lewis was silent but nodded his head, sad that she was not aware of what was going on.

"Do you believe me?"

"Yes."

"Good." Monica gave him another hug. "You'll see. Tomorrow will be just fine."

23

The next night, Nate found himself in his kitchen, phone in hand, telling himself the plan was not supposed to have gone as badly as it had.

For the rest of the day yesterday, Nate had continued to drill Nathaniel, holding up the photos of Monica, asking, "Who is this, Nathaniel? Can you tell me who this is, son?" Finally, with uncertainty heavy in his voice, Nathaniel said, "Mommy?"

Nate paused for a moment, turned over the photo to take a look at it himself, and then said happily, "That's right. That's right! It's Mommy!" Nate picked up another photo, held it in front of the boy. "And who is this?"

"Mommy?"

"Yes!"

"And how about this one?"

"It's Mommy," Nathaniel said with confidence.

"Exactly!" Nate said, grabbing his son and giving him a hug. Maybe the first phase of his plan would work.

Earlier that day, sitting in the kitchen, he had filled in Mrs. Weatherly.

"Now you remember how this is supposed to go, right?" he asked her.

"Yes, Mr. Kenny. After I pick up Nathaniel from nursery school, I'll take him with me to run some errands. We'll stop at the bookstore, get him a book or two, and there I'll wait for you to call, letting me know it's okay for us to come home."

"Good," Nate said.

The idea was for Nate to be in conversation with Monica. There would be soft music playing upon her arrival, and maybe by the time Nate had made the phone call to Mrs. Weatherly, he would have offered Monica a glass of wine. His intention was not to get her drunk and into bed, but to soften her up, lower her guard just a little.

Mrs. Weatherly would walk in with Nathaniel as though she didn't expect Nate to have company, and that's when Monica would see the boy.

She would recognize him from when she had wanted to adopt him. It would probably pain her a bit, seeing the boy, Nate told himself. And then when Nathaniel called her Mommy, she would want to know why. Nate would tell her he always considered her the boy's mother even though they were divorced. If nothing else, it would be a good starting point for deeper discussion.

But things were not going as planned.

Earlier tonight, when Nate heard the doorbell ring, he quickly glanced at himself in the bathroom mirror and smoothed down the front of his shirt. He was dressed casually, the shirt unbuttoned at the collar. Instead of slacks he wore jeans, and loafers instead of the dress shoes he normally wore. Passing the living room, he lowered the volume of the jazz he was playing and opened the door.

Upon seeing Monica, Nate smiled brightly. She looked even

more beautiful than he had thought she would, wearing her hair down as he always loved it, and wearing only the slightest bit of makeup. But the smile fell from his face when, just beside her, Nate saw Lewis Waters.

Nate stood there, holding the door, not knowing what to say or do. He knew Monica was involved with this man, but considering the history between him and Lewis, Nate would never have thought she would have brought him along. Monica looked down at her feet, almost appearing sorry after she saw the expression on Nate's face. "Hello, Nate. I hope you don't mind that I brought Lewis with me?"

"No. That's fine." Nate's voice was low. He stepped aside and let Monica and Lewis enter his house.

"Come into the dining room," Nate said.

He closed the door and just stood there a moment, shaking his head. He turned off the stereo, breathed deeply, and exhaled before walking into the dining room.

"Monica," Nate said, standing behind the head of the dining room table. "It's good to see you." He reached out his hand. Monica took it and they awkwardly shook.

Nate glanced in Lewis's direction. "Lewis," Nate acknowledged coldly.

"Nate," Lewis said, sounding as though he still hated the man and wasn't trying at all to hide it.

"Can I get either of you something to drink?"

"Nothing for me," Monica said.

"Yeah, Nate. I think I'll have a beer. I know you got something expensive and imported in your fridge, don't you?"

Nate tried his best to display a smile. "I'll see what I have," he said, turning and leaving the room.

In the kitchen, Nate picked up the phone and dialed Mrs. Weatherly.

"Don't bring Nathaniel home yet. Not until I call you back, okay?"

"Is everything all right, Mr. Kenny?"

"Everything is fine. I'll call you when you can come home."

Nate hung up the phone, grabbed a beer from the fridge, along with a bottle of water for himself, and headed back into the dining room. He placed a coaster down for Lewis, then set the bottle down on top of it. Just when he was about to sit, Lewis said, "Uh, you got a glass? I stopped drinking beer from the bottle about a year ago."

Nate gave Lewis a hateful glance, then headed back to the kitchen. The man was playing games, Nate thought as he pulled a glass from the cabinet. But Nate told himself he would be cordial, civil. He would discuss the things he had planned with Monica but make it very quick and then get them out of there. There was no way he could follow through with his original plan.

"Thanks," Lewis said, taking the glass from Nate once he returned.

Nate sat down, and again Lewis spoke.

"Where's your bathroom? I want to wash my hands first."

"Down the hallway, on the left," Nate said, pointing.

Lewis stood, but before stepping away from his chair, he leaned over and gave Monica a quick kiss on the lips. By the look on Monica's face, she was not expecting it.

After Lewis was gone, Nate just sat and stared at his ex-wife. "And you brought him why?"

"This is a business meeting. He can be here. He can hear this."

"But what's the point, other than to spite me? Will he know what he's hearing? The man can barely speak proper English. Will he understand what we're talking about?"

"I don't appreciate that, Nate," Monica whispered. "I'm in a relationship with that man, and I will not allow you to sit here and talk badly about him."

"A relationship. Of all the worthless, out of work, uneducated street people out there, you had to pick him."

"I didn't just pick him, Nate," Monica said, pulling her left hand out from under the table and showing Nate the ring. "I'm marrying him."

Nate was speechless. He understood she had probably been rebounding when she started seeing Lewis. She probably figured she knew Lewis, felt that some of the identity that Nate had created for him had to have been real. But he hadn't thought she was foolish enough to marry the man. All Nate could do was shake his head.

"You ain't liking that too much, huh, Nate?" Lewis said from the door of the dining room.

He took his seat beside Monica, casually draping an arm around her chair. "Nate, you ain't saying nothing."

"Lewis, that's enough," Monica said.

"Yeah, you better listen to her, or you might have to fool someone else into marrying you," Nate said behind clenched teeth.

"You ain't liking this 'cause you want Monica back?"

"Lewis," Monica said, "I told you—"

"Naw, baby. I already know the deal," Lewis said, looking around the room. "Lights all dim, too dim to be looking at paperwork. And when we came in there was soft music playing, which he quickly cut off after seeing me. What was that about, Nate? And look at him, his shirt all open. And I bet you got the fresh haircut just for this little meeting tonight, didn't you?"

"You don't know what you're talking about," Nate said.

"I don't? Tell Monica you don't want her back."

"Lewis, would you stop this? Or maybe we just need to leave," Monica said.

"Fine. I don't want to be here anyway," Lewis said, smiling. "But first I want him to look you in the face and tell you he don't want you back."

Monica stood, shaking her head, and grabbed her purse.

"This is my house, and what you want means nothing," Nate said.

"Just like I thought," Lewis said, standing up from his chair, beside Monica.

"I'm sorry, Nate," Monica said. "But I really think we need to be going."

"Fine," Nate said, standing. "You know where the door is."

Monica headed toward the door, but Lewis stopped just in front of Nate. "I ain't no fool. I know you want her back, but you ain't getting her."

"Lewis, come on!" Monica called from the front door.

"You hear me," Lewis said. "Motherfucker, you ain't getting her."

Nate turned to Lewis, his face calm, not at all rattled, and said very softly, "You wanna bet?"

Lewis looked shocked, as though he could not believe Nate would actually admit his intentions. He whipped his head around, as if to see if Monica had heard what Nate said, but she was still down the hall.

"I swear if you don't come with me now, you'll be walking," Monica warned.

"Run along, Lewis," Nate said, smiling. "You don't want your free ride to leave you."

24

On the way home, Monica drove.

Lewis tried to tell Monica what Nate had told him, explain to her that the man was really trying to steal her back, but Monica held up a hand. "Don't say nothing to me," was all she said.

While they put Layla to bed and showered, and while Monica dressed for bed, she was obviously still mad. She would not say a single word to Lewis.

Finally, once they were both in bed, the blankets pulled up to their chests, Monica stared up at the ceiling and said, "Why would you do that?"

"I was just trying to make you see the truth."

"What truth?"

"The man wants you back."

"What are you talking about? You of all people know the trouble he went to just to divorce me. Nate does not want me back."

"Why would he invite you over there?"

"I told you why. But that couldn't happen, because you were acting crazy."

"Monica, he told me!"

Monica paused, as if weighing the possibility. "No. He did not say that."

"What? I'm lying?"

"You're saying what you think you need to in order for me to believe your story."

"Monica," Lewis said, sitting up, "I—"

"No, Lewis, you need to listen to this," Monica said, sitting up herself. "You say you want to marry me. Then there are things you're going to have to accept. Nate Kenny is no longer my husband, but I was married to him for four years. I own stock in his company, which means to some degree we are business partners. We will probably, one day, be friends. In order for you and me to stay engaged, I need to know that you're cool with that."

Lewis crossed his arms over his chest, stared up at the ceiling, not saying a word.

"Lewis, I'm serious. If you're not cool with this, then we probably need to take this ring back."

"Naw," Lewis said, glancing angrily at Monica. "I'm cool."

Later that night, Lewis sat in front of Monica's computer. It was 1:04 A.M.

After Monica made Lewis accept her terms, she clicked off the bed lamp. Minutes later, Lewis felt her dozing, then falling completely off to sleep. He could not follow her. His mind was far too troubled with what had happened at Nate Kenny's house. The man was not expecting Lewis. He could tell by the initial expression Nate had when he first opened the door. He thought it would be an evening with just him and Monica. Lewis was sure.

But what troubled Lewis more was wondering why Monica

didn't tell Nate that she had gotten engaged until tonight, or that she was bringing Lewis to begin with. Maybe Monica had an interest in getting back with him, too. Maybe she was trying to decide at the last minute if she would bring Lewis or not, at least give herself an opportunity to hear what her ex-husband had to say to her before deciding what to do.

Lewis told himself no. That couldn't have been the case. It was all Nate Kenny. The man finally realized he had made a huge mistake giving Monica away, and now the fool wanted her back. Lewis opened the photo software on the computer and dumped the photos he had on the digital camera onto the hard drive. This was the camera he and Monica kept in the bedroom. The camera they occasionally used to take dirty pictures and sometimes video when they got in that mood.

After doing a search to find Nate Kenny's business e-mail address, Lewis opened up three of the photos, smiled, and attached them to the message he was sending to Nate.

"You wanted to see your ex-wife. Tomorrow morning, you gonna get your wish."

Lewis pressed Send.

25

This morning in front of their house, Freddy and Kia had helped Freddy's mother step gingerly out of the car after picking her up from the hospital.

Last night in the emergency room, a haggard, boyish-looking doctor had pulled Freddy aside.

"Mr. Ford, your mother was worked over pretty badly. Along with the scratches and bruises she sustained during the attack, she fell pretty hard on her hip. We X-rayed it. It's not broken. I gave her some medication, because she's still in a substantial amount of pain. But what I'm even more concerned with is the bump she took to her head when she fell."

"What bump?" Freddy said, worried. "Is she going to be all right?"

"Yes," the doctor said. "But the MRI shows she has a mild concussion, and I think I want to keep her here overnight. Is that okay?"

If he could find the motherfucker who did this to his mother,

Freddy thought, trying to control the anger he was feeling. "Yeah, okay," Freddy said. "Thank you, Doctor."

The doctor took Freddy to see his mother.

Freddy stood in the doorway, staring at her in the hospital bed, lying under the white sheets, her head wrapped in bandages, her eyes closed. She was so silent, so still, that if the doctor hadn't told Freddy she was alright, he would've thought she was dead.

There was a tube in her arm, a bedside machine that beeped every now and then. Freddy was afraid to enter, scared that he would approach the bed, find that his mother had passed away. But when he stepped closer, she slowly opened her eyes, and a smile spread across her dry lips.

Freddy took his mother's hand. "This is never gonna happen again, Moms. I'm gonna get us away from there. I promise."

"I know you will, son," Freddy's mother said, sounding weak. "And I'll be able to help. You know why?"

"Why, Moms?"

"Because I got the job," his mother said, her voice a whisper.

Kia had come up to the hospital after Freddy had called her and he told her what had happened. But after they had returned home, Freddy stayed in the living room while Kia put her jacket in the closet. She stopped halfway down the hall, turned, and saw Freddy just standing there as if he didn't know where he was.

"Freddy, you okay?"

He didn't answer.

She walked into the living room, took his hand. "Freddy, I said are you okay?"

He did not answer right away, didn't even look at her. A moment later he said, "I need to step out."

"Where are you going?"

"It's not important," he said, moving toward the front door.

"Freddy, what are you doing?" Kia said, following behind him.

"I'll be back later. Don't wait up, okay."

"But—"

He opened the door, gave Kia a quick kiss on the lips, then left.

Now, this morning, as Freddy held on tight to his mother's arm while walking her from his car to the sidewalk, she said, "Easy. My hip still hurts."

"He said it wasn't broken," Freddy said.

"What did that boy know? He looked young enough to be your son."

Freddy looked across at Kia, who had his mother's other arm, and smiled. "It's good to have you back, Moms."

"I ain't never been gone nowhere. Now hurry up and get me in the house before *The Price is Right* comes on."

"Yes, Moms," Freddy said, slowly walking his mother toward the house.

Out of the corner of his eye, Freddy saw a tall, thin man, about twenty-five years old, walking toward them. The man's hair was a mess, his clothes filthy and torn. He walked slowly toward them as though he was thinking, planning.

Neither Freddy's mother nor Kia seemed to have been paying any special attention to the man, but Freddy's mind was racing. He asked himself if things had gotten so bad where robberies were attempted at ten in the morning, right outside his house. The dirty-faced man walked even closer, was twenty feet away, fifteen, when Freddy said as calmly as possible, "Kia, you got Moms?"

"Yeah. What's wrong?"

"Nothing," Freddy said, his voice low, as he let go of his mother, reached behind him, grabbing something out of the waist of his jeans. He quickly stepped the three feet over to the man, grabbed him by the collar, and pressed a gun to his head.

"Fred, what are you doing?" his mother said, frightened.

"What the fuck you want?" Freddy yelled, his hand now around the man's throat.

The man threw his hands in the air. "Nothing. Nothing!"

A woman on her porch across the street and a man lowering himself into his car both stopped, gawking at Freddy.

"You walking up like you trying to rob us. What the fuck you want?"

"Freddy, don't!" Kia yelled.

"You the guy looking for the man who robbed your mother last night, right?" the man said, trembling. "Said you'd pay forty dollars."

"Yeah, that's me," Freddy said, slowly lowering the gun.

"That's what I'm here for. I know who it is."

26

Nate's secretary, Sandra, handed Nate the clipboard, waiting for his signature on the letter she had just printed. Nate scribbled his name on the bottom, and passed the board back.

"Thank you, Mr. Kenny. Your one-fifteen appointment has just arrived."

"Thank you, Sandra. I'll be with him shortly," Nate said, watching the woman till she stepped out of the office and closed the door. Nate turned back to his brother.

Tim had come by half an hour ago to get the details regarding Nate's meeting with Monica last night.

Nate filled him in on all the ugly details, how Nate had wanted nothing more than to wrestle Lewis to the ground, strangle him till his eyes popped out of his head.

"She says she's going to marry him," Nate said.

Nate looked bad today. His suit was slightly wrinkled, his hair barely combed. When he turned back to face his brother, dark circles hung under his eyes from his restless night before.

"Tim, to be honest, I couldn't believe it."

"Why not? He was the guy who stuck by her when you decided she wasn't worth your time anymore."

"How many times are you going to rub that in my face?"

"As long as you continue to think she's the reason you two divorced, when it was actually you."

Nate rubbed a hand across his unshaven chin. "I want to get back at her for what she took from me. I no longer care who's to blame. But to tell you the truth, if she marries this fool, I should really consider the job done. She obviously doesn't know it, but Monica's life will go to hell with Lewis."

"Then leave it alone," Tim said. "Let what happens, happen."

"No. I don't want it to go that way. I want to know that I'm personally responsible for whatever pain she feels."

"Why don't you just leave her and Lewis alone? He obviously cares for her."

Nate stood beside his desk, looked down at his computer, thought for a moment before saying, "Come here. I want to show you something."

Tim walked over and stood beside the desk as Nate pecked away on the keyboard. He pulled up his e-mail account, clicked on an e-mail labeled "FOR YOUR COLLECTION!!!"

An e-mail from Lewis Waters opened. Nate scrolled down to the tiny paperclip icon, then turned to look at his brother. "If the man cared about her at all, would he have sent me this?"

Nate clicked the paperclip, and a photo of Monica and Lewis, both naked, filled the screen. Monica lay on her back, rump elevated in the air. Lewis straddled her, on hands and knees, pushed deep inside her. Nate could not see the expression on Monica's face, which was turned away from the camera. He was thankful for that. Lewis, on the other hand, faced the camera, smiling, sweat dripping from his brow.

Tim turned away and stepped back, as if the image sickened him. "Damn, Nate. I'm sorry."

"There are two more. Do you want to see them?"

"Hell no. Delete them."

"No," Nate said. "I'm saving them. They might come in handy."

Tim turned away from Nate, crossed his arms, exhaled, then faced him again. "So. What now?"

"Nothing changes. I continue as planned."

"Which means what?"

"I don't know. I think I call this bastard, arrange a meeting or something, lay it out there. Tell him I want my wife back and tell him to step away. I make him an offer he can't refuse. If he agrees, I continue working on getting back what's mine."

Tim shook his head. "In my opinion, you're still wrong about this."

"I haven't asked for your opinion. I need to get this man's number and set this up. Daphanie's back in two weeks, and I don't have time to be questioning myself."

Nate reached for his phone, preparing to assign Sandra to the task of finding Lewis's number, when it rang.

He punched the lit plastic cube and said, "Yes, Sandra?"

"Call for you on line four, sir."

"Who is it?"

"A Mr. Waters. Shall I take a message?"

Nate looked up at his brother. "No, no. Put him through."

"Yes, sir."

Tim stepped closer, stood over the phone's speaker.

Nate spoke. "This is Nate. Who am I speaking with?"

"You know who this is, Nate," Lewis's voice came through the speaker. To Nate it sounded as though the man had a smile on his face. "You get the pictures I sent you?"

"Yes, and they disgust me."

"They don't disgust me and Monica. We're into that, taking pictures during sex, looking at them afterward. Sometimes we do video, watch it on TV."

"What do you want?"

"Easy, easy there, Nate. We're just having a friendly conversation. No need to get feisty."

"Why are you calling me?"

The line was quiet for a long moment. Nate looked up at Tim. Tim hunched his shoulders. They heard Lewis breathe heavily into the speaker. "You aren't slick, Nate. I know you want Monica back."

Nate paused now, wondering how to answer, and finally said, "And what if I do?"

"Then we should meet, talk about it."

"I agree. Where?"

"Taylor's. I assume you remember the place. It was our favorite last year."

"I do. Time?"

"The sooner the better. Half an hour," Lewis said.

"How about later? I have a meeting in—"

"See you at one thirty, Nate," Lewis said, hanging up the phone.

27

Nate told himself he would be cool about this as he grabbed the handle to the door of Taylor's Bar. He would take the tiny table in the back, as he did more than a year ago when he first met Lewis here. Nate would order himself a scotch rocks, cross his legs, and wait patiently for the boy.

But upon stepping into the darkened bar and heading toward his usual table, Nate saw that Lewis was already there.

Nate halted in his tracks. The smell of cigarette smoke drifted around him. Lewis looked directly at Nate, smiled, and waved him over. Nate stepped toward the table. On it, Lewis had a bottle of beer set on a coaster before him, and on the other side was a dark drink in a short glass. Nate assumed it was the scotch he would have ordered.

"I thought you said you stopped drinking beer out of the bottle," Nate said.

"Naw." Lewis smiled, raising the bottle and taking a sip. "I just wanted to see you jump." He lowered the bottle. "Have a seat," Lewis said, nudging the chair across from him with the toe of his shoe, then gesturing toward it.

Nate sat. "I assume this is mine?"

"Scotch rocks, right?" Lewis said, in good spirits.

"Right." Nate picked up the glass with two fingers, examined it.

"Go ahead. I ain't spit in it or nothing."

Nate took a sip. It was good. The boy had obviously gotten the brand right. Nate settled into his chair a little more. It was early afternoon, so only a few patrons sat at the bar, hunched over their drinks.

Lewis took a swallow of his beer and then leaned over the table closer to Nate. "So how many times did you jack off to those photos of my girl?"

"What kind of sick motherfucker are you?" Nate said, keeping his voice down.

"I ain't sick, Nate. I just want you to know what's what. Things ain't the way they used to be, and what you really need to know is they ain't ever going to go back to being the same."

"Why are you with her?"

"What kind of question is that?" Lewis said.

"If it's the money, I got money."

Lewis laughed, banged the table with the flat of his hand, as though he could not control himself, then said with a straight face, "It ain't the money. Don't get me wrong, Nate. The money's nice. Whatever me or my child wants, Monica gets. But it's way more than that. It's love, Nate."

"You're just some down-on-his-luck thug off the street, looking for a warm spot for him and his bastard child to lie down in for a while," Nate said, feeling himself getting riled. "What the hell do you know about love?"

Lewis frowned and then worked a smile back to his face. "I ought to fuck you up for that comment, but I'm working on controlling my temper," Lewis said. "What I know about love is that when you have it, you don't pay some thug off the street to fuck your wife so you can lose it. I know that when a woman loves you, wants to give you everything she can, you don't kick her ass to the curb just because she can't have your fucking baby!" Lewis said, raising his voice.

Two of the men drinking at the bar looked over their shoulders at Lewis.

"I know that it's fucked up of you to try to come back and put yourself in that woman's life after she's finally able to get over your punk ass."

"I still love her," Nate said.

"Don't matter, 'cause she don't love you. Now get outta' here." Lewis raised his hand for the bartender. "Another beer," he yelled across the room, then slumped back in his chair.

Nate didn't move.

"You act like there's more to say. We done, motherfucker. Pull up from my table."

"Look, I'm sorry that got out of hand, and I'm sorry for referring to your daughter that way. That's not what I came here for."

"Then what?"

"I want to . . . ," Nate started, pausing, while the bartender set Lewis's beer down on the table. Lewis pulled a five and a single from his wallet and gave it to the bartender.

"Go on," Lewis said, taking a drink from his beer.

"I came here to ask you to leave her alone. Whatever you need, I'll provide for you. I'll set you up like I did last time, a place for you and your daughter to live. I even know the head of a construction company. He'll put you on right now, give you a steady income. You can start all over. It'll be a good life. All you have to do is leave Monica alone and promise not to come near her again."

"That's it?" Lewis said.

"That's all."

Lewis sat up in his chair, rubbed his chin like he was seriously thinking it over. "And you'd do all that. Buy me a house and everything?"

"Yeah," Nate said, feeling like this man might actually be willing to consider his proposition.

Lewis paused for another moment, then finally said, "The answer is no."

Nate stared at Lewis for a few seconds. "I see," he said, then dug into his back pocket for his wallet. "How much for the—"

"I got that. It's already paid for."

Nate stood, slipped the wallet back in his pants. "I asked my question, and you gave me an answer. I guess I'll leave now."

Lewis stared up at the man, emotionless. "Naw," Lewis said.

"What?"

"I don't believe you. I know who you are, been on the receiving end of what you'll do to get what you want."

"I don't know what you're talking about."

"Last year, I remember lying in an alley after getting my ass beat almost dead. Three, four men standing over me, wearing masks and all black. I was bleeding out my mouth, ribs felt broke, wondering if I was gonna make it, wondering who would do that to me. Then one of those men bent over, looked down at me, and pulled off his mask. He said not to fuck with his wife no more, or else next time I wouldn't live through it. That was you, Nate, remember?" Lewis said, looking up at Nate, a little bit of the smile still left on his face.

"Yeah," Nate said, his voice soft.

"A man that does all that to get what he wants doesn't just walk away after being told no."

"Things have happened. I've changed."

Lewis chuckled a little, took another sip. "Let's hope so, Nate. Because if you haven't, this time it's gonna be you looking up from the ground, bleeding."

28

Freddy sat low in his car behind the steering wheel, watching the man across the street.

"He tall, like six five, and skinny." The voice of the man from this morning echoed in Freddy's head.

"He like forty years old, always wears a dirty-ass T-shirt and blue pants. He got marks all over his face, and he walk wit' a limp. Everybody call him Notty."

This had to be him, Freddy thought, watching the man limp up to a boy standing on a corner, no older than fifteen. Notty handed the boy something, the boy handed something back, and Freddy knew it had to be drugs.

The man from this morning told Freddy that Notty was a junkie, had knocked more than a few old ladies over the head to keep himself high. Freddy grabbed his gun off the passenger seat of his car, slid it behind him in the waist of his jeans, then got out. He waited for two cars to pass, keeping a close eye on Notty, then crossed the street.

Notty was heading toward an alley, probably to shoot up,

Freddy thought. He followed the man, looking both ways before he stepped into the alley.

Freddy walked slowly, some thirty feet behind. The alley was filled with trash, boxes, Dumpsters. The buildings on either side had all been abandoned; broken windows dotted the facades. No one was in the alley except Notty and Freddy. Fifty yards into the alley, Notty stepped to the left, around a corner and out of sight.

Freddy continued walking, a little quicker now, till he got to a point only a few feet from where he'd seen Notty disappear.

He pressed himself against a wall, very near to Notty, and listened. Freddy heard the man breathing hard, heard him rustling about.

Pulling the gun from his jeans, Freddy exhaled, then jumped out from behind the wall, pointing the gun in front of him. Notty looked up, only slightly surprised. He was sitting on a crate, a rubber tourniquet tightened around his bicep, his teeth clamped down on the butt end of a hypodermic needle.

"What's up, motherfucker?" Freddy said. He didn't know why, but for some reason he was shaking, felt scared. Not of the man, but something else.

"Who is you?" Notty said after pulling the needle out his mouth. He was calmer than Freddy felt he should have been.

"You robbed my old lady."

"I robbed a lot of old ladies. That's what the fuck I do. Now I'm tryin' to get high here, and unless you got some specific bidness wit me," Notty said, standing, all six foot five of him, and stepping right in front of Freddy's gun, "I suggest you carry yo' little ass on."

Freddy stared at the man from behind the gun, both his hands shaking, causing the barrel of the gun to shake as well. Notty smiled, exposing three gaps where missing front teeth should have been. "Little bitch," Notty said, dismissing Freddy. "Tell your moms to stay off my streets, and next time she'll be all right." He moved back around to what he was doing and Freddy quickly reared back, swung the gun, and struck Notty as hard as he could across the jaw. The tall, wiry man stumbled on his feet, the band still tight around his bicep.

Freddy swung again, a wide sweeping blow, catching the wavering man on the side of the skull. Notty dropped to the ground. Freddy threw himself on top of him, straddled him. Notty threw up his arms, trying to block the blows Freddy was raining down on him.

He pounded Notty's forearms with the butt of the gun till they fell, then he slammed the gun down against the man's head, his face, his chest, his shoulders.

Freddy wielded the gun in a blind fury, till blood coated the gun, till he felt it splatter on his bare arms, on his face. The man stopped struggling, lay still under Freddy's weight. Freddy continued to assault him, yelling, pounding him with his two fists wrapped around the gun, over and over and over again.

Finally, the gun was over Freddy's head, about to come down once more, but Freddy stopped himself.

He was spent. He looked down at Notty's face. It was covered in blood, swollen, cut, unrecognizable.

Freddy didn't know if Notty was dead or alive. He rolled off him, stood, and then nudged the man with the toe of his work boot.

Notty did not move. Freddy kicked him again, and the man coughed, stirred, then moaned in pain.

Freddy pointed the gun down at the man's face.

The one eye of Notty's that was not swollen shut focused on the weapon. He slowly raised an arm, as if preparing to defend himself against a bullet.

Freddy stared down, his finger on the trigger, slowly applying more pressure. Suddenly he released it.

"You ever fuck with my moms again, you're dead."

29

Later that night, Nate was on the phone in his home office, talking with Abbey his investigator.

"So exactly what do you want from your ex-wife?" she asked Nate.

"I would like my money back. I just don't know how I'd go about getting it."

"We could do the same thing with her as we did with Tori. Instead of using one of your guys, maybe you could persuade her current boyfriend to work for you."

"No. That's what got me into all this to begin with."

"We could find someone to hack into her accounts and just take the money that way," Abbey suggested.

"That's just outright robbery. No, I won't stoop that low."

"Then it seems we'll have to take some time to think more on how to access her funds. But tell me this, is there anything as important to her as the money?"

Nate leaned back in his chair, rubbed a hand over his hair. "All I can think of is her business. When we were married, she always talked of having her own business. I would think that's very important to her."

"Is there some way that you could acquire it? I could find out if there are any back taxes owed on the property, if she's behind in any payments, check out the real-estate contracts, see if there are any loopholes. Maybe you can come in and take the buildings from under her."

This was all starting to sound pretty low down and underhanded to Nate, but he knew these were things he might have to do; he might have to do even worse.

"Sure, check all of that. Get back to me, tell me what our options are," Nate said, knowing there would be few, if any.

"Sure, Mr. Kenny. Good night."

Nate hung up the phone, closed the computer file he was working on, and opened up his e-mail account to check for new messages.

Nate hadn't heard from Monica after their brief meeting yesterday. He wondered what would happen if he called her at that moment. What would he say? What would be his new approach? He wasn't sure.

He would have to give that some more thought, he decided, glancing at his list of new e-mails. To his surprise, he saw another e-mail from Lewis. And yes, there was another tiny paper clip symbol beside it.

There was no subject. Nate scrolled down. There was no message either.

He moused the pointer arrow down to the attachment, held his finger just above the clicker, trying to decide if he really wanted to see what had been sent to him this time. He decided he needed to face it.

Nate clicked on the attachment, opening it up. The screen went black, and the video play screen popped up. Nate clicked the play arrow.

He saw a grainy close-up of Monica's eyes, her hair hanging

in her face. Then she moved back away from the lens, coming into focus, as if she had just clicked the camera on.

She smiled and moaned, bit her bottom lip as she retreated farther from the lens. Her sensual cry came through the speakers on Nate's desk. It sent a pain through his body he had not expected.

As the shot opened, Nate saw that his wife was naked, dripping with sweat, saw that somebody was behind her. It was Lewis. The man's deep voice spilled from the speakers now. He knelt behind Monica, grabbing her by her hips, ramming himself into her. Nate could hear the sweaty, slapping sounds of skin each time they collided.

"Shit baby, shit baby, shit!" the man yelled.

"Oh, god, oh god!" And that was Monica.

Nate turned away from the screen, shut his eyes tight, but he still heard their cries and moans.

He had to see this, deal with this, he told himself. It will strengthen his resolve to do whatever he had to do to get back at Monica for what she had put him through, what she was putting him through now. Nate turned back to the screen, slowly opened his eyes, clenched his teeth, and tried to watch as his ex-wife endured what looked to be the punishment Lewis was doling out to her. Then suddenly, Nate lunged across his desk, grabbed one of the speakers, yanked it from its input, and slung it across the room toward his office door. He did the same with the left speaker. Now there was no sound. He looked down at the screen again.

Lewis pulled out of Nate's wife, hard and dripping.

Monica turned to face him, crawled near him, and grabbed him between the legs.

"No," Nate said softly to himself.

Monica eagerly brought her face close, opened her mouth, was about to take the man in, but Nate quickly clicked the pause button.

The two bodies froze, Lewis, bushy headed, sweaty, naked on his knees, his erection jutting out before him. And Monica, on hands and knees, holding the man in her fist, her eyes looking up at him, her mouth open, seemingly wanting nothing more than to please this fool. What had this man done to his wife? Nate thought. What would she think of him if she knew that at this moment, Nate was viewing this recording?

Would she change her mind about marrying him?

Nate clicked off his computer and grabbed the car keys that were beside him on his desk, thinking maybe he should go find out.

30

"Lewis," Monica said, nudging him.

They were sitting on the living room sofa, watching a movie, Lewis's arm thrown around Monica's neck, his head resting on her shoulder.

"Wake up!"

"What?" Lewis said, quickly lifting his head, blinking weary eyes, and wiping the back of his hand across his lips.

"You keep falling asleep. Why don't you just go up to bed?"

"What time is it?"

"Five minutes till ten," Monica said, after glancing at the clock.

"But the movie, it's almost over."

"It's only halfway through. Go to bed, Lewis. I'll be up when it's over."

"You sure?"

But before Monica could answer, her cell phone started ringing.

"Who's calling me this late?" she asked aloud, pulling herself

from the sofa and walking over to grab the phone off the enter-
tainment center shelf. Monica looked at the caller ID. She didn't
recognize the number but flipped the phone open and said,
"Hello."

There was no response.

"Hello," Monica said again.

"Monica," a voice said. It was Nate.

Monica's heart suddenly started to race.

"I know that Lewis is probably with you, so just act like
you're talking to Tabatha."

"Tabatha," Monica said, her voice shaky. "What's going on,
girl?"

"I need to talk to you," Nate said.

"Can't it wait till tomorrow? Lewis and I are watching a
movie."

"I don't care about that. I need to talk to you now. I need to
see you."

"That's crazy," Monica said, feeling uneasy, looking over and
seeing that Lewis was staring right at her.

"I know I shouldn't be calling you, but I need to talk. Can
you get away?"

"No. I told you that—"

"Tell him Tabatha's car broke down. She got it towed and
you're going to pick her up and give her a ride home."

Monica couldn't speak, just held the phone to her ear, thinking it was going to slip, considering how much sweat was now
coating her palm.

"If you don't," Nate said, "I swear, I'm coming over there to say
what I have to say, and we can just deal with it all at your place."

"Where did it break down?" Monica suddenly said.

"Good. I'll be at the park over on Clark Street. You remember the one we always used to go to?"

"Yeah. I know where that is," Monica said, glancing nervously at Lewis. "Okay, bye."

"So who was it?" Lewis said.

"Tabatha."

"I thought you said you ain't recognize the number."

"She called from a pay phone," Monica said, thinking quickly. "Because her cell was dead."

"Is she okay?" Lewis stood, walking toward Monica, concerned.

"Yeah. She just needs me to pick her up." Monica mechanically walked toward the closet to grab her coat and bag.

"Then I'll go with you."

"No!" Monica said, spinning, overreacting. "I mean . . . you have to stay here and watch Layla. She's asleep. Wouldn't make sense to wake her when I'm just going to go pick up Tabatha, drive her home, and come right back. You know what I mean?"

"Yeah," Lewis said, not seeming to believe her. "I know what you mean."

Fifteen minutes later, Nate's cell phone rang.

"Hello," Nate said.

"Where are you? It's dark and I don't see you. I'm not getting out of this car if you aren't out there," Monica said.

"Hold on." Nate stepped out of the swing he was sitting on, then walked toward the middle of the park and waved an arm toward Monica's car. "Do you see me now?" he said into the phone as he headed toward her car.

"Yeah."

Nate examined Monica's Jaguar as she climbed out of it.

"See you bought yourself a new car."

"No. It was your money, so I guess you did," Monica said. "Why the hell are you calling me?"

"I need to talk."

"We did all the talking we needed to do at your place."

"No. There's more." Nate started walking back toward the swings.

"Where are you going?" Monica said, looking around as if worried she'd be kidnapped if she remained there alone. She quickly followed behind Nate.

"Remember this park? We'd come here all the time, just sit, watch the kids play, and dream about the family that we'd have."

"I remember. But that was then."

"The family we could have had if you would have just let me get you pregnant right after we got married, like you promised."

Monica halted behind him. "I didn't come here for you to badger me about a mistake I made years ago."

"I know," Nate said, turning. "I'm sorry. I didn't come here for that, either. I want you back, Monica. It's that simple."

Monica looked at him strangely. She did not speak for a moment, and then finally said, "Then Lewis was right. He said that's why you wanted to meet."

"Okay, so what? It doesn't negate the fact that I've been doing a lot of thinking and like I said, I want you—"

"You can't have me back. I'm fucking engaged!"

Nate looked away, chuckled a little. "Are you in love with him?"

"That's none of your business."

Nate walked right up on her, asked the question again. "Are you in love with him?"

Monica stared directly into Nate's eyes but did not answer.

"I see," Nate said. "So, do you still have feelings for me?"

"Not the kind of feelings that would make me want to come back to you."

"What changed?"

"You. The shit you did."

"You know why I did it."

"Because you're a selfish bastard."

"No. Because I wanted children and you stole that from me."

"If you see me being unable to have children as stealing something from you, then so be it. But fact is, nothing's changed, so why in the hell would you want me back?"

"Something *has* changed."

"What?"

Nate wanted to tell her about Nathaniel, that he had adopted the child, but this wasn't the time. Seeing the boy with her own eyes would be much more powerful than just hearing about him.

"I have. I'm a different man. You come back to me, you'll find that out. I promise," Nate said, taking one step closer to her.

"I can't."

"Lewis," Nate sighed. "He's nothing, probably was a thief, a drug dealer, a purse snatcher before I found him. But the most important thing I want to ask you is, what does he add to your life? What does he bring that you don't already have? Can you grow with him?"

"I don't have to answer those questions for you. All I'll say is that he's a good man, and he has a beautiful daughter whom he's entrusted me with."

"I see," Nate said, nodding his head. "It's the little girl. You can't have any children, so you've taken her as your own. You love the child, don't you?"

"With everything in me," Monica said, honestly.

"So it really isn't because you love him," Nate said, coming even closer to her.

"I do," Monica said, not taking a single step back.

"Not the way you loved me. You can't."

Nate stared deeply into Monica's eyes, felt he was making some sort of connection. "We were together four years, not like you and Lewis. We married each other because we loved each other, not because you were frustrated and I was needy." Nate placed himself right in front of his ex-wife, their bodies practically touching. "Your marriage will be based on last resort, ours was on love."

"If you loved me, why did you—"

Suddenly, Nate slipped a hand behind Monica's neck, pulled her into him, and pressed his mouth to hers. For the slightest moment, he felt no resistance at all. Her lips parted, his tongue touched hers, and then she pulled away, stepped back, and slapped him hard across the face.

Nate stumbled backward, tripped and almost fell to the grass in the middle of the darkened park. He recovered, rubbing the side of his face. "I'm sorry. I shouldn't have done that."

Monica stood there, breathing heavily, anguished, near tears. She didn't speak.

"What are you thinking?" Nate said, concerned.

Monica wiped at her eyes, and then said, "I never want you to come near me again. Do you hear me?"

"But Monica—"

"Do you hear me?" she yelled.

"Yes."

She turned and stormed off toward her car.

After Monica peeked into Layla's room to check on her, she slipped quietly into her own bedroom without turning on any of the lights. Lewis was there in bed, sleeping.

Monica walked cautiously across the carpet, over to the chair in the corner, and quickly disrobed. As she reached around to unclasp her bra, a quick image of Nate kissing her in the park flashed through her head. She shut her eyes, removed and dropped her bra to the chair, pushed down her panties, and slid into a nightgown. Monica climbed into bed with Lewis, hating the fact that the image had skirted through her mind at least a dozen times on the drive back home. Monica settled in, turning on her side, away from Lewis. She closed her eyes, then jumped as she felt a hand on her hip.

"You okay?" Lewis said, nuzzling up behind her.

"Yeah. Just tired is all." Monica inched just the slightest bit away from her fiancé and pulled the blankets over her shoulder, preparing to deal with the thoughts she knew she'd be wrestling with all night.

"How is Tabatha?" Lewis asked.

"Huh?"

"Tabatha. Her car stopped. You went to pick her up, right?"

"Oh!" Monica said, completely forgetting about the lie. "She's . . . she's fine. She should get her car back in the morning."

Lewis paused, and then finally said, "That's good."

31

Nate lay in bed, the lights off, the blankets kicked halfway off the bed. The cordless phone was pressed to his ear, held in place by his shoulder, as he slid his fist quickly up and down his erection.

"Do you feel it, baby?" Daphanie said, her voice throaty, sensual. "I'm riding you, riding that dick!"

"I feel it!" Nate said, stroking himself harder, on the verge of exploding.

"I'm about to come for you, baby," Daphanie said, panting. "You wanna come for me? Please come for me, baby."

"I'm going to . . . I'm going to," Nate said, feeling his body tightening, the orgasm tunneling through him, about to spill out of him. "I'm coming!" he yelled, trying to contain the explosion within his fist.

"Me too! I'm coming, too!" Nate heard Daphanie cry on the other end of the phone, thousands of miles away. "Oh, baby. Oh, baby," she purred. "I miss you so much."

"I miss you, too," Nate said, feeling the fluid trying to seep out of his closed hand. He glanced at his alarm clock. It was 1:42 A.M. "Hold on a second," Nate said. "It's not long after midnight here. You aren't at work, are you?"

He heard Daphanie chuckle into the phone. "I needed it now, baby, and my office door is locked. Besides, my meeting isn't for another five minutes."

"Woman, are you crazy?"

"Only for you, baby. I was thinking, maybe next weekend I could fly back. It would cost an arm and a leg, and with flight time I would only be there about eighteen hours, but it would be—"

"No!" Nate said, a little too quickly. "I mean, I might have to head to the West Coast for this buyout thing next weekend, and I would hate for you to travel all that distance and me not be here."

"You don't miss me?"

"Like you wouldn't believe. But two weeks will pass before you know it."

"Okay. You're right," Daphanie said, still sounding disappointed. "Let me get cleaned up before someone comes banging on my door. Love you, sweetie. And give Nathaniel a kiss for me."

"Sure thing, baby. Love you, too," Nate said, pulling the phone from his ear and ending the call.

In the bathroom, standing before the sink, washing himself off, the smile that had been on his face after hanging up from Daphanie quickly disappeared. Although he had loved hearing from her, was crazy about what a sexual being she was, Nate was angry. He tried to deny it, but he knew he was thinking about his ex-wife more than he should, considering that the woman he had fantasized about while pleasuring himself wasn't Daphanie, but Monica.

32

I hate him," Monica said, pacing back and forth across the alley in back of her store.

Tabatha stood casually against the brick wall behind Monica, puffing on a cigarette. "You don't hate him."

"I do," Monica said, stopping in front of her friend, looking her square in the eyes. "I fucking do."

"Because he kissed you."

"As if he hadn't already disrespected my relationship by calling me like that, saying he didn't care that I was engaged to Lewis—he goes and kisses me."

"Did you like it?"

"What?"

"You heard me. Did you like it?"

"I won't dignify that question with a response. To think that I was trying to help him with his company, he goes and does something like that."

"It's not that big a deal, Monica. The man kissed you. You guys did that all the time when you were married."

"When we were married," Monica clarified. "I'm pissed! Give me one of those cigarettes."

"No. I will not allow a young innocent to start this disgusting, life-threatening habit," Tabatha said, coolly blowing smoke out of her mouth and nose. "Could it be you're pissed because you have questions about Lewis, now that Nate is trying to stake his claim?"

"Fuck Nate's claim. He has no claim!"

"But what if he's really trying to get you back. You don't want to think about it? You had a great marriage before the baby thing came up. Now that that's over, you don't think you all could recapture what you had?"

"What the fuck is it with you and Nate?" Monica said, turning to Tabatha. "I'm with Lewis now. I'm going to marry Lewis."

"And once you're married, you'll still have all the problems that you two have been having. You'll still have the arguments, the differences you have, the fact that you question if he's enough, if he does enough, will he ever amount to anything? I'm just saying, with Nate, you won't have those questions."

"I know I won't. Because, like I said, I'm with Lewis."

"Fine," Tabatha said, waving the conversation off and changing the subject. "You think Lewis suspected something last night?"

"I don't think so. What do you think?" Monica said.

"Well, he called my cell phone just like you said he would—to see if what you had told him was legit. It's a good thing you called me and let me know not to answer. How did he respond when you got back?"

"He was pretty much asleep. He asked me were you okay. I told him yeah, and that was it."

"Good," Tabatha said, flicking her butt across the alley. "Then you have nothing to worry about."

33

Lewis sat in front of the reception-area computer screen at Freddy's uncle's management company. He typed in a Web site address and waited for the screen to display.

"Yes, I'll let him know," Freddy said, then hung up the office phone. He walked over to Lewis, stood behind him. "What are you doing?"

From the counter, Lewis picked up last month's Sprint cell phone statement he had taken from Monica's home office that morning. He typed in her account number. "What does it look like I'm doing?" Lewis said.

"Paying a bill. But you don't pay bills. Where would you get the money?"

"From your girlfriend," Lewis said. "I ain't paying no bills."

Lewis clicked on a tab and a call history list appeared.

"Aw, dude," Freddy said, seeing the list. "You checking Monica's cell phone records. She said she went to get Tabatha last night. Why can't you just believe that?"

"'Cause I know it ain't true. I could tell by the funny way she was talking on the phone that something was up. I ain't crazy," Lewis said, looking at the long list of ten-digit numbers.

"Nobody saying you are. Just trust the woman, 'cause I bet she's being up-front with you."

Lewis looked over his shoulder at Freddy, a serious expression on his face. "Then you'd lose." Lewis clicked on a number, highlighted it. "That's last night's date, 9:56 P.M. You see that incoming number? Look at this piece of paper."

Freddy looked at the paper on which Lewis had earlier jotted down a number from his outgoing cell phone call list.

"That's that motherfucker Nate's cell number. And again," Lewis said, pointing at the screen, "Twenty minutes later. She called his ass again. I told you, Freddy. What did I say? She's cheating on me!"

"She's not cheating on you. She was gone for an hour. What could she have done in an hour?"

"You said it only takes you five minutes to bust a nut."

"Well . . . ," Freddy said, hunching his shoulders. "That still don't mean nothing. He could've called without her even expecting it. Maybe she lied to you because she didn't want to have you thinking it was something more than it was. Maybe she just went to tell that fool to never call her again."

"If that happened, she could've just told me," Lewis said, standing from his chair.

"But she didn't. And it's probably all over now. Just leave it alone."

"I told that motherfucker some shit would go down if he pursued this," Lewis said, walking through the office, slamming his fist into the palm of his other hand.

"Relax, dude. I'm sure there ain't nothing to it."

"Naw. He forcing my hand. I gotta do something."

"Leave it be, man. Leave it be!"

Lewis walked quickly back over to Freddy, stood in his face. "Who's the most important person in the world to you?"

"My moms. You know that."

"For me, after my daughter, it's Monica. Your moms got jumped the other day? I know you gonna look for the fool who did that."

"Yeah. I guess I probably will."

"And I know you gonna teach him a lesson when you find him."

Freddy didn't answer, just looked away for a moment.

"So what you expect me to do when I know this punk ain't doing nothing but trying to pull my damn card? When I told him to expect consequences if he acts a fool. Just what do you expect me to do, Freddy?"

Freddy shook his head, dragged a hand down his face, then reluctantly said, "Handle your business."

"You damn right! And I'm gonna want your help on that, you know."

"So what you talking about?"

"You know what I'm talking about. Beatin' that motherfucker down."

Freddy shook his head. "Man, I don't know if all that's required. Maybe you should just give him another warning."

"Hell with a warning. I did that. It's time to deliver. You down or what?"

"All right," Freddy said. "But what are you gonna do about Monica?"

Lewis lowered his head, sighed sadly. "I don't even feel like looking at her, knowing what I found out. It's best I just stay away from her till we handle this business with Nate."

34

M r. Ford," the youthful-looking secretary said from behind her desk, "Dr. James will see you now."

Freddy lifted himself from the chair in the reception area and walked toward the hallway leading to the attorneys' offices. He wore a white shirt, a blue tie, and black slacks and shoes, all bought from Target yesterday and packed and carried with him today to work. For the past two days he had been calling Kia's father at work, unable to get him. He decided there would be no other way but to go down there and see him face to face.

Freddy stopped at the office door, read what was before him: Alexander James, J.D., Ph.D., Attorney-at-Law. "Whatever," Freddy said to himself, and then knocked.

"Come in," a voice instructed from behind the dark, wooden door.

Freddy entered the huge office, paneled in the same dark wood as the door. In the center of the room was a desk. A large man was standing behind it, wearing a pin-striped suit and glasses.

"Have a seat," Dr. James said. "I have five minutes for you. Next time you'll call and make an appointment."

Freddy took the seat before the desk. "I tried to make an—"

"What is it you want?" Dr. James said, sitting, pulling his glasses off, and devoting all of his attention to Freddy.

"You can't stop paying Kia's tuition."

"I can do whatever I want. And as long as she's seeing you, I will."

"You'd stop her from getting her education just because you don't like me?"

"That's correct."

"She's having my baby."

"She hasn't given birth to it yet."

Freddy looked intently at the man, understanding that he had not given up on the hope of Kia aborting Freddy's child. Freddy clenched his teeth, trying to stop himself from voicing just what he thought of the man before him. "Mr. James, I love your daughter."

"It's Dr. James, and I don't care how you feel about her."

"I'm doing right by Kia, Dr. James," Freddy said, trying to appeal to the man. "I'm working every day. I've taken classes. I plan on opening up my own real-estate company. I'm going to be a success. I'm going to make your daughter proud of me. I don't know why you won't just give me a chance. I haven't done anything wrong."

Dr. James put his glasses back on, reached into a bottom desk drawer, pulled out some papers, and set them on his desk. "I'll tell you what you've done. Close to twenty years ago, you killed your own father. You were sent to a mental institution for the next six years, and after that term, you were wrongly proclaimed cured. You went to high school, graduated with

straight D's, then started and either left, or was fired from—"
Dr. James silently went down the list, counting to himself "—
sixteen jobs, before working for your uncle. Now let me tell
you what you haven't done," Dr. James said, looking Freddy
squarely in the face. "You have not gotten an education. You
have not worked a job requiring intelligence beyond the
eighth-grade level. You have not secured your own housing.
You have not distinguished yourself as being anything other
than the average, do-nothing, learn nothing, hand-out nigga
on the street that plagues not only the black community, but
the black race. And you definitely have not earned the right
even to stand in the same neighborhood as my little girl, let
alone impregnate her, fool her into believing there is a future
with you, which will ultimately ruin her life. Now you have the
nerve to come down here, sit before me, and tell me who you
are, what you're going to do, when I've known since I first laid
eyes on you, you aren't capable of accomplishing anything,"
Dr. James said, removing his glasses and standing again. "Get
out of my sight before I'm forced to do something I may
regret."

Freddy did not move from his seat, did not flinch, and just
stared up at the big man. Dr. James had just made a threat.
Freddy did not have his gun, but upon walking in, he had noticed the huge, brick-like paperweight that sat on Dr. James's
desk.

A split-second image of himself, straddling the big man
behind his desk, bashing his head in with the blood-covered paperweight, flashed through Freddy's mind.

"Are you getting up, or do I need to help you?" Dr. James
said, starting to move from around the desk.

Freddy slowly rose from the chair, turned, and headed quietly for the door. He opened it, but did not leave before saying,
"I came here trying to earn your respect. You don't want to
give it to me. That's cool. Everything I need, Kia gives to me.

But I'm just telling you, things gonna be kind of crazy at the family reunions, cause I'm gonna ask Kia to marry me one day, and something tells me she's gonna say yes."

Freddy smiled at the look of shock on Dr. James's face, then gently closed the door.

35

The next morning, Monica opened her eyes but did not feel Lewis's body beside her. Yesterday evening, she had called him for the fifth time at Layla's request, before Monica and the little girl had sat down to eat dinner.

She rang his phone, but no one answered. Lewis didn't want to speak to her, Monica figured.

At midnight, she lay in bed, falling off to sleep. The phone rang. Monica turned, reached over, pressed the receiver to her face.

"I'll be home later." Lewis's voice was deep. He sounded sad. "Is Layla okay?"

"She asked about you. Are *you* okay?"

It took him a moment before saying, "I'm cool. I'll try not to wake you when I come in."

Monica wanted to talk some more, but Lewis hung up.

Now when Monica walked into the kitchen after showering and dressing for work, Layla was in her high chair, Lewis sitting beside her, both eating the breakfast he had made them. Lewis didn't look up.

"Morning, Monica," Layla said.

Monica walked over, stood between Layla's and Lewis's chairs. She kissed the child and then pressed a hand onto Lewis's shoulder. "Can we talk?" she said softly to him.

Lewis set his knife and fork on the rim of his plate. "I got a lot of stuff I have to do today. Can it be this evening?"

"Sure," Monica said.

She did not eat, not wanting to deal with the attitude Lewis obviously had. Monica simply kissed Layla on the cheek good-bye, grabbed her purse, and walked out to her car.

After stepping out of the house, Monica noticed an aging, pale green Ford sitting across the street.

She had seen that car at least three times before. What struck her as odd was that the car was never empty. There was always an older lady with graying hair sitting behind the wheel, staring out at Monica. As the same lady was doing now.

Monica stopped in midstride, thinking of walking across the street and approaching the woman, but deciding against it. She had better things to worry about than some lady who probably spent all of her days sitting in front of one stranger's house or another.

An hour later, Monica pulled her car up to the curb and stopped on the west side of the park where she had met Nate the other night. There was something going on with Lewis. He had one of his attitudes, and Monica was just not in the mood to be babying him. She wondered if it had anything to do with the other night when she supposedly picked up Tabatha.

Sure it did. He was mad that she didn't take him with her, but he couldn't have known the real reason for that.

He would just have to get over it. She wasn't going to let him stress her out, and that was one of the reasons Monica came back out to this park, to relax and forget about that stuff before work. Monica looked out the window at the vast grassy area, shaded by huge oak trees, and the towering Chicago high-rise condominiums. It was 7:30 A.M. The time when parents took their children for walks before school and seniors marched in couples, getting their daily exercise. Monica stepped out of her car and started to stroll slowly down one of the paved paths that led through the park, toward the swings, where parents stood watching their children play.

All of a sudden, Nate came to mind. She wondered if she had been too hard on him. Monica stopped at an empty bench and sat down, feeling sorry she had said those things to him. She breathed deep the fresh morning air. After another couple of minutes, she stood, told herself she would walk through the play area, probably wave at a few of the kids, and decide whether this was a place she could take Layla in the future.

As she walked, she thought that maybe later she would ring Nate and apologize.

He was once her husband, and just like he said, if things had worked out, it would have been the two of them standing just outside that play area, like the parents Monica was watching right now.

She was fifty or so feet away from the yelling, laughing kids playing on the monkey bars when she took a second look at one of the parents. At first Monica thought the tall, brown-skinned man resembled Nate just a little, but now she realized it was him. Monica closed the distance between them by half. He had not noticed her, for he seemed deeply occupied with the play of the children.

She wondered what he was doing here amidst the group of a

dozen or so parents. Then she remembered how Nate had told her, when they thought she was pregnant, that he used to go to the window of the newborn nursery and watch the babies, eagerly anticipating the birth of his own.

That's what he was doing now, Monica believed, watching the children play, still wishing he had his own. Monica felt momentary failure deep within her. She forced it away, walked closer to her ex-husband, and said, "Nate?" Nate turned, appearing more shocked than she expected. He quickly looked back out toward the children playing, then back to her as she approached.

"What are you doing here?" she asked.

"Just . . . enjoying the morning. I still come here sometimes," he said, sounding uncertain.

"I can understand why."

There was a long moment of silence, and then Monica said, "About the other night. I didn't mean what I said. You know . . . the part about . . . I . . ."

"Don't worry about it," Nate said, trying to smile but failing. "I understand. You were mad. So it's fine. Okay?" Nate said, glancing over at the children again.

"Okay, good. I was going to call you today and tell you, but this works out just fine," she said, smiling.

"Yeah."

"Okay then, I'll see you around."

"Yeah," Nate said.

Monica turned, hearing the kids behind her still yelling, their voices loud, one of them calling, "Daddy!" to one of the parents.

Monica was glad she had seen Nate this morning, but something didn't seem quite right with him, so she decided she would make sure he was fine. When she turned around, she saw Nate lift a child from over the short rail that bordered the play area and set him on the ground in front of him. Nate looked at the child's hands, pulled a packet of Wet-Naps from his pocket, kneeled down, and started to clean them.

"So who is this?" Monica said, after she had walked back unnoticed by Nate.

After looking up, Nate quickly stood, holding on to the boy's hand. He didn't speak a word.

"Nate?" Monica said, looking at the little brown-skinned, curly headed boy. She felt that there was something very familiar about him.

"Mommy!" the boy said all of a sudden.

Shocked, Monica looked at Nate, then back at the boy.

"Mommy!" he said again, and instantly Monica knew who the child was.

"Nathaniel?" she said to Nate.

"Okay, Nathaniel," Nate said, picking the boy up in his arms. Nathaniel smiled at Monica with his huge, dark eyes.

Monica was crushed. "It's him, isn't it?"

"I'm sorry I didn't tell you. It was supposed to happen the other night, but . . . I wasn't expecting your guest, and . . . I didn't want my son around him."

"Your son," Monica said wistfully, taking one of the boy's hands in hers.

"You're my mommy," Nathaniel said again, squeezing two of Monica's fingers.

"Why is he saying that?" Monica asked.

"Because it's what I've always told him."

"Why?"

"Because it's what I believed should have been. I'm sorry," Nate said, sounding sincere. "Maybe I shouldn't have told him that."

"No," Monica said, shaking her head, feeling emotions she wasn't comfortable with. "Why now? When I came to you when our marriage was failing . . . when I brought the idea to you . . ."

"I know," Nate said. "But I was wrong then. When you left, I realized how much. So I adopted him, and I've never made a better decision in my life. When I told you the other night that I was a different man, Nathaniel is the reason why."

Monica just stared at Nate with his . . . son. The happy family she should have been a part of, but wasn't. She felt tricked by Nate yet again. For some reason she felt left out. "What am I supposed to say to this, Nate?"

"I don't know."

"Should this mean something to me?"

"I don't know."

"It can't. It doesn't," Monica said, feeling a single, thin tear roll down her cheek. "Nothing has changed. This means nothing to me."

"I know."

"I'm happy for you, though."

"Thank you."

"Good-bye, Nate. Good-bye, Nathaniel," Monica said, turning, quickly walking away, faintly hearing the child ask his father, "Why is Mommy leaving?"

36

All day, Monica found herself thinking about Nate and his son, Nathaniel, the boy who could have been her son as well.

She had also been thinking about the conversation she'd had with Nate the other night in the park. She had been bothered so much by these two things that at lunch Monica left the store and found herself sitting in Tabatha's living room, talking to her friend on her day off. Monica had told Tabatha how she had bumped into Nate this morning, how she had met his adopted son.

"He just seemed different," Monica told Tabatha. "He seemed settled, and content, and more fulfilled than I've ever seen him."

"So?" Tabatha said.

"He seems the way I knew he would have been if I would have given him the child he wanted."

"And how is that?"

"I don't know," Monica said, smiling uncomfortably. "Perfect. He was a good man before, but there was always something missing, that thing he longed for. Now . . ."

"With Nathaniel, he seems to have found it," Tabatha finished for Monica.

"Yeah."

"I say again, so?"

"I know I told you that I don't want you to talk about my situation with Lewis anymore, but I want you to tell me what you honestly think of it. I want you to tell me how I'm perceived by our friends, by our business associates."

Tabatha stood from the sofa. "Why would you want to hear that? You aren't going to do nothing but marry Lewis anyway."

"You don't know that."

"You're scared," Tabatha said, sitting back down again. "You're frightened to death of being alone, otherwise you wouldn't be with Lewis. You two have nothing in common."

"We both like the same foods. We like some of the same TV shows. And every now and then we have a good time together."

"You probably have that in common with every other man in Chicago, Monica. What do you have in common that matters? You have a master's degree, he has a high school diploma. You own your own business, he works part-time. You like to talk business and politics, he likes to talk sports and rap music."

"That doesn't mean I can't love him," Monica said defensively.

"No. It doesn't mean that. But relationships are difficult enough with someone you share similar interests with. Why make things harder for yourself with someone like Lewis. Monica, look," Tabatha said, scooting closer to her on the sofa. "You wanted to know what people think of the man you chose to be with. After being with Nate, people think you're slumming. They think you've taken in a charity case, someone less than what you deserve, because you've been hurt and you don't want the risk of being hurt again by someone on your level."

"That's not true," Monica said.

"The reason why Lewis doesn't like accompanying you to

business functions is because he has nothing to say. He feels out of place around all those executives and corporate folks, talking about things he has no clue about." Tabatha paused for a moment, looking at her friend with compassion. "Monica, you marry this man, all he's going to do is keep you from going as far as you can go."

"That's not true."

"You might want to expand your business, but he'll try to stop you, because he won't want you to become more successful than you already are. You might want to go back to school to get your Ph.D., but he might not want you to, because the gap in your education is already wide enough."

Monica dropped her face in her hands. "It sounds like something Nate said the other night. He asked me did I expect to grow with Lewis? I couldn't answer him."

"I think Nate still loves you."

"Don't say that. I don't need to hear that right now."

"Why not? Because you still have feelings for him? Because you know he's a better man than Lewis could ever be, even after the stunt he pulled last year?"

"No," Monica said, looking up at Tabatha. "Because Lewis accepted me when Nate didn't. Because Lewis gave me his child when he knew I couldn't have one of my own. I can't abandon him just because he doesn't have a degree or watch CNN. He was the man who was there for me during a time when I had no one else."

"I'm sorry to say, but that time has gone, baby, and maybe Lewis should be gone too. You know what I mean?"

Monica looked up sadly at her friend but did not say a word.

37

Wearing their blue work shirts, their names sewn onto the breast pockets, Lewis and Freddy painted the basement window frames of a twelve-unit apartment building Freddy's uncle managed.

Freddy had been quiet for the better part of the day.

The words that Kia's father had said had been constantly ringing in Freddy's skull since his meeting with the man. He had repeated the insults almost verbatim to Kia last night as they lay in each other's arms.

"Don't ever listen to a word he says, okay?" Kia said, her soft hand caressing the side of Freddy's face.

"But is he wrong?"

"You're doing things, baby. You are."

"Enough to be with someone like you?"

"Yes," Kia said.

Freddy didn't believe her. But oddly enough, Freddy found himself both thankful to and resentful of the man. The negative things Dr. James had said to him would only make Freddy work harder to prove that fool wrong. But the way he'd looked at Freddy, the way he spoke down to him, reminded Freddy of the way his own father used to treat him. He should have grabbed the man in his office, squeezed him around the throat till he took back every negative word he had said. But Freddy shook that idea out of his head.

Violent thoughts were not good. They only triggered more violent thoughts. The image of Notty's bloody face flashed through Freddy's mind.

Even though he had beaten the addict down days ago, the image still haunted Freddy. Now, when Freddy looked down, he had to tell himself the splotches of white paint on his hands and arms weren't red, weren't blood from the man he had almost killed.

"Why you so quiet over there?"

Freddy glanced at Lewis, then turned back to the up and down motions of his paintbrush. "I'm just not saying nothing."

"Naw. It's more than that. What's up?"

Freddy set his brush on the edge of the can of paint, stood from his knees. "I'm thinking you should rethink this beating you planning on giving, ol' boy."

Lewis stopped painting, set his brush on the rim of the same can. "You ain't punkin' out on me, are you? That ain't like you, man."

"Naw, I ain't punkin' out. But what did the man do? Make a phone call 'cause he interested in your woman. He deserve a beat down for that?"

"Yeah," Lewis said, walking over to Freddy. "Hell yeah. And payback for when he got me."

"And what if it get out of hand? What if you climb on that fool, whuppin' him so good that you can't stop yourself, and you look down and find you almost killed him?"

"That's why you gonna be there. To pull me off before that happens."

"And what if it goes the other way? Say he whuppin' on you?"

Lewis smiled, laughed a little. "Guarantee that won't happen. But again, that's why you gonna be there."

Freddy shook his head, looked down at his hands again, attempted to rub the white spots from his wrists. "Tell you the truth, I don't know what good gonna come from this. Maybe you should give this a little more thought, not do it today."

Lewis shook his head, seeming disgusted with Freddy. "I tell you what. Today, after I get off work, I'm going to this man's house. I'm going to hang in the bushes, just like he did me. And when he comes home, I'm gonna jump his ass and beat him down till all he can do is crawl to his phone and dial nine one one, just like he did me. Now you either gonna be with me, or you ain't."

"Lewis, you don't know what you could be starting by doing this. Something tells me you ain't just gonna whup his ass and he gonna just go away."

"Freddy—either you with me, or you ain't."

Freddy paused, and then said, "Yeah. I'm with you."

38

Four hours later, when Nate pulled up in his driveway, he was happy, almost merry.

It was because of what had happened this morning with Monica.

After being introduced to Nathaniel, after hearing the boy call her Mommy, and after the look on her face, Monica told Nate that none of that made any difference, that nothing had changed.

Nate didn't believe that. Monica had been moved. A wall had come down somewhere within her, which he knew would ultimately make his job easier.

Even though Nate wasn't ready at the moment it took place, Monica had finally met Nathaniel, and she liked him.

The only problem was that Nathaniel had instantly taken a liking to Monica as well. The boy could not stop talking about "his mommy" on the way to nursery school this morning.

It was the reason why Nate had called Mrs. Weatherly from work and told her that he would pick up his son today.

Nate wanted to see if it was just a passing infatuation. He worried that if his son got too attached to Monica, Nathaniel might truly be hurt once Nate followed through with his intentions and Nathaniel could no longer see his "mother."

Nate looked up into the rearview mirror at his son, strapped in his car seat.

"I like Mommy," Nathaniel said. To Nate's disappointment, it was something Nathaniel had been saying the entire trip home.

"Do you like Mommy?" the child asked.

"How about I answer that question a little later, because right now, we should go inside," Nate said, pulling his key from the ignition.

"Okay, Daddy."

Nate pushed opened the door, stood, closed it, and reached out for the handle on the back door when he heard the flapping sound of quickly moving rubber-soled shoes racing toward him.

Nate spun around to catch the blurred glimpse of a fist flying at him.

He was struck across the jaw. Pain erupted in his head, stars exploding behind his eyes, as he fell to one knee.

Nate tried to recover, attempted to rise, but was kicked in the gut.

He flipped over onto his back, his head cracking against the concrete.

Nate thought he would vomit, or black out, but he fought not to lose consciousness.

His son was in the car, and there was a man, maybe two, on top of him now, beating him. Nate had no idea why, but he turned over on his stomach and tried to pull himself to his hands and knees, tried to fight back.

Thoughts started to run wild through Nate's head. He was worth millions. Maybe the thugs beating him were trying to take his son, hold the child for ransom.

Nate managed to lift himself to his knees, his forehead pressed against the ground, the taste of blood in his mouth, spilling over his lips.

He raised his head, opened his eyes to see a man standing over him wearing a black ski mask.

"My s—" Nate attempted to say, to tell the man that his son was in the car. But the man jumped, kicking Nate in the face.

Nate whirled on his knees in a half circle, blood spraying from his mouth, his arms flying out before him. He crashed on his belly again.

"Ain't you gonna get some of this?" Nate heard the man say to his accomplice.

Then Nate thought he heard the sound of his son crying. Nate began crawling toward the car, worried that Nathaniel would be heard, yanked out, taken from him. He was thankful for the dark tint on the glass, hoping they would not see the boy.

Nate crawled some more, his mouth full of blood now. He spit and slowly opened one of his swelling eyes.

He saw another man wearing a mask, standing hesitant some ten feet away from him.

Nate reached out a hand to him, as if feeling that the man wanted this no more than Nate did. Feeling as though this man could save him.

But his hand was stomped on by the first assailant.

Nate screamed out in agony, feeling a bone snap under the pressure. His cry was cut short as he was kicked in the stomach again, in the ribs over and over. Finally he was dealt an overwhelming blow to his head by the man's boot.

This time the world went silent, except for the sound of his rapidly beating heart. He no longer heard the man yelling, nor his son screaming. Everything was threatening to go dark, but Nate fought again to stay conscious. He could not black out, knowing that his son could be gone when he awakened.

Nate stared out of his ballooning eyes. He saw a pair of legs in front of him, and then farther away, the pair of legs belonging to the other man.

The man closest to Nate came nearer, stooped down so that he could be almost face to face with Nate—eye to eye.

"I told you not to fuck with her no more, but you didn't listen," the man said through the black mask. "You think things are the same, but they're not." The man peeled the black mask up from under his chin to fully expose his identity. It was Lewis.

He said, "Don't make me come back here," and then he spat in Nate's face.

Nate watched the man stand and walk away.

The other man remained a moment longer, shook his head, then obediently followed when he was called.

Suddenly, Nate heard his son crying again.

He turned, his head spinning, trying to locate the car.

Nate winced in extreme pain, turning himself toward the sound. He could not lift himself, so he desperately reached out for the door handle, his mind filling with anger and frustration, because he knew he would not reach it.

The beating was too much. The pain was too much, and the world was fading out around him again. He continued to extend his trembling hand toward the car, a puddle of blood flowing freely from his mouth and accumulating on the ground beneath his chin.

He could make it, Nate kept telling himself, but he knew better. He felt his senses leaving him, his eyes closing, and as he lost consciousness, his body falling limp in the driveway, Nate prayed that his son would be okay.

39

When Monica stepped into her house from work some time after nine o'clock, she found Lewis in the living room, his feet kicked up on the coffee table, watching BET music videos, smoking a joint.

"Dammit, Lewis," Monica said, closing the door and walking into the room. "I told you I didn't want you doing that stuff in this house."

"What are you talking about?" Lewis said after blowing smoke from his nose and putting out the joint. "You weren't saying that when we were doing it together."

"That was once," Monica said. She grabbed the remote from beside him on the sofa and changed the channel to MSNBC. The wisecracking Keith Olbermann was talking about the 2008 presidential elections.

"I was watching videos."

"That's all you ever watch," Monica said, sitting.

"Well I don't want to hear about no damn presidential elections. That ain't got nothing to do with me."

"It would if you voted."

"Well I don't, so can we watch something else?"

Monica clicked the TV off. "What was up with you this morning?"

"Nothing."

"No. It was something. You didn't say a word to me at breakfast."

"Everything was cool."

"No it wasn't," Monica said. "Why can't you ever just tell me what's on your mind?"

"Because there was nothing on my mind."

"Fine," Monica said, standing. "I'm getting a bottle of water. Do you want anything from the kitchen?"

"No."

When she returned, Monica sat back down next to Lewis, took a swallow from her water, and said, "So how's school going?"

"It's good."

"You doing okay in your classes?"

"Yeah," Lewis said, sounding the slightest bit irritated.

"Do you not want to talk about this?"

"There are a thousand other things we could talk about."

"Suggest something."

"I don't know. I'm just sayin'."

"How about what you plan on doing once you finish school."

Lewis turned to Monica, gave her an incredulous look. "You serious?"

"Yeah, I'm serious. Have you thought about what your plans are?"

"I don't know. Freddy and I are thinking about starting a real-estate company, or maybe I might open up my own barber shop. I haven't given it much thought."

"You think you might want to start?"

Lewis pulled himself from the sofa, stood in front of Monica. "What the hell is this? Are you my counselor now? Is this career day or some shit?"

"No. Nothing like that. I just think the future is important, and I thought we'd talk about it, considering we're going to get married."

"Well, I'm fine, alright. Just let me worry about my own future, okay?" Lewis said.

"Okay," Monica said. "I won't ever ask you about it again."

40

Nate sat on an emergency room bed, behind the door of a small exam room, wearing a blue hospital gown.

He had been given a shot of some sort of painkiller, but he was still in agony.

Nate had been sent through a battery of tests after arriving at the hospital. X-rays of his skull, his arms, hands, and ribs had been taken. Nothing was broken. His ribs were bruised, which was the pain he felt when he breathed. A CAT scan had been taken of his head, which revealed a concussion.

Nate had gotten a glimpse in the bathroom mirror after he had been treated. Even with the bandage covering part of his face, he could still see how badly he had been disfigured.

His bottom lip had been cut open, needing several stitches. His left eye was bruised so badly it required a patch, while the right had just enough swelling that he could only partially open it.

The rest of his face was covered in blue and black bruising.

"You got roughed up pretty badly, Mr. Kenny," the petite

Asian physician told Nate. "The swelling will go down after a few days, the bruising in about a week, and then you should be back to normal."

"And the pain?" Nate said, looking and sounding as though his mouth were packed with gauze, even though it wasn't.

"I'll get you a prescription for that, and then we can let you go. Okay?" the doctor said, patting Nate on the shoulder.

"Okay," Nate said, watching the doctor step out of the room and close the door.

Nate had been waiting, rocking himself, trying to endure the pain silently, wondering how long it would be till he could see his son.

He looked up when he saw the doorknob turn.

Tim walked in, worry on his face. "What the hell happened?"

"Where's my son?"

"Nathaniel's fine. He's in the waiting room with Mrs. Weatherly."

"I want to see him."

"He can't come back here."

"I want to see him!"

"The doctor said she'll be right back with your prescription, then we'll go and you can see Nathaniel then, okay?" Tim stepped closer to Nate. "What happened?"

"I thought he was going to kill me, Tim," Nate said, glassy eyed, his voice low. "He just kept on kicking me, and I thought he was going to kill me, right there in front of my son. That bastard!"

"Do you know who it was?"

"It was Lewis," Nate said, wincing.

"Are you sure?"

"Positive. It was broad daylight, and he came to my house, beat the hell out of me, and left me there. If it wasn't for Mrs. Weatherly coming out and finding me . . ." Nate lowered his head.

Tim placed a hand on his brother's shoulder. "Nate, everything is going to be fine."

"No," Nate said, looking up. "Not for him it's not. He's going to pay for this."

"What do you mean?"

"I'm going to make sure that Monica leaves him. Then I'm going to take everything he has. I'm going to make him wish he were dead."

41

F reddy sat at the kitchen table after washing the dishes from the frozen pizza that he and Kia had finished eating not long ago. Before him sat an envelope he was anguishing over. He had gotten it from the mailbox when he walked in this evening.

It was his scores from the real-estate licensing board test. This would determine whether or not he had passed, whether he had his license and would be one step closer to fulfilling his dream or would continue to be the do-nothing nigga that Kia's father had called him.

That was how Freddy felt that moment, how he felt all day after watching Lewis beat up that Mr. Kenny guy.

Lewis was trying to urge Freddy on, but Freddy didn't want any part of that. He was scared that he would get in there, throw one blow, deliver one kick, have it start getting good to him, and then find out that the guy was dead.

So Freddy stayed on the sidelines, watched. And he was glad

he did. He reminded himself he didn't need any more violent contact with anyone else for a long time.

What he needed to be doing was concentrating on his future, which was why he was so worried about what was in the envelope. Freddy picked it up and thought of not opening it, because something was telling him that he had failed. He had never really accomplished anything, so why would this be any different?

But then again, Freddy told himself, that was maybe because he had never tried anything, never put forth an effort to achieve anything. This time was different. He had taken the course, studied for his test, and finished as one of the top five students in the class.

Remembering that gave Freddy the confidence to tear open the envelope and look at his scores, whatever they might be.

He held the page in his hand, scanned it nervously, finally locating the score.

He had received an 83 percent. Passing was 75 percent.

Freddy held the sheet in both fists, smiling, a tear almost coming to his eyes. He just couldn't believe it.

All of a sudden, he shot up from the chair and practically ran through the house, down the stairs, and into the basement, where Kia lay in bed, watching television. Freddy jumped into bed with his girlfriend.

"What are you running around here like a five-year-old for?" Kia asked.

Freddy thumbed down the TV's volume with the remote, turned to Kia, and said, "I told you I was gonna make something of myself."

"Yeah, and I believe you."

"Well, I want to give you a little proof," Freddy said, handing Kia the letter.

"What's this?"

"For the past few months, I've been taking real-estate classes. I didn't tell anybody until I was sure I passed the test."

Kia looked up from the sheet of paper, a smile spreading across her face. "So since you're telling me, that means . . ."

"That's right, baby," Freddy said. "That means I passed."

"Woohoo, baby!" Kia said, throwing her arms around him, squeezing him. "Prove my daddy wrong, sweetheart. Show him what you got!"

Freddy leaned out of the embrace so he could look into Kia's eyes. "Are you proud of me, baby?"

"Prouder than you can ever know."

42

As Monica walked the path through the park after the third morning in a row of not seeing Nate, she told herself this would be the last time. This had become her before-work detour, parking the car at the exact time she had before, getting out, strolling along, and acting as though she was not looking for Nate and his son.

Monica waved at the graying senior couple in matching sweatsuits she had seen for the last three mornings. She moved in the direction of the swings and monkey bars where she had seen Nate before. Children had played there as they had the other mornings, parents standing along the outskirts, lovingly watching them. From that distance, she could not see Nate.

Monica looked nice today, wore her hair pinned up, a curl hanging in her face. It was the way Nate used to like it, but as she looked in the mirror this morning, she had tried to convince herself that it had nothing to do with her choice. She stopped when she saw a man she thought was Nate sitting at a bench on the other side of the play lot. She walked over to him. He was looking away, intent on the kids running around in the play area before him. Monica sat down without him knowing, then said, "This was going to be the last time."

Nate turned, and immediately Monica noticed the bruises on his face, the blackness around both of his eyes.

She gasped. "What happened to you?"

Nate smiled, hesitated for a moment, then said, "I was out with Tim and his wife the other night and a man said some obscene things to her. Tim was in the bathroom, and I couldn't let it slide. I punched the guy, he punched me back. Before I knew it, Tim comes out, joins in, along with the rest of the bar."

Monica reached out, touched the side of his face. "How does it feel?"

"Better now."

Monica quickly pulled her hand away.

"What's in the bag?" Nate asked, nodding at the Toys "R" Us bag she was holding.

"It's a little something I picked up for Nathaniel. Did you bring him?"

"Mommy!" Monica turned to see Nathaniel running across the grass toward her. She stood up, walked a few steps toward the boy, and then stooped down. Nathaniel ran into her arms, hugging her around the neck.

"Mommy!" he yelled again.

"I bought you something," Monica said, sitting back down and handing Nathaniel the gift-wrapped box out of the bag.

"Can I open it?" Nathaniel asked Monica.

Monica looked to Nate. He nodded his head.

"Sure," Monica said, smiling. "Open it."

Nathaniel tore the wrapper open as Monica watched happily.

He lifted the top off the box, dug through the tissue paper, and said, "Wow!" after pulling out the red fire truck. "Can I play?" he asked.

"What do you say?" Nate said.

"Thank you."

Nathaniel kissed Monica on the cheek and ran back over to the other children playing, the fire engine in his arms. Monica sat back on the bench beside Nate quietly, and they watched Nathaniel, as if they were the proud parents.

"He still calls me mommy. Why haven't you stopped him from doing that?"

"You don't seem to mind."

"But it's not true. And I'm not coming here anymore. The only reason I came today was to tell you that."

"You could have called," Nate said.

"I had the gift for your son."

"That was very sweet of you."

Monica moved as though she was getting up to leave. "I really need to be getting to work."

"No, you don't," Nate said, looking out at the children. "You're the boss, right? You go in when you want, just like me. How's that going, anyway?"

"I own three stores. Employees, merchandise, insurance, complaints. Sometimes it can be a complete pain in the ass."

Nate turned to her. "But you love it, don't you?"

Monica smiled. "Wouldn't trade it for the world."

Nate smiled with her. "I know."

Monica had not seen that smile in more than a year, had forgotten how warm it could be. She felt herself trying to recall the last time she felt like this with Nate, but then forced herself to stop. She turned away from him abruptly, saying, "But all that might change today. I get my quarterly reports, and who knows, tomorrow the whole thing might be shut down."

"I don't think that's the case. But if you ever need any advice, or just want to talk about your next move, you know you can bring that to me."

Monica nodded her head, smiling gratefully. "I truly appreciate that. Sometimes it's hard making people understand what you go through as the big boss, so I might just do that."

Monica stood. Nate did not.

She extended a hand to him. "Well, this will be the last time I'll be seeing you here, okay?"

Nate took her hand. "Okay."

Monica did not let go, but looked over her shoulder at Nathaniel playing, then turned back to Nate. "I just want to say— your son . . . you're different . . . better. I'm proud of you."

"I could make you prouder if you gave me a chance," Nate flirted.

"Oh, I bet you'd love to try."

"Of course I would."

Monica paused, thoughtfully. "No. Like I said, this is what it is. Okay, Nate?"

"Okay."

Monica let go of his hand, turned and walked away. She only looked back at Nathaniel twice.

43

Three days later, Abbey Kurt pulled her Audi sedan over to the curb in front of the small rehabbed house. She eyed the FOR SALE sign on the neatly cut front lawn.

Three days ago, Mr. Kenny had slowly walked into her office with the assistance of a man he had introduced as his brother, Tim. Mr. Kenny's face was bruised, and by the way he walked, he appeared to be in a significant amount of pain. Abbey quickly stepped from around her desk to help Nate into a chair.

"I need to intensify this," Nate told Abbey once he was settled. "The man Monica is involved with—"

"Lewis Waters," Abbey said. "His name came up in my research. I've already done some quick checking on him."

"Deepen that. As deep as you can go. And not just with him, with whoever he knows, immediate family, distant relatives, past employers, friends—you name it. Whoever he knows, I want to know better. I want every available avenue open to get to this man."

Abbey started her work moments after Nate and his brother left and did not stop until three days later.

She did extensive work on the Internet, went down to city hall for records, visited grammar schools and high schools. She made phone calls, walked the streets of the neighborhoods where Lewis had lived, talking to people, gathering information on the man.

Abbey found out that he had been born on the West Side of Chicago to a single mother. The father had been in and out of the house, and when Lewis was five years old, the father had left, never to return.

Lewis's mother lived on welfare while working odd jobs at grocery stores, a pawn shop, and a number of bars. Lewis was an only child and had a rough upbringing. He was in and out of school, barely graduating from both elementary and high school.

He had been arrested for a number of petty crimes—drug possession, vagrancy, destruction of public property—all before he was eighteen years old.

Lewis was either kicked out or left his mother's house soon after that, and he bounced around from place to place for the next few years, working only when he needed to, staying with whatever friends or girlfriends would have him.

Abbey could not find specific information regarding exactly where those places were. But checking the Department of Motor Vehicles Web site, Abbey found that Lewis had registered his license to an Ida B. Wells Homes housing address some three years ago.

She dug up information on a Selena Wells, to whom the apartment was registered. There was a baby born, Layla Waters, a few months later at Cook County Hospital.

Two nights ago, Abbey had leaned back from eight straight hours in front of her computer screen, pulled her glasses off, and rubbed her eyes.

Her phone rang. She glanced at her desk clock. It read 10:01 P.M.

"This is Abbey Kurt," she said, softly.

"How's it coming?" It was Nate, checking her progress.

"Very well, Mr. Kenny. So far, I've turned up a lot of useful information. But I'm sure there's much more. I just stumbled upon a friend of Lewis Waters. His name is Freddy Ford."

"Good," Nate said. "Follow up on that, and let me know what you uncover."

"Yes, sir."

The following morning, Abbey stood before Nate in his office. He was looking through a manila file she had compiled.

"And that's a photo of the friend I was telling you about last night, Freddy Ford. The two have been friends since second grade. They both struggled in school, both had minor criminal records, and currently, they both work for a real-estate management company Mr. Ford's uncle owns."

"Does this Freddy Ford have a father?"

"He did, but when Freddy was eight years old, his father died in an accident at home. I dug deeper to find out just what that accident was, and it turns out that this Freddy Ford killed his own father. After asking around his neighborhood, I was told it was because the man was abusing Ford's mother. You're looking at the death certificate right now," Abbey said. "From that point on, after the father's death, his mother struggled with paying bills, for household necessities, so on and so forth."

Nate looked up. "Did you find out where this Ford lives?"

"Yes, sir. The address and a photo of the house are right there," Abbey said, leaning over and sifting through the paperwork for Nate. "I checked the status of the house, and there were outstanding taxes that had not been paid in more than two years. One month ago, a real-estate investor, his name is in the file, took ownership of those delinquent taxes."

Nate pulled the page with the investor's name and information. He smiled, saying, "It seems their grace period for paying these taxes has already ended."

"That's correct," Abbey said.

"Is there any indication as to why they didn't pay?"

"Freddy's mother has been out of work for two years, I believe. She has been drawing disability for that period. I don't have the exact figure, but I'm certain it's not substantial enough to pay the taxes. Honestly, I don't believe they are even aware the taxes have been bought from under them."

"Good work, Abbey. I want you to continue digging this stuff up. I'm going to try to contact the investor who holds the taxes on the Ford house and see if I can work something out. I'll call you and let you know what the next move is."

Abbey sat up straight in the Audi. She powered down the window when she saw a man wearing a blue work shirt and jeans step out of the house.

Abbey took off her glasses. "Excuse me," she called to the man she recognized as Freddy Ford. "May I speak with you please?"

Freddy walked across the lawn, smiling as he came closer to the car.

"Do you know who's selling this house?"

Freddy leaned an elbow on the roof of Abbey's Audi. "I am. Why, you want to buy it?" he joked.

"No, but my employer does. If it's still for sale, I know he would be interested in the property."

"Yeah, it's still for sale."

"May I have your card?"

Freddy patted himself down and pulled out a single dog-eared business card, a dirty thumbprint on the face. He handed it to Abbey. "You can reach me at that number. It's my cell."

"Mr. Ford," Abbey said, reading the card as though she did not already know his name. She extended a hand out the window. "I'll contact you later today to give you the address where I would like for you to meet my employer and discuss the sale of the house. Does that work for you?"

"Oh yeah," Freddy said, smiling and nodding. "That works just fine."

44

Monica sat at one end of the dinner table, Lewis across from her, Layla in her high chair at the side of the table.

Monica sat there listening to whatever Lewis was talking to his daughter about, while they ate the cheeseburgers Lewis had made them all for dinner.

She sat silently, feeling content, overjoyed actually, a simple smile on her face.

"Okay," Lewis said, setting down his greasy half-eaten cheeseburger. "You been smiling all night and haven't said a word. What's up?"

"You really want to know?" Monica said, feeling as though she was going to burst if she didn't tell him.

"Of course, baby."

"I got my quarterlies back today, and you won't believe it. We sold sixteen percent more clothing and merchandise than we did last quarter. Our spa services are up even higher—twenty-one percent. Do you believe that? This surpassed even the annual goals that my accountant and I had set, which is just insane," Monica said, excited. "You know what? Nothing tells it better than the actual report," she said, getting up from her chair and leaving a less than enthused Lewis and his daughter at the table.

Monica returned and leaned in beside Lewis, shoving a number of computer pages in front of him, lined with column upon column of numbers and percentages.

"See, last quarter, the margin we set was attainable, but we still didn't meet it. But this one, here," Monica said, pointing. "Wow! I don't know what happened—but we made it and even passed it. This opens the doors for who knows what. Maybe I can do some radio ads, maybe even TV. And with the extra money, I can probably expand the stores even more, build an addition, look at the property next door. Or maybe even open another location. You know what I mean?"

"No, Monica," Lewis said, handing back the pages. "You're at work all day, and sometimes well into the evenings. You talk about your business all the time, now you saying that we got to hear about it even when we're eating."

"I just thought that you'd want to know about the report."

"Baby, I'm glad you met your gains, or margins, or whatever, but to tell you the truth, I could not understand a word you were saying. Layla, could you?" Lewis asked the child.

The little girl hunched her shoulders and shook her head.

"See," Lewis said. "Nobody knows what you're talking about but you. So can you put the papers away for right now so we can finish eating, and then maybe we can talk more about your work another time?"

"Yeah," Monica said, disappointed. "I can do that."

45

The next morning, Freddy stood before Nate Kenny, wearing a shirt and tie. He had Kia tie it for him this morning, after he showered.

"What's the special occasion?" Kia asked while she, Freddy, and his mother ate breakfast.

"I'm going to meet the man who wants to buy that rehab today," Freddy said, smiling. "I'm telling you all, this is going to be it. This is going to be the beginning."

Kia pushed back her chair, came over, and wrapped her arms around Freddy's neck. "I'm so happy for you, baby. You sure this man wants to buy it?"

"The woman I spoke to yesterday said her boss definitely wanted it. She called me last night and told me to meet them this morning. I'm gonna go myself, make sure it's the real thing, and then I'll tell my uncle. After that, it's on, baby."

Freddy's mother smiled silently from across the table. She had been feeling good enough to climb the stairs, but not to start her new job, yet.

"Moms, what you thinking?" Freddy asked.

"That I'm just so proud of my boy. I always knew you'd make a success of yourself."

But now, standing in Nate's office, hearing what the man just told him, Freddy knew his mother would have lost what little pride she'd had in Freddy.

"Did you hear what I said, Freddy? Someone purchased the unpaid taxes on your house. Did you know they had not been paid?"

"No," Freddy said, his voice soft, his head lowered, his fists clenched at his sides.

"You should have," Nate said from behind his office desk. "I'm sure your mother received countless notices. Do you believe she ignored them, thought everything would be just fine if she paid them no mind?"

"I don't know."

"Freddy, let me assure you. Everything is not just fine." Nate rose from his chair, walked around his desk, past Abbey, who was standing off to the side, back straight like a soldier.

"The gentleman who bought the taxes does that for a living. I called him, and he was more than happy to sell them to me. There is always a grace period given in order for the owner of the property to try to scrape up the money to save his or her home. But since your mother has been out of work, we both know that she wasn't able to do that."

Freddy looked up angrily at Nate for speaking so harshly about his mother.

"That period has expired, and just days ago, I bought your house," Nate said, smiling. He reached back onto his desk. "Here is the deed." Nate handed it to Freddy.

All Freddy saw was his address, and he handed it back to the man. He felt himself becoming even angrier.

"What the fuck do you want with me?"

"Temper, temper, Mr. Freddy Ford," Nate said, pacing in

front of him. "Do you know how I got these scars and bruises on my face?"

"No. How would I?"

"I was jumped, in broad daylight, in the driveway of my own home. I was jumped and beaten, while my almost-three-year-old son sat in the back seat of my car and had to watch it."

Freddy's eyes widened the slightest bit at the mention of this news.

"That's right, you didn't know that, did you?" Nate stopped in front of Freddy, looked him in the eyes. "I know you were the other man that was there, and I appreciate you not contributing to the beating I was given. And because I am grateful, I will allow you not only to serve my needs, but to benefit from that service."

"What are you talking about?"

"You are Lewis Waters' best friend. By now you should know exactly who I am, and what's been going on between he and I for more than a year. He had made the mistake in thinking that he no longer has to worry about me, that my wife is his and he will never lose her. Freddy, I don't have to tell you how wrong he is. I'm going to take back my wife," Nate said, walking behind him. "And then take away everything else of importance to him." Nate rested a hand on Freddy's shoulder. "And you're going to help me."

"Fuck you," Freddy said, turning and starting toward the door.

"Mr. Ford!" Freddy heard the woman call his name as he reached for the doorknob.

Freddy turned.

"Mr. Kenny is not finished. It would behoove you to stay for your own sake, and the sake of your family."

Freddy stepped back to the place where he'd been standing.

"Freddy, let me make this simple for you," Nate said. "You help me out, do what I tell you, and I will sign over your house to you. Meaning you will no longer have to pay the back taxes. You will own the home, free and clear. But, if you don't do exactly what I say, or if you try to warn your friend of what's going on, mention a single word of this to him, I will put you, your little pregnant girlfriend, and your mother out on the street. Then I'll have that heap of a house condemned and bulldozed, as it should've been years ago. Do I make myself clear, Mr. Freddy Ford?" Nate said, standing over his shoulder, his voice no higher than a whisper.

Through painfully clenched teeth, Freddy said, "I need time to think about this."

"You have a day. Now get out of my office."

46

After work, Freddy and Lewis sat in Freddy's car parked on a street in Lewis's old neighborhood, sipping Coronas.

Freddy was melancholy, picking at the label of his beer, taking the occasional sip. "You ever think about your old man?"

Lewis pulled the bottle down from his lips, shifted toward Freddy in his seat. "Me? Shit, my old man left when I was like five. Hadn't thought about him since."

Freddy tore off a corner of his beer label. "Sometimes I still have dreams about mine, about him laying there, his face all pushed in, covered in blood."

Lewis stared at Freddy but did not speak a word.

"Sometimes, I can't get it out of my head."

"Just don't think about it."

"It ain't as bad as it used to be," Freddy said. "Remember before they found out what really happened and sent me away, when you walked into the bathroom at school and found me crying? I thought you'd think I was crazy or a punk when I told you that I'd been doing that every day for the past week."

"Naw. You were going through something. That was your father. Regardless of how foul he was for beating your moms like that, I knew you was still sorry he was gone."

"And I appreciated that." Freddy took another drink from his beer. "Remember after they let me come back home, my moms would have to damn near kick you out of my crib every night, because you'd be there until like midnight?"

Lewis smiled a little. "I was afraid you'd do something stupid like try and hang yourself, or jump out the window or something. You were my best friend. I wasn't about to let that happen."

"If it wasn't for you, I don't know if I would've gotten through that. I owe you, man," Freddy said.

"That's what friends are for, right?" Lewis said.

"That's right. Drink to that."

The two men tapped the butts of their beer bottles together and took a drink.

"But look at us now," Lewis said. "I got a beautiful little girl, and I'm about to marry a millionaire. And you just got your real-estate license, about to have a baby with the finest future lawyer at UIC. And we ain't gonna even talk about the real-estate business we gonna open once we sell this first rehab. Sky is the limit, baby. That ain't too bad for two poverty-stricken kids, growing up without fathers."

"Yeah," Freddy said, trying to mask his sadness. "Not bad at all."

47

When Freddy got home, he went straight upstairs to see his mother. He was angry, wanted to yell at her about the situation with the house, demand why she didn't tell him about the tax notices. They could've gotten the money from somewhere, asked for an extension, something! But upon walking in his mother's bedroom door, seeing her laid up in bed, nodding off to sleep, Freddy knew he could not bring himself to scold her.

He sat beside her on the edge of the bed. She opened her eyes, smiled at the sight of her son.

"Did you sell the house?"

"No, Moms. The man wasn't serious."

She placed a hand on Freddy's, squeezed it. "It's gonna be all right. There'll be another buyer."

Freddy smiled, then said, "Can I ask you something?"

"Anything, baby."

"If someone is trying to pressure you into something that

you know will hurt a friend of yours, would you do it, knowing that if you don't, there'll be bad consequences?"

"I didn't even have to hear the rest of the question before I knew the answer, son. If it's truly a friend of yours—a real friend—never let anyone pressure you into anything that can hurt that person. How I see it, there are no consequences that bad to make it worth losing a good friend."

"I think there are, Moms."

"The consequences will pass. A good friendship lasts forever."

Freddy thought about what his mother said a moment longer, and then a smile spread across his face.

"You know what, Moms? I think you might be right." Freddy leaned over, kissed her on the cheek. "I'm going downstairs to see what's up with the future mother of my child."

"You do that, Fred."

Freddy hopped off the bed and walked toward the door.

"And Fred," his mother called.

"Yeah?" Freddy turned, the smile still on his face.

"My boss called today," his mother said, looking down at her hands. "He said he couldn't wait any longer on me. He had to fill my position. I no longer have that job."

Freddy lowered his head there in front of his mother, feeling the pain and sorrow he knew she was trying hard to hide from him.

Downstairs in his basement apartment, the phone rang.

Kia moved to answer it, but coming down the stairs, Freddy said, "Don't. It's just another bill collector."

Freddy walked over to Kia, hugged her tight.

"What's wrong, baby?" Kia asked.

"Did you know Moms lost her job?"

"I know. She told me. I called her employer, practically begged for him to wait for your mother to get on her feet. He asked how long, but because I didn't know, he said he just couldn't."

Freddy pulled away from Kia. "I can't pay for everything with just the money I make."

Kia followed behind him. "I would say that I could take out some loans to help, but since my father isn't paying my tuition anymore . . ."

"No. It's okay," Freddy said.

"Maybe I can get a job, or postpone my last year until—"

"No! This is my mother's house, but I'm supposed to be the man. You're in school. You do school. This is my responsibility. I'll take care of it."

"But how?" Kia asked desperately.

"Don't worry. I'll find a way."

48

Last night, after his mother told him about her losing her job, after Kia tried to offer postponing school to help him maintain the household, Freddy called the number Nate had given him.

He stood over the phone at almost eleven o'clock, the living room lamp burning dimly beside him. With his voice filled with guilt, he said, "What do I have to do?"

"Take down this address and show up tomorrow at twelve-fifteen P.M." Nate said.

Freddy grabbed the pen from the end table and started writing.

The next day, Freddy sat uncomfortably in the bar of the InterContinental Hotel on Michigan Avenue. The room was huge, ceilings stretching high above him, the walls graced with old paintings by some Italian artist.

Men in business suits sat at tables, sipping cognac and smoking cigars, while Freddy sat at a back corner table, wearing dirty jeans, work boots, and his work shirt.

Nate sat before him, wearing his usual dark suit. He sipped occasionally from a glass of scotch.

Nate offered to get Freddy a drink, but Freddy declined, being on his lunch break. Freddy had been there for half an hour, reluctantly spilling his guts in regard to everything he knew about Lewis.

"And how does he get along with my ex-wife?" Nate asked.

"Like any other couple. Sometimes good, sometimes bad."

"When is it good?"

"When Lewis is fucking her. He wears her ass out whenever he can, as often as he can."

Freddy saw the muscle in Nate's jaw tighten, and he smiled to himself.

"I see. And when is it bad?"

Freddy wanted to lie, but as soon as he'd sat down, Nate had reiterated just how important Freddy's honesty was to him.

There was a manila file that sat on the table before Nate. His hand rested flat on it.

"There's more in this file about you than you probably know about yourself. I have even more information on Lewis. So if you lie to me, I'll know. If you withhold information from me, I'll know. And if that happens, what will happen next?" Nate asked.

"You'll throw my family out and tear down our house."

"That's right. I will not hesitate. You understand?"

Freddy understood completely, that's why when Nate asked him when Lewis's relationship with Monica was bad, Freddy answered, "Most of the other times. Monica sometimes deals with men with the business. Every now and then Lewis gets jealous. They fight a lot about that. And then they just don't have a whole lot in common."

"What do you mean?"

"All Monica seems to talk about is work, trying to expand her business, how much money she's making. Lewis doesn't like to hear about that. It makes him feel like he's not doing nothing."

"That's exactly what he is doing—nothing," Nate said.

Freddy ignored the comment, and continued. "Lewis watches sports, listens to rap music, and we play a lot of PlayStation Three. We smoke weed every now and then, and Monica doesn't like that."

"The fool doesn't try to better himself? Doesn't he know that she won't tolerate that for long?"

"He supposed to be in college."

"What do you mean, supposed to be?"

Freddy immediately regretted mentioning that. But went on and said, "Monica is paying for him to go to school, but he stopped going a little while ago."

"She doesn't know this?"

"No. He spends that time at work with me now, making extra money and saving it."

Nate smiled, shaking his head. "For what?"

"We want to start our own real-estate company. He wants to prove to Monica that he can be a success."

"He's trying to become the man he was pretending to be when he met Monica."

"I don't know," Freddy said. "Maybe."

"Why does she stay with him? What does she see in him?"

"She loves him, and she loves his daughter."

"The daughter. Layla is her name, right?" Nate said.

"Yeah. She cares for that girl like she's her own. Like the daughter she could never have."

"And Lewis knows this, doesn't he? He uses that to his advantage."

"He ain't using nothing. He's just happy Monica treats his daughter right."

Nate turned up his glass, swallowing the last of his drink, and then stood. "How do you feel?"

"I don't like what I'm doing. This is wrong, and I don't like that you making me do it."

"You better learn to like it. We have a long way to go," Nate said, pulling out his wallet. He laid a crisp new hundred-dollar bill on the table beside Freddy's hand.

"I don't want that."

"Don't be a fool. Your mother's not working, and you have bills to pay. This will keep something in your pocket. Do what you supposed to do, and there'll be more to come."

Freddy slid the bill off the table.

"Continue to keep your ears open when you're with him. And don't turn your cell off. I don't know when I'll want to talk to you again."

Nate walked away. Freddy was left there holding the hundred-dollar bill he wanted to tear in half, but knew he could not afford to.

49

The next morning, Nate sat on his usual bench at the park, watching Nathaniel play in the grass with the fire truck Monica had given him.

Nate glanced at his watch: 7:45 A.M. He wondered if Monica was going to appear.

As he did every morning, Nate came to the park with Nathaniel, but for the past two mornings, Monica did not show, and he had been starting to believe that she was serious about never meeting him there again. After he had gotten more information from Freddy than he had expected yesterday, Nate had returned to his office and dialed Monica at work.

"He misses you" was the first thing Nate said, after Monica had picked up.

It took her a minute to respond. "What do you expect me to do about that?"

"Visit us. Tomorrow morning at the park."

"You know I can't. I told you that."

"Tell my son. Maybe he'd understand it better coming from

you. When I tell him, he just crosses his arms, pokes his lip out, and says, 'But I want Mommy.'"

Monica laughed. "Sorry. You're the one who convinced him I was his mother."

"I didn't have to convince him. It's true," Nate said. "At least to me."

There was a thoughtful silence.

"Besides," Nate continued, "I want to talk to you about your stores. You never told me what your quarterly report looked like, and I think I have a business opportunity that you could benefit from."

"I don't know, Nate. I told you—"

"Think about it. If you decide yes, you know where I'll be."

Now, still sitting on the bench, Nate looked down the path Monica had come from the times she had visited. There was still no sign of her.

He took a sip of the coffee he had bought and felt to see if the cup he had bought her was still warm. It was.

"Is that for me?" Monica said, standing on the other side of him.

"If you keep on sneaking up on me . . . ," Nate said, standing and offering her a hug.

Monica looked at him oddly. "Nate, I'm not going there with you."

"You don't hug your male friends? Monica, please. I promise I won't cop a feel."

Monica allowed Nate to hug her. She gave him three friendly pats on the back.

They sat, and Nate handed Monica her coffee. "Carmel macchiato. Your favorite."

"You shouldn't have."

"And a French cruller," Nate said, offering Monica a small paper bag. "Also your favorite."

"There is no game to win, Nate. No points to score."

"I know that. I'm just being the wonderful man that I am."

Monica shook her head, sipping from her coffee. "Where is Nathaniel, so I can give him a hug?"

"He's out there playing with his truck, but let me have a minute with you first. Tell me about the report."

Monica smiled widely all of a sudden. "Oh, the profits we made this quarter, the margins—we did far better than I ever expected."

"Congratulations. That's wonderful!" Nate said. "Have you decided what you're going to do with the extra revenue? I know you're not just going to stick that in the bank."

"No. I'm thinking about putting it into advertising time. Or maybe expanding the store. Or I know this is crazy, but maybe even looking to open another one. The properties are just so expensive."

A huge smile spread across Nate's face.

"What?" Monica said.

"I can't believe this."

"What?" Monica said, more excited.

"A guy I know just came to me a few days ago about a few warehouses he's trying to unload. He said they were perfect for retail space."

"You're joking."

"No. And he said he would sell them to me for a song."

Monica eagerly scooted to the edge of the bench, "Do you think he still has them?"

"Only one way to find out," Nate said, pulling his cell from his pocket. He dialed his friend's number, waited for an answer, then said, "Bob, it's Nate. You still have those warehouses that you came to me with the other day? Only one left, huh?" Nate said, looking in Monica's eyes. "But it's the best one? Hold it then. I have someone who I think is very interested. Yeah . . . yeah. Now I still get the friendship deal, right? Good." Nate laughed, winking at Monica. "Okay . . . good, I'll get back with you later today."

Nate slapped his cell phone closed, then said to Monica, "He has one left. Just let me know when you want to check it out."

Monica practically jumped in Nate's lap as she threw her arms around him. "Thank you! Thank you!"

"Whoa, whoa!" Nate said. "I'm not going there with you, because there are no points to score."

Monica slapped Nate playfully across the arm. "Shut up."

"Ouch. Gentle. I'm still healing, remember."

They laughed together, and then they sat in an awkward moment of silence.

"What are you doing, Nate?" Monica asked, all of a sudden.

"What do you mean?"

"What do you want?"

If Nate were to tell her the truth, he would've said he wanted to expose Lewis Waters for the loser clown he was. He wanted Monica to kick his ass out of her life, not just because he knew that would bring pain to Lewis, but because Nate knew Monica took joy from raising the man's little girl. Nate would've told her that he also wanted to win Monica's trust, have her agree to come back to him, think that everything would be as it was before when their marriage was good. He would allow her to fall in love with Nathaniel. He would try to convince Monica to trust him with her money, her assets, possibly get her to sign a power of attorney over to him. He would take everything he could, all the money she had swindled from him and everything she had bought with it. And if he could not get hold of her possessions, her finances, then he would just leave her again. He would leave her and hope that the loss of the tie she had developed with Nate's son, and the loss of the love she had thought she had gotten again from Nate, would be too much for her to overcome. Nate wanted Monica to suffer horrendously and alone for the lies she had told him, for the years she made him waste with her without giving him children, and for the money she had stolen from him.

"Nate," Monica said, pulling him out of his thoughts. "I said, what do you want?"

Nate looked into Monica's eyes and said as sincerely as he possibly could, "Don't you know? I want you."

50

Later that afternoon, Monica sat in her office, just staring at her desk phone. Unbeknownst to her, Tabatha was standing just within the door and had been watching her for the last minute.

"I can't take it anymore! Are you gonna make a call, or what?"

"The annual Women in Business Ball," Monica said, tilting all the way back in her chair. "I haven't told Lewis about it yet. Is that wrong of me?"

"What are you waiting for? It's Thursday."

"I know. But if I have him go with me, would that be running the risk of—"

"Him acting like a baby, complaining about going? Then once he got there, drinking too much, talking badly about people, calling all the black folks white wannabes because they decided to go to school, work jobs, and make lots of money, and if a man happened to look at you too long, would you be risking

Lewis clubbing that man over the head? I'd say yes. You'd definitely be rolling the dice on that one," Tabatha said.

"I know all that. But I'm asking would I be running the risk of finding out that he really doesn't care about any of it? Before, when I thought it meant nothing to him, I just accepted it, told myself I had to deal with it. But now that I know that there is someone who feels as passionately about all this as I do—"

"You mean Nate?" Tabatha interjected.

Monica ignored Tabatha's interruption, saying, "I told you what Lewis said when I showed him our quarterlies."

"Yeah, that neither he, nor Layla, who might actually be smarter than her father, wanted to hear anything about it."

Monica stood, walked out from behind her desk. "Doesn't he know how important all this is to me? And if he cared, wouldn't he act like it? Hell, even if he didn't care, shouldn't he at least fake it?"

"This is how he's always been. Why are you acting like this is new information?"

"I don't know," Monica said, turning in a circle, pushing her hands through her hair. "No. I do know. This morning I told Nate I'm thinking about another store and he just went and got in touch with someone he knows who's selling some retail space. He says he can get it for me for cheap if I'm interested."

"Wow," Tabatha said. "That's juice."

"It totally just came out of nowhere. But just with that one gesture, I could tell that he really wants me to succeed with this. It felt like he sincerely cared. And that made me wonder. Shouldn't I be getting that feeling from the man I'm about to marry, not the man I just divorced?"

Tabatha just sat there, looking up at Monica. "You're right."

"So what does it say about a man who doesn't care about

something he knows the woman he's supposed to love cares about?"

"Hmmm. Or you could ask," Tabatha said, grinning, "what does it say about a woman who doesn't care about a man who loves the same things the woman he once loved cares about?"

"What?" Monica said.

"Think about it. You'll get it eventually."

51

The next morning, Abbey sat, her cell phone pressed to her ear, beside Nate in the first-class section of a United airliner, preparing to take off for St. Louis. The day before, she had done a more detailed search on Selena Wells, Lewis's deceased girlfriend and the mother of his child. What Abbey discovered was that Selena had family in St. Louis, a mother named Salesha, forty-five years old, and a sister named Salonica, thirty years old. The sister had two fifteen-year-old twin daughters named Lena and Lois. The family lived in relative poverty.

Abbey was able to turn up spotty employment records for both of the women, but nothing solid, and no sign that they were working now.

Abbey had presented this information to Nate yesterday, before he left his office for home.

"Have you contacted them?" Nate asked, walking with Abbey from the break room back toward his office.

"I called only to verify a working number and to see if they still resided at the address I had."

"And do they?"

"Yes, Mr. Kenny, they do."

Nate stopped, waited for one of his employees to pass before he spoke. "It sounds like they could use some money."

Abbey nodded. "Yes it does."

"I want you to call them again. I want you to tell them we're from Chicago, that we have some information that could be financially beneficial to them, and that we're prepared to fly down and speak with them about it."

"Yes, sir. When should I arrange for our travel?"

"Book the flight for tomorrow morning. That will give me enough time to think about how I can make these two work for us."

Abbey closed her cell phone, slid it into the seat-back pocket in front of her.

"Are they still expecting us?" Nate said.

"Yes, sir. The mother, Salesha, kept asking, Are they going to get paid? Did they win the lottery or something?"

Nate laughed a little, thinking to himself, Not the lottery, but if they do what I say, they will get lucky.

52

Abbey parked the big rented Buick in front of a dilapidated frame house. Paint peeled from its aging surface, bedsheets hung in the windows, and trash was strewn over the weed-infested front lawn.

"This is the place?" Nate said with a frown, as he looked through his passenger-side window.

"It's the address I have, sir."

Nate stepped out of the car, wearing a brown suit and black tie. Abbey exited, wearing a skirt suit that closely matched the color of Nate's outfit.

She reached into the backseat, grabbed her briefcase, carried it around the car, and stood beside Nate on the sidewalk.

"Well," Nate said.

A boy wearing a long white T-shirt and a black do-rag whisked between Nate and Abbey on a bike much too small for him.

Nate continued. "Time to do what we came here for."

They walked up the path toward the house, climbed the

creaking, rotten wood stairs, and stood on the big front porch. Nate looked for a doorbell but only found two exposed wires snaking out from a small hole.

He knocked on the door, looked at Abbey, then stood, waiting. Yells of children and a barking dog could be heard in the far-off distance.

A moment later, the locks on the front door clicked undone. The door opened, and behind it stood a woman wearing a large pink T-shirt, boxer shorts, and fluffy Tasmanian Devil slippers. She ran a hand over her wild hair and said, "You Mr. Kenny?"

"Yes, ma'am," Nate said. "I'm Mr. Kenny, and this is Ms. Kurt. We phoned you from Chicago to—"

"Yeah, yeah," the woman said, smiling, showing the gaps from a couple of missing teeth. She pushed the screen door open. "Come in. Come on in."

Half an hour later, Nate and Abbey sat on a soiled living room sofa, drinking Kool-Aid out of plastic cups. The woman who answered the door was Salesha, the mother. Her daughter, Salonica, had been introduced not long after Nate and Abbey entered.

Salonica was painfully thin. She greeted them wearing skin-tight blue jeans and a halter top that exposed so much of her midriff that the bottom of her bra could almost be seen. She extended a hand to Nate, every finger adorned with a gaudy silver ring. "Nice to meet you." Nate took her hand and shook.

She had brought her two twin girls out to meet the visitors. Salonica stood between them, a hand on each of their shoulders. "This is Lena, and this is Lois."

Their hair was parted down the middle of their scalps, pigtails hanging from either side of their heads. They were both pregnant.

"They doin' real good in school," Salonica said. "Because I tell 'em, you don't keep them grades up, I'm gonna get rid of them babies you carrying faster than you can say free clinic."

Nate smiled uncomfortably and took a sip of his Kool-Aid.

After the girls left, Nate got down to business. He told the women that he knew the man who had dated Selena.

"Yeah, we know him. Lewis Waters, right?" the mother said.

"That's right," Nate said. "He's raising your granddaughter, correct?"

"Yeah. So what?"

Nate turned to his investigator. "Abbey," he said.

Abbey opened her briefcase, pulled out two plane tickets, and handed them to Nate. He then set them on the coffee table before Salesha and Salonica.

"I want you to fly to Chicago and tell Lewis Waters you want custody of your grandchild."

Salesha turned to her daughter, and they both started to laugh.

"Mr. Kenny," Salesha said, "do you see the house you walked into? I ain't holding all the money I have for home repairs because I got it in stocks and bonds. There ain't no money. That's why this place look the way it looks. I already got two grandchildren I can't half feed, and they about to have two more children of they own. What do we need with another mouth around here always begging for food?"

"He's not going to give the child to you, Ms. Wells. I can assure you of that. But I want you to ask him all the same. I want you to pressure him, tell him that you believe your daughter died because of him. I want you to tell him that you'll take him to court, fight for the child if you must. He won't want to do that, trust me. The little girl is not only very important to him, but instrumental in maintaining the situation he's in."

"So what happens when he keep on telling us no?" Salonica said.

"You'll tell him that you can make a deal. You tell him if he gives you thirty thousand dollars, you'll leave."

"Thirty thousand dollars!" The mother practically screamed. "We getting thirty grand! How he gonna get that?"

"Don't you worry about it. He'll find a way, I'm sure. And yes, once he gives you the money, then it's yours to keep."

Both women stood from their chairs, hugged each other, and bounced around the living room, screaming.

"But it's up to you," Nate said, raising his voice over the celebrating women. "You hound him so much that he feels he has no choice but to give you what you want."

"Oh, don't you worry," Salesha said, out of breath, her heavy breasts heaving under her T-shirt. "Once we roll into Chi-town, all hell gonna break loose."

53

Her jeans around her ankles, her torso bent over the kitchen table, her palms grabbing the edges, Monica gritted her teeth, groaning as Lewis continued to pound himself into her from behind.

She had already come twice. Her inner thighs were wet with her orgasms, and now she was urging Lewis to finish. Monica pushed back into him, opening herself up, then clamping down around him, trying to squeeze the pleasure out of him. She felt him grab on tight to her, felt his body stiffen, and then he cried out, shooting himself inside her. He slumped over her, huffing and sweating.

Monica eased out from under him.

"What are you doing? Don't," Lewis said, grabbing her, trying to hold her in place.

"My legs are tired, standing like that," Monica said, pulling up her jeans, fastening them. "Besides, Layla might wake up and come down."

"You know that girl sleeps hard," Lewis said, falling onto one of the kitchen chairs, his pants and underwear still around his ankles.

Monica turned around to see him there, exposed. "Pull your pants up."

"Ain't you gonna get a cloth to clean me up?"

"What?"

"C'mon," Lewis pleaded.

Monica went to one of the kitchen cabinets, grabbed a clean hand towel, went to the sink, ran it under cold water, wrung it out, and then slung the twisted cloth at Lewis.

"Hey!"

"Wash your own balls!"

Monica stomped out of the kitchen.

Lewis yanked up his pants.

"What's going on with you?" he said, catching her and taking her by the shoulders.

"The annual Women in Business Ball is Thursday. Are you going with me?"

Lewis rolled his eyes, slumped his shoulders, and whined, "Not another one of those things."

"That's what I thought," Monica said, shaking free of his grip. "Don't even worry about it."

"You know how I am at those things. You gonna have me standing in some corner, looking crazy, while you laughing it up with John, Bill, and Ted, talking about shit I don't understand."

"I said forget it. It's cool," Monica said, standing in front of Lewis, her hands on her hips.

Lewis just stared at her, a guilty look on his face. "Naw, it ain't cool. You promise me if I go, you won't leave my side."

"I can't promise you that, and you know it. There are people I have to talk to."

"I know." Lewis sighed, shaking his head. "All right. I'll go."

"Let me know if I need to pay you, or if this is interrupting one of your TV shows."

"Damn, Monica, I said I'll go, alright?"

"Thanks for taking time out of your busy schedule," Monica said, walking out of the room.

54

M an, that's like the twelfth game in a row I whupped your ass in," Lewis said to Freddy.

After his little tiff with Monica, Lewis had stopped at the store, bought a twelve-pack of beer, and headed over to Freddy's house. They sat in front of the TV, downstairs in his apartment, playing Mortal Kombat.

"I'm killin you," Lewis said. "You gonna play, or am I gonna have to spank you a hundred to zero?"

"It's almost midnight," Freddy said. "Ain't your girl gonna be looking for you?"

Lewis took a swig of his beer. "Man, we had it out. She wants me to go to some business ball thing to celebrate all the folks who making more money than we are."

"What business ball thing?"

"It's this annual thing she wants me to go to with her."

"When?"

"Thursday."

"Where's it at?"

"Why all the questions?" Lewis said. "You want to take my place or something?"

"Naw. I was just curious."

"It's at the Hilton downtown I think she said."

"Oh," Freddy said, fidgeting with his controller. "So you ain't gonna go?"

"You know I don't want to. But this supposed to be such a big deal, so I told her I would."

Freddy grabbed his beer while he stared at Lewis playing the game. "Everything all right with you two?"

"Same old, same old," Lewis said, working the controller, not taking his eyes away from the screen. "You know how it goes."

"You ever think of leaving Monica?"

Lewis mashed the pause button on his controller, then turned to Freddy. "What?"

"I mean, you the one who saying that things are never going right between you two."

"I didn't say *never*. I said sometimes they ain't going right. Are things always perfect between you and Kia?"

"No."

"You getting rid of her anytime soon?"

"Naw," Freddy said. "But you don't like going to her work things, you don't want to hear about her job. Sounds like you might be happier without her. And you never know, you might find somebody who you got more in common with."

Lewis put down his game controller, got up from his chair, and sat beside Freddy on the sofa. He looked his friend directly in the face and said, "What the fuck are you talking about?"

"What?"

"You tell *me* what."

Freddy said nothing. Lewis continued to look into Freddy's eyes, and then he smiled a little. The smiled widened, he laughed, and said, "You fuckin' with me, right? You fuckin' with me."

Freddy started to smile, forced a phony laugh for Lewis. "Yeah, that's right. I'm fuckin' with you."

"I thought so," Lewis said, going back over to his seat.

The smile quickly left Freddy's face as he watched Lewis sit back down and take two swallows from his beer.

"Stop playing games," Lewis said. "Grab that controller so I can whup your ass some more."

55

Lewis pulled his Land Rover into the garage, clicked the remote, and heard the door roll down behind him. His head was buzzing slightly from the six beers he'd consumed at Freddy's place, but he felt good. His dash clock read 12:53 A.M., so he figured Monica would be long asleep. He was thankful for that; because she hadn't rung his cell once that night, Lewis knew she was still mad at him.

She'll sleep it off and be fine in the morning, he thought, grabbing the door handle and preparing to step out of the truck when his phone started ringing.

"Who the hell?" he said, checking the caller ID.

The screen read PRIVATE.

"Hello," Lewis said after flipping the phone open.

"Lewis," a strangely familiar woman's voice said.

"Who is this, and why you calling my phone at one in the morning?"

"We just arrived in Chicago on the red-eye."

"Who is this?" Lewis said, losing patience.

"I should take offense that you don't remember me, boy. This here is Salesha."

Lewis closed his eyes, every muscle in his body tightening.

"You there, Lewis?"

"Yeah, I'm here."

"Salonica here, too."

"Hey, Lewis!" he heard the daughter yell into the phone.

"What brings you all to Chicago?" Lewis asked.

"You know I want to see my grandbaby."

"Salesha, you can't just be popping up out of thin air, expecting me to drop everything just so you can see Layla."

"Really? Why not?"

"Because—"

"Because what? We flew all the way up from St. Louis to see our baby, and we gonna see her. You gonna tell me what time is good tomorrow, or should I come knocking on your door tonight?"

"You don't know where I live, Salesha."

"You wanna bet I can't find out?"

"All right," Lewis said, stepping out of the truck and slamming the door. "Tomorrow. You have to give me your number so I can call you and tell you when."

"That's all right. We'll call you first thing in the morning and get that info then. Have a good night, Lewis."

"Bye Lewis," he heard Salonica yell into the phone again.

"Good-bye," Lewis said.

56

Freddy lay sleeping peacefully in his bed beside Kia when he was suddenly jarred awake by his ringing phone. He flipped in bed and blindly groped for the cell phone on the nightstand.

"Hello," he said, his voice groggy as he glanced at his alarm clock. It was 6:00 A.M.

"Do you have more information for me?" It was Nate on the other end.

"What? It's six in the—"

"I know what time it is. Did you talk to Lewis yesterday? Do you have more information for me?"

Freddy turned to his side to see if Kia had awakened. She had not. Freddy peeled back the blankets and gingerly slid out of bed.

"Hold on a minute," he said.

He walked through the almost pitch black space into the bathroom, closed the door, and clicked on the light.

"We talked yesterday," Freddy said, his hand cupped over the phone, his voice hushed.

"And . . . ," Nate said.

"He was over till after midnight. He and Monica must've had a fight or something. She wanted him to go to some dinner party gala thing, and he doesn't want to go."

"When?" Nate said, sounding very interested.

"On Thursday."

"Where?"

"The Hilton on Michigan."

There was silence for a long moment while Nate thought this over.

"Mr. Kenny?" Freddy said after waiting another moment.

"You said the two of you watch sports. Does he watch basketball?"

"Yeah," Freddy said, as though the question was a stupid one.

"The Chicago Bulls play this Thursday at home, do they not?"

"I think they're playing against the Lakers."

"Would he rather do that than go to this gala Monica is asking about?" Nate asked.

"Who wouldn't?" Freddy said, thinking he heard movement outside in the bedroom. He moved as far away from the door as he could.

"When you speak to him today, tell him you have tickets."

"But I don't."

"You will. And make sure he goes."

57

Shortly after eleven o'clock that morning, Monica sat behind the elevated reception station of her store.

Tabatha stood beside her, ringing out a customer she'd sold three suits to.

"That's right," Monica said, continuing what she was saying after the customer paid for his purchases. "I don't even know what time he came in last night. But I know when I rolled over and last looked at the clock, it was twelve thirty and he wasn't back yet."

"So you think he's sleepin' around on you?" Tabatha quickly said. "I knew you couldn't trust—"

"Of course not! He was probably at Freddy's, playing video games and drinking, but still, he could have come home at a decent hour, especially after acting like he didn't want to go to the gala."

Tabatha sat beside Monica. "Forget him. Take me."

"We keep going to these things together, folks gonna think we're a couple."

"Then take—"

"Don't even fix your lips to say it, girl," Monica said.

"Okay. Then did Lewis even try to apologize this morning?"

"He was knocked out when I got up. I dressed and fed Layla, and I got us out of there, not saying a word to him. He's the one messing up. Let him come to me."

Just then a delivery man walked up to the counter with a wrapped bouquet of flowers.

"Speaking of messing up," Tabatha said. "Look who's trying to fix things. Can I help you?" Tabatha said, leaning over the counter to take the delivery.

"Sign here, please," the young man in shorts and a cycling helmet said.

Tabatha signed and set the flowers on the counter before her. "At least the boy has enough sense to know when he's wrong."

Monica smiled, waved Lewis's gesture off, and said, "I ain't even interested in those. But go ahead and open them. See how creative he got."

Tabatha tore the white paper away from the flowers to expose a dozen fully bloomed peach-colored roses.

"Beautiful. Okay, then," Tabatha said. "Lewis knows a little about what he's doin'."

"Wow. Peach-colored roses. Those are my favorite. Lewis doesn't even know—hold on," Monica said, standing. "Give me the card out of there."

Tabatha plucked the card out from between the stems. She handed it to Monica. "I gave that boy too much credit, didn't I?"

Monica opened the envelope, read the card, and a slight smile appeared on her face. She pulled something else out of the envelope and started laughing.

Tabatha stole the card from Monica, and read it aloud. "Please!" it said. "We've never made cookies before and we need all the help we can get. Signed, the two Nates."

Monica passed Tabatha the other item that was in the envelope. It was a snapshot of Nate and Nathaniel, wearing aprons. Their hands, noses, and cheeks were covered in flour and cookie dough.

"Well, this is just the cutest thing in the world," Tabatha said, turning to Monica. "Tell me again why you aren't in this photo, right there between these two handsome guys?"

"Because Nate is an uncaring, insensitive, evil man," Monica said.

"Oh yeah, that's right," Tabatha said. "Looking at this picture, I remember now."

58

It was after 1:00 P.M. and Lewis sat at the corner table of an empty, run-down fast food joint. He wore his work shirt, jeans, and work boots. His head was resting heavy in his hands, his temples starting to pulse with pain brought on by the meeting he'd had not long ago.

This morning, the ringing from Lewis's phone had pierced his brain like a railroad spike.

"Hello," he said, still in bed under the sheets, his head throbbing from all the beers he had consumed last night.

"Lewis, it's Salesha. You need to be meeting me and Salonica at ten o'clock."

"Meeting you for what?" Lewis said, sitting up in bed, wiping the sleep out of his eyes. He noticed Monica was gone.

"You just do."

"It can't be at ten. I'll be at work."

"You get a lunch break, right? Make it at noon."

"Where?" Lewis said, not certain he was even going to show.

"We gonna be getting our hands and feet done, so meet us at the salon on Forty-first and Cottage Grove."

"Yeah, whatever," Lewis said, preparing to hang up.

"Lewis," Salesha said, her voice much more businesslike now. "I'm serious. This ain't no bullshit."

"Yeah."

At noon, Lewis walked up to the salon, saw Salesha and Salonica in the window looking like twin prostitutes. Huge frozen curls were stacked on top of their heads and sprinkled with glitter. They looked like Christmas trees.

They wore tight T-shirts, miniskirts, and strapped high heels, the straps crisscrossing up their thin calves.

Lewis pulled open the door, and Salonica said, "We can't talk in here. Let's go to your car."

He followed them to the truck. Lewis clicked the keyless remote, watched the two women get in, Salesha in the front seat, the daughter in the back.

Lewis climbed in afterward. "What's this about?"

"Ain't you happy to see us, Lewis?" Salonica called from the backseat.

"Yeah."

"Haven't seen you since my sister's funeral, and all you got to say is 'What's this about?'"

"I'm sorry," Lewis said. "But it's always something with you, so I just want to get to it."

"Fine," Salesha said. "We want Layla."

"She's in day care right now. But I told you, I'll work out a time when you can—"

"Naw. I think you're misunderstanding us. I ain't sayin' we want to see her. I'm saying we want her. I want my grandbaby back," Salesha said.

*　*　*

An hour later and Lewis still couldn't believe Salesha had the nerve to ask him that. He looked up at Freddy, sitting across from him.

"And what did you tell her?" Freddy said, a soda cup in his hand.

"I told her hell the fuck naw, and to get her and her daughter's country asses out of my truck."

"Damn," Freddy said sadly, shaking his head. "What you think they gonna do?"

"She said they weren't gonna take no for an answer. They said they're gonna keep hounding me, ringing my phone. I told them to try it."

"You try giving them a few bucks to go away? You know that's all they probably—"

"I ain't giving them shit!" Lewis said, shooting up from his seat, raising his voice. "Give them money for what? So I can keep my child? Naw, yo'. It ain't like that. Trust me when I say that, Freddy. It ain't going down like that."

A Korean man, the obvious owner of the fast food joint, looked out over the counter as if expecting trouble.

Freddy noticed the owner eyeing them. "Dude looking at us like we about to rob this place." Freddy stood and said to the owner, "What the fuck you lookin' at? We paid for our nasty-ass food. Can't we eat it without your supervision?"

The man ducked back behind the counter.

Freddy sat back down. "Don't stress it, Lewis. You need something to take your mind off this nonsense, and you know your boy, Freddy, got what you need."

"I don't need nothing," Lewis said, his head in his hands again.

"You don't need to see the Bulls spank the Lakers' asses on Thursday?"

"For real?" Lewis said, perking up. Then deflating he said, "Naw, Monica's thing is on that night, remember?"

"Dude, sometimes you gotta do something for yourself. When was the last time I been able to get us tickets to a Bulls game?"

"Like two years ago," Lewis said.

"And when was the last time you went to one of Monica's things?"

"The last time she had one. I gotta go every time she has one."

"So you deserve a break, right?" Freddy said.

"Yeah, you right. Thursday night, we on!"

59

Monica sat on the living room sofa, her elbows on her knees, her palms pressed together, brought to her face as though she were praying. She wasn't. She was angry.

She had spent the evening out with Tabatha, partly because she needed a drink, and partly because she didn't feel like dealing with Lewis. When she pulled into the driveway, it was only minutes before nine o'clock.

She had left Nate's roses at work. But Monica slid the little snapshot out of her purse and looked at it for the umpteenth time that day and smiled.

She should have called Nate and at least thanked him for the flowers, for the lovely photo and the little bit of joy it brought her. But she didn't. She was engaged to Lewis, she had to keep telling herself, and she didn't want Nate to start thinking that would change.

But considering what a complete ass Lewis was being right now, Monica thought maybe he didn't appreciate her devotion to him.

She slipped the photo in between some envelopes in her glove box, knowing it might not be safe from Lewis's eyes if left in her purse. When she entered the house, she searched for Lewis. He was in Layla's room, sitting at the girl's bedside, staring down at her, the night-light burning dimly beside them.

Monica stood at the door for a few moments, knowing Lewis sensed her there, knowing he'd heard her car outside, heard her close the front door, climb the damn steps. But he didn't turn around.

"Lewis," Monica said, her voice low, careful not to wake the sleeping child. "When you're done, I'd like to talk to you downstairs."

She heard Lewis give a sigh he obviously did not try to hide.

"Lewis, did you hear me?"

"Yeah. I heard you," he said, but did not look away from his daughter.

"How long will that be?"

"I'll be down in a minute."

Monica looked up when she heard Lewis finally descending the stairs and realized it had taken him fifteen minutes, not the one minute he'd promised.

He stood in front of her, and said, "What?"

Monica unclenched her jaw to speak. "What were you doing up there? I asked to speak to you almost twenty minutes ago."

"I was spending time with my daughter." His tone was defensive. "I can't do that?"

"I didn't say that. It's just that I asked to speak to you, you said it would be only a minute, but you lied."

"So now I'm a liar because I want to sit with my daughter?"

"You're putting words in my mouth," Monica said.

"I'm putting them back in your mouth, because they never should have come out."

Monica was silent, shocked by Lewis's harshness. She nodded her head and smiled sadly a moment, as if letting it all roll off her back, then said, "We still need to talk."

"About what?"

"About how you reacted when I asked you to go to the gala with me. I want to know why—"

"We don't have to talk about that, because I ain't going."

"What?" Monica said.

"I ain't going. I got some stuff on my mind. I'm feeling kind of stressed."

"I'll say."

"Whatever. I'm not going," Lewis said, walking toward the front door.

Monica followed behind him. "But you said you would."

He turned to face her, just feet from the door. "Why you always want me to go with you to those things? People talking about stuff I don't understand, looking at me, talking shit, like because I don't want to do what they do, be who they are, then I'm less than," Lewis said, getting angry. "I don't know them people, don't like them people, so fuck them people!"

"I'm one of those people."

Lewis looked as though he didn't know just what to say. "Don't ask me to go to none of those things no more, okay?"

"Fine."

"You going to be here for Layla?"

"I'm not going anywhere."

"Then I'm going out for a drink. Don't wait up," Lewis said, opening the door and walking out.

Monica didn't move for a full minute.

Afterward, she went straight to her purse, pulled out her cell phone, dialed a number, and when her call was answered, she said, "Hello, Nate."

60

Two nights later, wearing a silver sequined backless evening gown, Monica walked into the Hilton's large, elegantly decorated ballroom.

The hall was busy with men and women dressed in tuxedos and beautiful formal dresses. They stood, sipping from champagne glasses, chatting and laughing, as big band jazz played in the background.

A man stopped in front of Monica. "You look amazing tonight," he said. It was William Keys, one of her customers. He worked at the Benston law firm downtown.

"Thank you," Monica said, taking the hug he offered her. But her mind was somewhere else. As she hugged William, she was glancing over his shoulder, scanning the room for Nate.

"Well, gotta mingle. See you around okay?" William said.

"Yeah, okay," Monica said, walking deeper into the room.

She had called Nate back, the day after she had first asked him to go with her to this event. Monica was uncertain if she should have gone through with it, and Nate picked up on that right away.

"Is everything all right? You sure about wanting me to go with you?" he asked.

"I'm positive," she said, sounding far less than certain.

"I'm not going to ask why your fiancé isn't going."

"Good. Don't. You want to come with me or not?"

After a short pause, Nate said, "Sure. Yeah, I'll go."

Monica filled Nate in on the details, where and when to meet her, then quickly got off the phone.

Now, walking slowly through the throngs of people, a wineglass in her hand, Monica realized how short she'd been with him and wouldn't have blamed him if he just didn't show.

After smiling, greeting, and chatting with at least a dozen people, Monica found a velvet-cushioned bench to sit on.

She turned up her glass and swallowed the last of her wine.

"Easy. You gotta pace yourself if you don't want to end up drunk and have some man take advantage of you."

Monica looked over the rim of her glass and saw Nate looking incredibly handsome, wearing his black tuxedo, standing before her. He had gotten a fresh haircut, a close shave, and every crease and corner of his suit was razor sharp. His teeth gleamed, and his cufflinks and the Cartier watch he wore sparkled.

"I was starting to worry that you wouldn't show," Monica said.

Nate reached out, took Monica's hand, and said, "That's something that you need never worry about again."

Nate seemed to be having a wonderful time. The two had engaging conversations with other couples and groups, talking about everything from politics to world events to, of course, business. There were so many people who knew Nate, had known Monica from when they were married, and they smiled when they saw the two of them together.

While dancing, Monica's hand on Nate's shoulder, she asked, "Why do people keep smiling at us?"

"What people?" Nate said, his palm pressed softly into the small of Monica's back.

"Your friends, Barry over there, and some of the people we used to hang out with."

"They see us and think we've gotten back together."

Monica and Nate danced and drank and chatted for the entire three hours of the event. Afterward, they stood outside in the warm Chicago spring evening, waiting for the valet to take the tickets Nate held.

Nate turned to Monica and smiled. She smiled back, pulling her silk shawl up over her shoulder, then looked away.

A young man hurried over to Nate. "Your ticket, sir."

Nate gave the man one ticket, and the red-jacketed valet ran off.

"You only gave him one."

"That's because I want you to come with me."

"Nate, no," Monica said.

"Before you say no—"

"I already did. We aren't going to—"

"We'll drive to my house, you can spend fifteen minutes with Nathaniel, and I'll drive you right back. When I told him I was going out with you, he made me promise I'd bring you back, even if only for a moment," Nate said. "Please, Monica."

Monica glanced down at her watch. It was only fifteen minutes after ten o'clock. Lewis would not be looking for her. Yesterday he had admitted that Freddy had gotten tickets to a Bulls game, and that's where he would be. Monica couldn't believe he'd actually admitted that to her.

"Okay, but only for a few moments."

When Nate and Monica walked into his house, Mrs. Weatherly was sitting in the living room, reading a romance novel by the light of an end-table lamp.

She stood, smoothed the front of her dress, smiled, and then walked over to meet the couple.

"Mrs. Weatherly," Nate said, his hand at the small of Monica's back again. "This is Monica, my . . . well, you know who she is."

Mrs. Weatherly extended a hand. "Very good to meet you, ma'am. I've heard so much about you . . . from both of the Nates."

Monica shook Mrs. Weatherly's hand and smiled, thanking her. "Please, call me Monica."

"Mr. Kenny, Nathaniel fought like a champion, but he just could not stay awake till you got back. I know he would love to see the two of you. Should I wake him?"

"No, Mrs. Weatherly, let him sleep." Nate turned to Monica. "I'm going to walk Mrs. Weatherly back to her house in the back, but please, go on upstairs and see Nathaniel. His room is the first door on the left."

"No. I'll just wait—"

"Monica, please. It's fine. I'll be right behind you. Okay?"

Monica smiled, nodded her head. "Okay."

After Nate and Mrs. Weatherly walked out, Monica slowly climbed the stairs to the second level.

Nathaniel's door was open. She stepped into a room decorated with items seemingly from every cartoon ever created. A dim blue lamp glowed at his bedside. Monica walked quietly up to the boy's small twin bed and just stood over him.

He lay on his back, his face turned toward her, wearing white Spider Man pajamas. Monica sighed, in awe at his beauty.

This was the child she had sought out, the child she had found, had wanted so badly to mother, and here he lay, just before her, and she could do nothing but admire him. If things had gone the way she wanted them, the way she planned—no, no! Monica told herself not to get caught up in that. It was over. The decision had been made. She had left Nate, and she could never go back. But couldn't she? She was standing in this room, in her ex-husband's house, over the boy who believed she was his mother.

She was not certain, but she believed Nate still loved her and would take her back if she even hinted that she was interested. Against her will, she allowed her mind to take her there, to the days in that possible future, where they would be a family. She would raise this boy, love him, as she would love Nate again.

She suddenly felt a pain, the loss of what she'd had with Nate, and a longing for what she knew she could never have with Nathaniel.

Monica reached out, smoothed her hand against the boy's curly hair. She touched his fat little cheek, then leaned over and kissed him lightly. When she leaned back, she felt Nate's presence. Not at the door looking in, but behind her, right behind her. She could feel the warmth of his breath on her neck. Then she heard a whisper that sounded like his voice, saying, "I miss you so much."

Monica stood frozen, feeling the slightest kiss on the curve of her skin, between her shoulder and her neck. It sent a warm chill across the entire surface of her body, but still she did not move. When she finally turned around, not a half a minute later, there was no one there.

* * *

After Monica descended the last stair, she saw Nate in the living room, pulling his tie from around his neck, laying it on the table. He turned around as though he had not been upstairs at all. "So, you have a good visit with Nathaniel?"

Monica just gazed at Nate, not knowing what to feel. "Yes," she said, her voice soft.

"He's gonna throw a tantrum finding out that he missed you."

"Tell him I'll see him again," Monica said, walking up to Nate, looking at him as if expecting him to clarify all the uncertainty in her head.

"So you ready to go?"

"Yes," Monica said, the dreamy quality still in her voice.

"Then I'll take you to your car."

Half an hour later, Monica stood outside of Tabatha's door, waiting for the woman to answer.

When her friend finally opened up, she said, "Girl, what are you doing here? I thought the gala was tonight."

"It was. It's over," Monica said, sounding as though she were in a mild trance. "But I have a problem."

"What is it?"

"I'm think I'm falling in love with Nate again."

61

The next day after work, Lewis pulled up into the parking lot beside Kenwood Academy High school. He was alone in his truck, even though he had told Salonica and Salesha he would bring Layla to see them.

Over the last four days, the two evil women had been ringing Lewis's phone day and night, several times in a single hour. Most times he tried to ignore their calls. Sometimes he would answer them.

"Hello!" he answered a day ago, his hand gripping the phone so hard he thought he would crumble it in his palm.

"We're not going to leave you alone till we get Layla back."

"FUCK YOU!"

That was the tone of their conversations lately.

Lewis told himself not to worry. They had his phone number because he had given it to them during Selena's funeral. He had thought about changing it but knew he would have to deal with questions from Monica. Besides that, he told himself he would not be forced into changing his life around because two crackhead lookin' women were trying to cause him stress.

"Talk all you want," Lewis said, during another short, angry call. "You don't know where I live or where I work, so to hell with you!"

But yesterday, while driving into work, Lewis noticed a burgundy Ford 500 in his rearview mirror that wouldn't move from behind him.

Lewis took turns he normally wouldn't have, sped up, slowed down, and then, irate, finally stopped in the middle of the street. The car pulled up beside Lewis's truck, the window powering down.

Salonica was behind the wheel, silver tooth shining when she opened her mouth. "We don't know where you live, but we can find you. Give me back my niece, and you won't have to go through this no more."

"Just do what the girl says," Salesha screamed from the passenger side.

Lewis thought about jumping out of the truck and pummeling the both of them, but he sped off instead. And then, this morning, while hugging Layla before handing her off to Ms. Becker at day care, Lewis looked up and saw the same burgundy Ford parked at the curb, just behind his truck.

"I love you, baby," Lewis said to Layla. "Monica will pick her up this evening," Lewis said to Ms. Becker.

He waited as the woman escorted Layla into the building, watching as Salesha and Salonica watched him from their car. After Layla was out of sight, Lewis took off running toward the Ford. Salonica put the car in gear and raced away.

After that incident, Lewis felt as though he had only one option. Days ago, Freddy had mentioned the idea of paying off the women. Lewis objected to the idea then but ended up going to the bank anyway to see if he could withdraw a sizable amount from Monica's account. As he had known, his name was on her account. He had all the documentation that was needed, and he was informed by the banker that he could withdraw whatever he needed from the account whenever he wanted.

Lewis assumed ten thousand dollars would make them forget about their desire to have Layla back. Something told him that was the only reason they were after him in the first place.

He had to take care of this matter and soon, because things had been crap for him and Monica for almost a week now. At first they had been arguing, but now they didn't even do that, which was worse. They barely said two words to each other. They came and went without alerting the other, neither seeming to care.

The only thing that kept them talking was the plans they had to negotiate regarding Layla's pickup and drop-off, and the other issues relating to her care. Lewis wanted to get all of this off his chest, just tell Monica everything about Salesha and Salonica, even though Freddy advised him not to.

"And what happens when Monica thinks there's a chance you might lose Layla?" Freddy said.

"What do you mean, what happens?"

"She can't have children of her own. I know she loves you, but don't you think Layla is one of the reasons she keeps you around?"

Lewis wasn't a fool. This wasn't new information to him. He didn't think Freddy was totally right, but, God forbid, if those foul skanks were able to steal Layla from him, he didn't want to wonder if Monica would let him stay around. So Lewis had arranged to meet the women and lied to them, telling them he would bring his daughter.

He drove slowly around the high school, to the back, and saw the Ford and the two women standing outside it. They stood next to one of the school walls, smoking cigarettes.

Lewis parked close to them and exited the truck.

Salesha took her last pull from her cigarette, threw it down, and ground it out with the tip of her high-heeled shoe. She looked past Lewis toward the truck, as if trying to look into it.

"Where's my grandbaby?"

Lewis heard what the woman said, but he was not listening. He just continued toward them, taking hard steps, jaw locked, fury burning within him. Then when he was right upon Salesha, he reached out, clamped a hand around her shirt, and forced her hard into the wall behind her. He heard the air push out of her mouth with the impact.

"What the fuck are you doing?" Salonica screamed, throwing wild open-hand slaps at Lewis. He quickly grabbed her and, as though she were a doll, threw her up against the wall beside her mother. There he held them both, struggling, kicking, trying to free themselves.

"Now you listen to me," Lewis said. "If you don't leave my child—"

One of Salesha's wild kicks caught Lewis in the groin, sending a pain through his body like he'd never imagined. He yelled out in agony and crumpled to the ground. His eyes shut, on his knees, his arms wrapped tight around his middle, he heard both women coughing, heard them moving around him.

One of them kicked him, tumbling him over on his side.

"Now you listen to me, motherfucker!"

Lewis opened his tearing eyes to see Salesha screaming.

"I said I want my grandbaby, and I'm going to get her. Or I swear, me and my daughter will make your life shit. Do you hear me?"

"Why?" Lewis coughed.

"What?" Salonica said, her hand around her throat.

"Why do you want her?"

"Because she's all we got," Salesha said. "She's all that's left after you killed Selena."

Lewis climbed back to his knees, the pain starting to subside the slightest bit. "I didn't kill her. She overdosed. You know that."

"Fuck you!" Salonica spat. "Fuck you!"

"She was with you and now she dead," Salesha said. "You the one we blame. Now we want what's left of her. We want Layla."

Lewis slowly rose to his feet, both hands on his stomach. The women took two cautious steps away from him.

"Is there any other way we can do this, because I ain't giving up my little girl. You ain't getting her."

"What other way you talking about?" Salesha said.

"I have money. I can give you money. Ten thousand dollars," Lewis said, defeated.

Salesha turned to her daughter Salonica as if for her input, then turned back to Lewis and said, "Make it thirty thousand and you got yourself a deal."

62

The next day at noon, Lewis walked into a Hyde Park McDonald's, carrying a fat brown envelope. He looked around, saw Salesha and Salonica sitting at a table.

Lewis took steps toward them, and then saw the man a few tables away stand up. He was shaved bald and wore a suit and sunglasses. He looked official, not like he'd know the likes of the two streetwalkers before him, but Lewis assumed he was there for them all the same.

"Have a seat, Lewis," Salonica said, nodding toward the chair. "I'm thinkin' that be a gift for us?"

Lewis was so troubled by all this nonsense that it seemed to be affecting all aspects of his life. He noticed he had been short with his daughter lately, impatient with all of the other things that would never have bothered him before. And he didn't even want to think about Monica. He'd torn her head off more times than he wanted to think about lately, ignored her, walked out on her. Last night, when Monica rolled over and said, "We don't have to discuss anything, we don't have to try to resolve any of our issues tonight, but I need some sex. Can you give that to me?" Lewis had rolled on top of her, tried to give her what she wanted, but he was so stressed by this business with Salesha and Salonica that he couldn't even get it up. Monica looked at him as though he was pathetic, then simply rolled over and went to sleep.

It was in that moment Lewis knew he had to get the women the money they had asked for. He just didn't know how he would get the thirty grand back into Monica's account before she realized it was missing. That was until this morning, when Freddy walked in the office much later than usual. He wore a cheek-to-cheek grin as he walked past the receptionist toward Lewis's desk and said, "Follow me."

Lewis pulled his heavy body from the chair, and met Freddy in the locker room.

Freddy was still smiling. "You're gonna pay those girls their money and let them take their asses back to St. Louis?"

"I told you, I ain't asking Monica for that. And I know I wouldn't be able to replace it without her knowing if I withdraw it."

"Yeah you will." Freddy took Lewis by his shoulders. "The house sold!" he said, faking excitement.

"The house sold?"

"It sold. A little while ago."

Lewis threw himself into Freddy, wrapped his arms around him, and squeezed. "Who bought it?"

Freddy hesitated a moment. "Does it matter? The house sold!"

"How much did it go for?"

"A hundred and twenty-five thousand."

Lewis did a quick calculation in his head, then all of a sudden became sullen. "My part only comes to half what they asking."

"But with my part, it takes care of all of it."

"Naw," Lewis said, shaking his head. "I can't—"

"Lewis," Freddy said, "I'm your friend. Your best friend. And no matter what happens, I got your back. Take my half of the money and pay them fools."

"Are you sure?"

"You know you don't even got to ask me that."

"Man, thank you, but you know you don't—"

"Lewis, I got your back," Freddy said, staring him in the eyes. "You hear me? No matter what goes down, I got your back."

Lewis paused for a moment. "Okay."

Freddy released Lewis, smiled some, and then said, "Go to the bank and take care of your business."

"You my boy. You know that? You my boy," Lewis said, gratefully.

Now, sitting down at the McDonald's before the two women, Lewis slid the envelope across the table. Salesha grabbed it, shoved it in her oversized purse, and smiled. "I don't even got to count this, because I know you learned your lesson about me and my girl, right?"

Lewis nodded. "Right."

"Then I guess we'll never see you again," Salesha said, standing, throwing her purse over her shoulder.

She walked from behind the table. Salonica smiled and did the same.

"Bye, Lewis," Salesha said.

Lewis turned his head away, saw the big man in the suit follow behind them. He watched as the two women got in the rented car and drove off.

The man seemed to disappear after he had walked out the door. Where he went, Lewis did not care. Lewis smiled to himself, because all of a sudden, life had just gotten a lot better.

63

Monica rolled over on her back after making love, her body still tingling from the three orgasms she'd just had.

She smiled, reached out with arms that felt too weak to hold her up. "That was wonderful," she said. "It's been so long, I almost forgot how good you were."

Nate leaned over her, kissed Monica softly on the lips, and said, "I was starting to believe it would never happen again."

Monica gave him an odd look, leaned away from him, and pulled the sheet up over her bare breasts. "It wasn't supposed to. It's wrong for me to be doing this right now, and I know that. I just couldn't stop thinking about you, so I came over."

Nate lay next to her. "I'm glad you did. It's what I've been wanting since the first day you came by. I missed you so much," he said, kissing her on the shoulder.

"Don't do that."

"What's wrong?"

"I know it's been longer than a year, but I still ask myself, how could you have just given me away to another man like that? Let him make love to me while we were still married?"

"I never wanted that to happen. He was supposed to tell me, get my permission before he had sex with you, but he didn't. If he would have told me, I would have stopped him, because by then I had changed my mind about all of that. When I found out, it was too late. Can you ever forgive me for that?"

Monica turned to Nate, slid her body closer to his. "You weren't the only one who was wrong. Just because you set me up to sleep with another man doesn't mean I had to. I could have told him no. I could have resisted, waited till you realized you really didn't want to divorce me. We would still be married. Can you forgive me for that?"

"I already have," Nate said.

There was a long, awkward moment of silence, which prompted Nate to ask, "So what's next?"

Monica waited a long moment before saying, "I know he's been put to bed already, but I really would like to see Nathaniel before I go."

Fifteen minutes later, they had both showered. Monica put her clothes back on, Nate slid on his robe and pajama bottoms, and the two stepped into Nathaniel's room to watch him sleep.

Monica stood, shaking her head, smiling. "I still can't believe you did it. Nate the father."

"I know. I'm a dad now. I can't believe it myself sometimes."

"He is so beautiful. Just look at him. I wish I could hold him."

"You can," Nate said.

"No, no. I shouldn't. I'll wake him."

"My son sleeps like a rock," Nate said, scooping Nathaniel up from the bed and gently placing him in Monica's arms. The child shifted a little and wrapped his arms around Monica's neck but never woke up.

"He's so adorable. I just want to take him home with me and never let him go."

"Come back to me and you won't have to."

Monica looked at Nate as though she was upset by the comment.

"Don't act shocked by what I just said. You know what I want, and I've hinted around enough. Obviously the thought has crossed your mind. We've become close as friends again. We've made love, and you're here, holding my child as if he were your own. So why not?"

"Because Lewis—"

"I don't want to hear about Lewis," Nate said, loud enough to almost wake the child. "You know you have no future with him. Just leave him."

"I can't!" Monica said, carefully handing Nathaniel over to Nate. "I agree, we have become close again. I like it. And I'll even admit, if I weren't involved with Lewis right now, I would probably be running home to pack my things so I could come back tonight. But I am with Lewis. And even though I know we aren't all that compatible, I can't just forget the fact that he's been there for me. I can't just discount that all of a sudden because now you want me back."

Still holding his son, Nate lowered his head.

Monica drew near, kissed the child on the cheek, then Nate softly on the lips. "I have to go before it gets too late."

After Monica parked her car in front of her house and got out, she stopped. The old Ford was across the street again, the aging woman was sitting there behind the wheel as always, just staring at her. This was getting creepy. Before, Monica had only seen the car during the day. It was after nine at night, and there she was again. Monica decided she would finally have to find out what this woman was up to.

Monica looked both ways, then took a step into the street.

All of a sudden, the Ford's engine roared to life, the head-lamps flicking on. Monica hurried toward the car and saw the woman shift the car into gear. She ran up to the window. "Who are you? Why do you keep—" But the woman sped off.

64

The next evening, Tim came by to see how Nate was doing. The two men had been talking, Nate telling Tim that everything regarding Monica was going exactly according to plan.

"And you're still going through with that?" Tim asked, sounding disappointed.

"You think I like doing this?" Nate said, standing. "Do you think I like deceiving her yet again? Having her think that there's something here, that there may be a future for us, knowing that once I get what I want, I'm just going to toss her ass away like I did the first time?"

"Yeah. I think you're enjoying it," Tim said.

"I don't enjoy having to keep my feelings in check."

Just then, the phone rang. Nate walked over to his desk, glanced at the caller ID. "Shit. Not now."

"Who is it?" Tim asked.

"International call. It's Daphanie."

"Go ahead, playboy. You're the man who has to have two women. Pick up the phone."

Nate picked up the phone and spoke to Daphanie for all of five minutes. For the entire time, his tone lacking enthusiasm, he stared at his brother. Finally he said, "I'm sorry, honey, but I really need to be going. I have some work that has to be completed by tomorrow."

Tim sat, his arms crossed, and just shook his head.

"Sure. I got a second to consider one last thing," Nate said. "What's that?" He listened intently, then closed his eyes at the news he had just heard, as though it was something that he just couldn't handle at that moment. "Yeah," Nate said. "I know. Why not? You're right. Why wait? I'll think about us getting married when you get back, okay? But let me go. Okay. Me, too. Bye." Nate hung up the phone.

His eyes still on his brother, Tim didn't say a word.

"What are you looking at?" Nate said.

"You've told me before that you could see yourself marrying Daphanie someday."

"Yeah, so what?"

"I'm not getting that impression now."

"You don't know what you're talking about."

"Before the phone call," Tim said, "you said something about not liking to keep your feelings in check. What feelings? Feelings for who?" Tim stood up, walked over, and sat on the corner of Nate's desk, smiling a little. "Could you be having feelings for Monica? Could my brother actually still have a heart in there, and it's being melted by the woman he used to love and knows he never should have gotten rid of?"

"Dammit!" Nate said, slamming his fist on the desk. "I want my money back, and I want to hurt her for what she's done to me."

"But . . ."

"But . . . we're getting closer. And I think . . . I think, yes, I might still have feelings for her."

"That's what I'm talking about!" Tim said, hopping off the desk, opening his arms. "Give me a hug!"

Nate shook his head and hugged his brother, then fell back into his chair.

"So what happens now?" Tim asked.

"She won't leave me as long as she's with Lewis. So I have to give her reason to leave him, and that means keep doing what I'm doing."

"Continue to blackmail that boy who has nothing to do with this nonsense between you and Lewis?" Tim said. "That's not a good idea, Nate. That man does not deserve to have his home and family threatened. I would really reconsider that if I were you."

"You don't have to tell me what I'm doing is wrong. Tori pulled a gun on me in California for this nonsense. So I know. But once I get my wife back, I'll be through with it. And if it makes you feel a little better for this boy I'm blackmailing, if he continues to act right, maybe I'll throw him a little something extra in the deal."

65

Freddy sat in his basement apartment, brooding, all the lights off, candles burning around him. He thought about what he had just put his best friend through, the lies he'd told him, the predicament he knew he would be putting Lewis in after all this was over. Kia sat next to him on the bed, just staring at him. The lights were off, not because he'd turned them off, but because the electric company had shut them off for late payment.

"I gave them the money before they closed today, and they promised the power would be back on tomorrow," Kia said.

"I'm so sick of this," Freddy said softly, angrily to himself.

"Baby . . ."

Freddy turned to Kia, a look of disgust on his face. "You want to know why we're poor like this? Why we've always been poor like this, since I was eight years old?"

"Why, Freddy?"

Freddy paused for a long moment, then said, "I never told you, because I been afraid of how you would react."

"Just tell me."

Freddy swallowed hard, then said, "My father ain't die in no car accident like I told you. I killed him."

"What?"

"He was beating my mother. Like almost every day," Freddy said, not looking at Kia, but staring straight ahead. "I thought he was gonna kill her. So one day, I came home for lunch, because I knew he'd be in his room sleeping. I grabbed my baseball bat, and I killed him in his sleep."

Kia jumped off the bed, released Freddy's hand, and backed two steps away from him. "You killed your father?" she gasped.

"We never been able to catch up without my father's income, so we been struggling since. Bills went unpaid, and the house taxes, and now some motherfucker went and bought those taxes out from under us."

"You got to pay those," Kia said, an urgent note in her voice. "After a certain period passes, somebody can come and buy those—"

"Somebody else already has. That's what I'm sayin'."

"Freddy, no."

"Yeah. And they telling me that if I don't do certain shit for them, against Lewis, then they gonna kick us out of this house and have it torn down."

"Who is this? You told him no, right?"

"I've been doing what he's been saying—I ain't got no choice! But something's tellin' me Lewis is gonna come out of this thing fucked up if I keep on."

"You can't do that to Lewis! He's your best friend."

"If I just keep on, the man said he'd give me the title to the house. It'll be all paid for, no back taxes, nothing. We'll be all caught up."

"That doesn't matter," Kia said. "You've known Lewis since you were eight."

"It does matter!" Freddy said, standing up. "Me and Moms

been poor as hell almost my entire life. She don't say nothing, but I know she blames me. I know it. Regardless what I say, I ain't nothing but a loser to her. I killed her husband, and all she got to show for it is bills she can't pay and a son who earnin' minimum wage. I do what this man tells me, I can give her a house. I don't, having me for a son, she would have not only lost her husband, but the house he bought her."

Kia stared at Freddy for a long while before standing and saying, "You're wrong and you know it." She walked over to him, took him in her arms. "You don't want to admit it, because you're scared. But you know if you were to tell your mother—"

"I'm not telling her this."

"Okay. But if she were to hear, you know she wouldn't want you to go through with this. You're a better man than this, Freddy. You aren't the type to let yourself be pushed around by whoever this is. My father is one of the top lawyers in this city—"

"I don't want to bring him into this."

"And I don't think we'll have to. I'm thinking the threat alone would be enough. All I'm saying, baby, is that there is a better way than to deceive your best friend like this. You know that, don't you?" Kia said, holding Freddy's face between her palms.

"Yes," Freddy said softly.

"Tomorrow, you tell this man, whoever he is, he can kiss your ass, and if he doesn't lay off, he will have an entire law firm camped outside his damn house. Can you do that for me, baby?"

Freddy smiled sadly, nodded his head. "Yeah."

66

Monica sat at her desk in her home office, looking at photos of the building that Nate's friend had sent her. A knock came at the door.

"Come in," Monica said.

Lewis stepped in, carrying a bouquet of a dozen roses wrapped in paper. He walked around her desk, laid them in her arms, and gave her a kiss on the lips. He stepped back and smiled.

"What's this?" Monica said.

"Things have been kind of rough for us over the past couple of weeks. It was because I was going through some things, but I'm happy to say that stuff is over, so now I want us to get back to the way we were."

Monica chuckled a little. "Just like that, huh?"

"Yeah."

Monica set the roses down. "The last serious conversation I had with you, I remember you saying fuck people like me and that you never wanted to go with me to another business function again."

"I didn't say fuck people like you. I said fuck the people at those functions and then you said you were one of them people."

"I see," Monica said. "That clears it all up. But just so I'm even clearer, I assume you don't want me to ask you to any other functions?"

"I'm not sure. I have to think about that."

"Well, you take your time. But while you do that, I want to ask you another question. Where is this really going between us?"

"What?" Lewis said, looking as though he had no idea where such a question had come from.

"The future. When I asked you before what you wanted to do after graduation, you seemed uncertain. So now I'm asking you what you want to do with me."

Lewis smiled, scratched his head a little. "I mean first we're gonna get married, right?"

"Right. But after that? The wedding is just the beginning. We'll have years and years to share our lives together."

"Then that's what I guess we'll do—share our lives."

"But my life isn't just sitting on the living room sofa, letting you fall asleep on my shoulder while we watch DVDs. I love Layla to death, but my life also isn't about just helping you raise her. And although it's good, my life isn't just having sex and taking nasty pictures with you, either."

"Where is all this coming from?" Lewis said, stepping closer to Monica, before she held out her hand to stop him.

"Right now," Monica said, turning her computer monitor toward Lewis so he could see, "I'm looking at a building I'm thinking about buying to expand my business. Do you think it's a good idea? Or will you not be cool with that, because you think it's going to take me away from the house more?"

"I don't know."

"I'm asking you, Lewis. I need to know. One of the reasons

why I always ask you to go to those functions with me is because I want you to know what I'm doing, know the people I'm doing it with. But you flat out told me that you want no part of that. And then when I get some of the most exciting news this year about my business and try and share it with you at dinner, you tell me you don't want to hear it."

"I'm sorry," Lewis said.

"Just tell me something. You don't want to be around the people I do business with. You don't want to be around me or them when I talk about it. What do you think is going to happen once we get married? You think I'll quit?"

"No. I never—"

"I won't stop talking about it. I won't stop doing it. As a matter of fact, if the business becomes more successful, I'll probably talk about it more." Monica stood from her chair. "Is that the kind of future you want? Have you thought about that?"

Lewis took a moment to think, stepped right up to Monica, placed his hands on her shoulders, and said, "I'm sorry for all of those things I said. I was going through something, but it's over now. About me not appreciating what you do and you wanting me to be a part of it—you never put it to me like this before. But baby, I love you. Do you hear me? I love *you*. And that's every part. You want me to go to your functions, I'll go. You want me to work for you, washing the windows at your store, sweeping and mopping, so I can learn what you do from the ground up, I'm right there. All I know is, I want to marry you. I want us to be a family and enjoy each and every day together until we get no more. How is that to answer your question about what the future holds for us?"

Monica smiled a little and said, "It definitely gives me something to think about."

67

The next day, Freddy sat in the passenger seat of Nate's Mercedes.

"Why are we stopping here?" Freddy said, looking out his window at the new townhome they were parked in front of.

"Just get out," Nate said, stepping out of the car himself.

That afternoon, Freddy had done as Kia told him and called Nate.

"Mr. Kenny, I was just calling to tell you I'm not doing this for you anymore. It's wrong, and I—"

"Yes you are."

Freddy was quiet for a moment, not knowing how to respond. "No. I said—"

"Freddy, we are at a very important junction where your

cooperation is imperative. Or do I have to remind you that I still hold the deed to your house, and I will—"

"I don't give a fuck about that," Freddy said, finally feeling as though he had had enough. "I said I ain't doin' it no more. You got me doin' this shit to my friend, and it's fucking with me. It ain't right!" Freddy said, sounding on the verge of tears. "You try and kick us out our house, I know some lawyers, and—"

"Freddy, Freddy. Hold on," Nate said, his voice soothing all of a sudden. "Let's not let this get out of hand, okay? So you said you won't do it anymore. Fine. But do me one favor. Let me take you somewhere, show you something, and make you a simple offer. You can say yes or no to it. Either way, I'll be fine with it. Will you do that for me?"

The phone still pushed up to his ear, Freddy thought a long moment, then said, "I don't got to do nothing? And I can say no if I want?"

"Absolutely."

"All right."

Nate opened the door of the brand new townhome and stepped in.

Freddy and Nate walked across the hardwood floors of the large living room, vaulted ceilings overhead.

"It has a formal dining room, as you can see," Nate said. "And up there is a loft area that overlooks this room."

Freddy turned, admired the beautiful new house. "Why are we here, Mr. Kenny?"

"Come on, follow me."

Freddy followed Nate through the rest of the house—looked at the kitchen with stainless steel appliances and the newly built deck out back. They then took the stairs down to the finished basement.

"You could stick a pool table down here or a nice flat-screen," Nate said. Then he showed Freddy the three large bedrooms, the two and a half baths.

Nate ended their tour out on the deck, overlooking the large backyard.

"Oh yeah," Nate said, pointing and smiling. "Two-car garage."

"This is a nice house," Freddy said. "But you still haven't told me why I'm here."

Nate cleared his throat and said, "The money Lewis gave to Salesha and Salonica, he stole out of Monica's account. I expressly bought your little rehab house so you could give him the money to replace the stolen funds he had taken. Which means since Monica most likely won't be getting her bank statement till the end of the month, she will never know what happened till then. But now I want him to steal from her again."

"What? Why?" Freddy said, surprised.

"I want you to tell Lewis what happened, that someone has bought the taxes out from under you, and unless you pay them in two days, your house will be taken and your family will be thrown out on the street."

"But how will I get the money back to him?"

"You'll tell him your mother has cashed in her insurance policy and you're expecting the check any day now."

"But my mother doesn't have an insurance policy," Freddy said.

"That's not a problem."

"Because I'm getting the money from you?"

"No," Nate said.

"Then how will I—"

"You won't," Nate said, smiling. "Freddy, this time Lewis will get caught." Nate stepped close to Freddy, took him by his shoulder. "I want my wife back, but she has to have a reason to leave her fiancé. This will be that reason."

"But what will happen to Lewis?"

"I don't know. I assume nothing. Monica knows Lewis doesn't have the money to pay her back, so at worst, she'll demand that he leave the house. She'll have nothing more to do with him."

"I don't want to do this," Freddy said.

"Are you certain? You stand to gain quite a bit if you do."

Freddy was certain, but his interest was piqued by what the man just said. "Gain what?"

A smile reappeared on Nate's face. "I think you already know."

Freddy felt the slightest weakness in his knees, felt his heart skip a beat. "You mean—"

"Do this for me Freddy, and this house is yours. Free and clear. I promise. But, as I said before, you alert Lewis as to what's going on, give him the smallest hint, then all deals are off." Nate extended his open hand to Freddy. "Will you at least sleep on it tonight? Call and let me know in the morning?"

Freddy looked down at Nate's hand, then up in his eyes before hesitantly pressing his palm into Nate's.

"Yeah," Freddy said, reluctantly. "I'll think about it."

68

That night, Freddy couldn't sleep. He lay awake tossing, thinking about the decision he had to make. With Kia in his arms, he told himself that he would tell Mr. Kenny that he would not take him up on his offer. His girlfriend was right. He couldn't continue to deceive Lewis. Freddy figured that even if he didn't do it Mr. Kenny would turn over the old house. At the very least, he and his mother would no longer have to worry about paying the taxes. It would be theirs again.

Satisfied with his decision, Freddy started to drift off to sleep. Suddenly he was awakened by the sound of gunfire cracking in the distance. It jerked him up in bed, his eyes wide open, looking around the dark room. He lay in bed listening, thinking he had heard movement above him in the house again.

Freddy felt his heart start to beat hard in his chest, felt sweat start to coat his brow. He thought of getting his gun, walking those stairs, and having to hope he wasn't going to find another intruder in his house. But he listened again and decided it was nothing more than his imagination terrorizing him.

The distant gunfire continued. Someone was probably getting killed, Freddy thought. As he drifted off again into a restless sleep, he asked himself, just how far away were they? A mile, a block, the next yard over?

Before his lids fully closed, Freddy knew what he had to do.

"That's what I'm gonna need. Fifty thousand," Freddy told Lewis the next day as they stood in the middle of the Evergreen Plaza mall. "I wouldn't be asking you if they weren't going to take the house tomorrow."

Lewis shook his head, acting as though his hands were tied. "You know the only place I can get that kind of money."

"I know. You did it before. Why can't you—"

"How am I going to get it back?"

"I told you. My moms cashed in her insurance policy. The only reason I'm asking you for the money now is because we had already expected her check to have come. We called the people, and they said they put it in the mail two days ago. It should be here by tomorrow, the day after, latest," Freddy said, looking his best friend straight in the eyes. "The money will be gone out of her account for a day, two—tops. I need this from you, man."

Lewis turned his back on Freddy, pushed his hands through his hair, turned back and said, "What if I just tell her what's going on and ask her for the money? She might give it to you."

"And what if she doesn't?" Freddy said. "Then the house is just gone, and my family is on the street. C'mon, Lewis. You know I'd do it for you. I gave you my end of that thirty thousand—"

"I know. I know," Lewis said, looking like he was about to agree to make the biggest mistake of his life. "You'll have the money back to me tomorrow, the day after at the latest, right?" Lewis asked, sounding worried.

"Right! I promise."

"Fuck!" Lewis said. "I'll get the money for you by this evening."

69

Nate had come by Monica's store, picked her up, and taken her to the building his friend wanted to sell her. They walked through the vacant old structure that had been a publishing company some thirty years ago. The space was vast. Huge windows let in lots of sunlight, and the hardwood floors were still in great condition.

Nate stood at one end of the third floor and watched as Monica walked about, mentally working out in her head how she would set up her new store in the building if she were to buy it.

"So what do you think?" Nate said, his voice echoing through the huge empty space. He walked toward Monica, the sound of his heels loud against the floor.

"I love it!" Monica said. "It's perfect. And the location . . . tell your guy I'll take it!"

"I don't have to do that," Nate said, digging into the pocket of his trench.

"Why not?"

"Because I already bought it," Nate said, waving the contract in front of Monica.

"No, you didn't," Monica said, shocked.

"Yes, I did."

"No."

"Yes."

"I want the building, but I can't take this from you." Monica dug into her purse and pulled out her checkbook. "Look, I'll write you a check right now for it."

"You sure you have enough in your account for that?"

"Yes," Monica said. "Of all people, you should know how much money I have. How much do I owe you?"

"In a week," Nate said. "I want my people to go over it thoroughly to make sure it's perfect before I transfer it to you. Till then, let me savor the thought a little longer that I bought you this building, okay?"

"Okay. But next week I'm paying for it. Like it or not."

"Think I can have a hug?"

Monica smiled, walked over, pretending to be shy, and gave Nate a hug. She looked up at the high ceilings, at all the options the building gave her in the design of the new store. She walked out into the middle of the room, spread out her arms, and spun in a circle. "Store number four, baby!" she shouted.

Nate stood by, a proud smile on his face.

"Kenny Corporation," Monica shouted to Nate, "get ready for a little competition, 'cause I think there's about to be a Kenny Corporation number two."

"How do you feel?" Nate shouted back, walking over to her.

"Wonderful!"

Right next to her, Nate said in a softer voice, "This is how you'd always feel if we were together again."

70

Lewis had stolen things before—a toy when he was a
child, a few things out of a neighbor's house, shoplifted
an item or two at the occasional convenience store when
he was a little older. But never before had he felt like such a
criminal.

As he walked toward the door to exit the bank, he felt that
the security guard was eyeing him, felt as if all the security cameras were swiveling around to keep him in sight.

He kept expecting someone to say "Stop! Wait!" Expected
someone to chase after him, tackle him in the bank's lobby, just
before the door, and wrestle away the fifty thousand dollars in
cash he had in the envelope in his jeans pocket. But a moment
later, Lewis was outside, walking toward his truck, where
Freddy sat in the passenger seat. Lewis climbed in, shut the
door, and wiped away the sweat that had accumulated on his
brow.

"You get it?" Freddy said.

Lewis dug the money out of his pocket, held it out to Freddy.

"Tomorrow, man. The day after at the latest. That's what you said, right?"

"Yeah, man. That's when I'll get it back to you."

"You promise?"

Freddy paused a little longer than Lewis thought he should have. "Yeah. I promise."

For a brief moment, Lewis thought not to let go of the envelope, then he finally surrendered it to his best friend.

71

I got it," Freddy said two hours later, standing at Nate's front door.

Nate opened the door, stuck his head out, and looked both ways, up and down the street. "You made sure he didn't follow you, right?"

"Yeah," Freddy said, feeling awful about what he was doing.

"Come in."

Freddy followed behind Nate through his huge, beautiful home. Freddy was envious. How could some people live this luxuriously when others like him and his moms were living in damn near squalor?

But that would soon change, Freddy assured himself as he was led into Nate's den. Once this was over, his family too would have a beautiful home.

Nate walked over to the far wall of the den and removed a framed oil painting from the wall, revealing a safe. He rolled the big dial, back and forth and back again, yanked on the handle, and pulled the safe door open.

Freddy peered over Nate's shoulder to see what was in there. He only caught a glimpse. But what he did see were numerous small stacks of bound crisp bills.

"You have the cash?" Nate said, extending a hand.

Freddy walked over to him, pulling the thick envelope out of his jeans pocket, and placing it in Nate's hand.

Nate sat the money in the safe. "I'll count it later to make sure it's all there."

"Okay," Freddy said.

Nate dug back in the safe and pulled something else out. "You want to see something?" Nate said, smiling.

"Okay."

Nate opened up a contract, set it on his desk, pointed down at it, and said, "That's the address to the house I showed you. There's my name as seller. And right there is your name as the buyer. Did I spell it right?"

"Uh, yeah," Freddy said, trying to stop himself from smiling. But he couldn't help himself. It appeared on his face as he thought how proud he'd feel once he showed his mother the house. Once he told her and Kia they would not have to live the way they'd been living anymore, in that neighborhood with the constant threat of being robbed, shot, or killed.

"I think your mother will be very proud of you once she sees it. What do you think?"

"I think you're right," Freddy said.

Nate stuck the contract back in the safe and closed the door. He stepped back to Freddy. "Give it about another week, all this will all be over, and you'll have your house. Okay?" Nate said, holding out his hand.

"All right," Freddy said, feeling a bit more comfortable now about shaking Nate's hand.

72

Three days later, at eight forty-five that night, Lewis sat in his truck, parked outside of Freddy's house, practically yelling into his cell phone. "Freddy, where the fuck are you, and why ain't you picking up your phone?"

The morning after Lewis had stolen the fifty grand out of Monica's account and given it to Freddy, Lewis had approached him at work.

"The check come yet?" he asked Freddy as they slipped on their work boots.

"Mail don't come until this afternoon. But I told Moms the second she get it to give me a call, okay?"

"All right. Let me know."

After work, Freddy found Lewis and told him that the check hadn't come. But he said it would definitely come tomorrow. At home that night, Lewis intentionally said very little to Monica. He stayed out of rooms she was in and told her he had a bad headache, retiring to bed much earlier than he normally would have, just to avoid speaking to her.

The next day, Freddy wasn't at work. Lewis knew this wasn't Freddy's day off, and when he asked the receptionist, she said, "Freddy called in sick this morning."

Immediately, Lewis thought something was wrong. It was no coincidence that on the last day Freddy had to pay back the money to Lewis, he was sick all of a sudden.

At 2:00 P.M. Lewis had called Freddy's cell phone. He got his voice mail. "Freddy, where are you, man? You got me hanging here and it's making me nervous. Give me a call."

Two hours later, Lewis hadn't received a call back, so he called Freddy's home phone. No one answered, not even a recorder.

"Shit!" Lewis said, sitting in his truck. He drove by the house, knocked on the door, and rang the doorbell, but no one answered. He walked around the house, peering in the windows to see if there was anyone there who just wasn't answering the door. After fifteen minutes of that, Lewis got in his truck and left.

That night, Monica asked Lewis what was wrong with him.

"What are you talking about?" He was outside, washing his truck in the dark. Of late, he was doing anything to avoid conversation with Monica, fearful she'd discover somehow just by his guilty facial expressions that he had done something terribly wrong.

"You've been avoiding me," Monica said. "I thought you said whatever you were going through was over."

"It is. I just wanted to wash the truck," Lewis said, nervously dipping his rag back into the bucket of soapy water.

"I see. Okay," Monica said, looking through him, knowing he was lying about something.

Now it was the end of the third day, and Lewis sat outside Freddy's house. Lewis glanced at the dash clock again: 8:48 P.M. Somebody should be home by now, he thought.

Lewis got out of the truck, walked up the stairs, approached the door.

"I don't know where Fred is," his mother said after letting Lewis in the house.

"He hasn't been at work the last couple of days."

"I know. He said he's been sick. But he left without tellin' me where he was going, and I don't know where he went."

"Are you sure he's not downstairs?" Lewis asked, thinking that maybe his mother was lying for him and all the while Freddy was down there, hiding in a closet.

"No. But Kia is."

"You mind if I go down and say hi to her?"

"Be my guest."

Lewis turned and for a brief moment thought about turning around and asking the older woman about her insurance check. But he decided not to, knowing this business was between him and Freddy, at least for the moment.

Kia was on the sofa, one of her law books open across her lap. She immediately got up upon seeing Lewis and walked over to him.

"Hey, Lewis. You looking for Freddy?" she asked.

"You seen him?"

Kia lowered her head. "He's been gone since I got back from school."

"He hasn't been at work."

"Yeah. He's had this stomach thing."

Lewis could tell something was wrong by the way Kia was talking to him.

"Has he told you about anything dealing with me and him?"

"No. Like what?"

"I don't know," Lewis said. He paused and looked at Kia, hoping she'd tell him something—that was, if she knew anything. "I guess nothing. I'm gonna take off," Lewis said, turning and starting toward the stairs.

"Lewis," Kia called, halting him on the first step.

"Yeah?"

She looked at him for a long moment. Lewis read guilt on her face. Kia looked as though she was on the verge of admitting something to him, then she simply said, "Uh . . . I'll tell Freddy you've been looking for him."

73

That night, Nate leaned against his kitchen counter, his sleeves rolled up, a towel in his hand, drying the dinner dishes after Monica had washed them.

Not only had she made dinner for him and his son tonight, but the evening before, she had taken Nate and Nathaniel out for ice cream, and then to their favorite park. It had been three days since he had gotten the money from Freddy, and Nate found it hard to believe that Monica had not noticed it missing yet. He guessed that since she had probably checked her account balance just the other morning, there was no need for her to check it again anytime soon.

He thought of suggesting the idea to her some way, but he knew that once she noticed the missing money, the ball would start rolling and the search for the money would be on, disrupting the calm nature of everything that was going on right now. Nate was enjoying the time they were spending together and knew that with each day that passed, each hour, Monica was coming closer and closer to deciding that she would come back to him.

Nate stepped behind Monica and wrapped his arms around her waist as she continued washing dishes.

"Why have you been spending this time with us lately?"

"You don't like it?" Monica said, peeping back at him over her shoulder. "I can finish these dishes and never come back if you like."

"You know that's not what I'm saying. It's just—"

"I don't know why, Nate. And I really don't want to understand it. Right now, I want to see you and Nathaniel, and I'm glad that you're letting me."

"And Lewis doesn't mind you being gone as much as you are?"

Monica shook her head. "I don't know what's going on with him, and I'm tired of guessing."

"So can I assume that all this extra time my son and I are getting means that you're considering what I asked you?"

Monica set the dish she was washing back down in the soapy water. She paused a moment, then turned in Nate's arms to face him.

Just then his home phone started ringing.

"I'm not getting that," Nate said.

"No. Get it. I'll remember what I have to say."

Nate hurried into his den, assuming he knew who was calling. He glanced at the caller ID; as he had thought, it read INTERNATIONAL CALLER.

Nate set his hand on the receiver but did not pick it up. This had been Daphanie's third call today, and she had called twice yesterday. Nate had not taken either of the calls and had not gotten around even to listening to her voice messages. He felt too guilty about the feelings he had for Monica to even begin to think about how he would confess this to Daphanie.

"Just somebody trying to sell me something," Nate said back in the kitchen, his arms back around Monica's waist. "You were saying . . ."

"I was saying what I've always said, that nothing has changed. I'm enjoying this. I love your son, and . . ." Monica smiled. "I might even have some feelings for you. But me spending time here doesn't mean that I'm making decisions about anything. It could mean that, but I just don't know. But seriously, would you rather I not come around anymore? Would that make things easier?"

"No. Harder. And I'm sure Nathaniel would kill me if he knew I was the reason 'Mommy' wasn't coming around. What I was thinking is that I want more time. Why don't you stay over a night?"

"Oh, no," Monica said, stepping out from Nate's arms. "What I'm doing is bad enough already."

"That's right," Nate said. "So what additional harm could one night together cause? Why not get a glimpse of what it would be like to be here with me and my son overnight like a family?"

"Nate, I told you—"

"Think about it. Will you at least do that for me?"

"Maybe," Monica said.

74

"What the fuck?" Freddy yelled the next night after Nate had finally answered the door, wearing his bathrobe.

Nate looked down at his watch and saw that it was almost nine thirty. "What are you doing here?"

"What do you mean? What am I supposed to do? Lewis has been ringing my phone, coming by my damn house, harassing my moms, my girl. When is this shit going to be over?"

"You told them not to say anything to him, right?"

"Yeah, I told them. But I ain't even been going to work. I can't answer my phone, because I think he might try calling me from another number. What the fuck do I do?"

Nate noticed that Freddy looked pretty haggard. He had not shaved, or combed his hair, and Nate could have sworn those were the same clothes he was wearing last time he had spoken with him.

Freddy was shaking his head now. "I don't know. I don't think I want to keep on with this. Just give me the money back."

"Come in here!" Nate said, closing the door behind Freddy. In the living room, Nate stepped very close to Freddy, looked him sternly in the eyes. "There is no giving back the money. You're in this now, do you understand that?"

"But I can't take this."

Nate grabbed Freddy by the shoulders. "This won't go on for much longer, I assure you. Keep out of sight and wait. Everything is going to happen as planned in a day or two. Somehow I'll get her to notice the money is missing and then it'll be all over."

Freddy shook his head, appearing on the verge of breaking down. In Nate's grip, the boy felt weak, fragile. "I don't know if I can keep this up. I don't know if it's worth it."

"You're getting a brand-new house!" Nate said, becoming annoyed with him. "You'll be able to move your family out of that horrible neighborhood, away from the shooting and thievery. Your family will no longer have to worry about that, and you'll no longer have to worry about them. You have a baby who's going to be born soon, don't you even care—" Nate stopped himself and looked at Freddy with disgust. "You want it to end. Fine," Nate said, stepping away from Freddy and turning toward his den. "You don't want the house. You want the money instead—I'll give you the money. Come back here, and I'll give you what you ask for," Nate said, walking away. But he stopped when he didn't hear Freddy behind him. "You want the money or what?" Nate said, turning back.

"Naw," Freddy said, looking as beaten and worried as he felt. "I need to do this for my family."

"That's right. You do, and you will. And when all this is over, you'll know you made the right decision. Alright?"

"Yeah, okay," Freddy said, still sounding uncertain.

Nate walked Freddy to the door, opened it, and watched the man step out. "The moment something happens, I'll let you know."

"Thanks," Freddy said.

Nate closed the door, parted the curtain beside it, and watched Freddy until he got in his car and drove out of sight.

Nate walked back upstairs, entered his bedroom, removed his bathrobe, and slid back under the sheets.

"Is everything alright?" Monica asked.

"Yeah, just a neighbor going out of town in the morning and he wanted me to keep an eye on his house," Nate said, sliding closer to Monica, wrapping his arm around her bare waist. "Now, where were we?"

75

Monica had told Lewis she would be back tomorrow afternoon, that she was driving down to Detroit early today with Tabatha to meet with some people about opening a store there. Lewis was glad she was gone. It gave him time to think without having to duck and dodge her around the house.

Now, at almost ten o'clock, Lewis sat in Monica's home office, looking at the computer monitor. He was online, on Monica's bank's Web site. He had her account page open, staring at her account activity, at the fifty-thousand-dollar withdrawal he had made five days ago.

He was shocked that after so long Monica still hadn't come to him about the missing funds. Lewis figured someone must have been looking out for him. But as he shut down the computer and reached over to click off the monitor, he knew something had to be done, and it had to be done by tomorrow.

76

Freddy sat in his apartment on the bed, staring at the television but not paying attention to what was on. The discussion he'd had with Nate not an hour ago was still on his mind. Kia stepped out of the bathroom after taking a shower. She wore a nightgown and was smoothing lotion into her hands and arms.

"Are you hungry? You want something to eat?" she asked Freddy.

"Naw, I'm good," Freddy said, paying Kia little mind.

"Are you sure, 'cause I know you didn't eat dinner."

"Goddammit!" Freddy yelled, standing. "I said I wasn't fucking hungry, I meant it. Okay?" After a moment, he sat back down, lowering his head, knowing he had made a mistake to yell at Kia that way. If she had decided to walk out of there that moment, Freddy wouldn't have blamed her.

Instead, she quietly approached the side of the bed and stood there. "You never told me what happened after you told that man that you wouldn't be helping him anymore."

Freddy's arms were crossed over his chest, a scowl on his face. He cut his eyes to glance at Kia but said nothing.

"Freddy, you need to talk to me."

Freddy clicked off the TV and pulled Kia over to stand between his knees. "I tried to tell him. But then he offered me something I couldn't refuse."

"No. Don't say that. There is nothing that he could offer you—"

"No, no. Just wait till I tell you."

Now Kia crossed her arms, looking angrily away from Freddy as though she wasn't interested in what he had to say next.

"A house, Kia. A brand-new townhouse, three beds and two and a half baths. No more living in the basement for us. And it's in a nice neighborhood. No more hearing gunshots at night and people breaking in."

"He's going to give you a new house for doing this?" Kia said, doubt in her voice.

"He showed me the paperwork with my name on it."

"And you believe him?"

"Yes. It's going to happen. I know it. All I have to do is—"

"Sell out your best friend," Kia answered for him.

Freddy was quiet.

"What's going to happen to Lewis after all this is over? Do you even know?"

"He'll probably lose Monica. But the way he was treating her, he was on the verge of losing her anyway. So one way or another it was gonna happen. At least this way, we get a new house, a new start, a new fucking life, Kia."

"But you lose your best friend," Kia said.

"Yeah," Freddy said, shame in his voice.

"And you're okay with that?"

"Goddammit, Kia!" Freddy yelled. He immediately apologized, calming some, then said, "I have no choice."

Kia stood there staring at him, shock on her face. She pulled his arms from around her waist and slowly backed out of the space between his knees. "Maybe that's all right with you, but not with me." Kia grabbed one of the pillows and the folded blanket on the foot of the bed and moved toward the stairs. "Maybe my father was right. Maybe you're not the man I thought you were."

77

Nate sat bolt upright in bed the next morning, breathing hard. He looked wide eyed in the direction of the bathroom. He heard the shower water going and figured Monica was in there under it.

Nate jumped out of bed, walked around the room, as if searching for something. He went to the windows, parted the curtains, looked outside as far down both sides of the street as he could see.

The dream he had this morning was so real that even now he quietly opened the bedroom door, looked down the hallway, and then took the stairs down to the first floor.

"Hello," he called.

No answer.

Nate quickly walked through the house, opening doors and peering into rooms to make sure that no one was there. Upstairs, he crawled back into bed, hearing that the shower water had stopped.

Last night, Nate had suddenly awakened out of his sleep. He

felt Monica sleeping peacefully beside him. He leaned over, blindly found her cheek, kissed her there, and was about to fall back off when he thought he felt a presence.

He continued lying there on his back, feeling only half awake, when he'd decided to raise his head. There, standing at the foot of the bed, Nate saw the shadow of a person—a woman. He could not tell for sure, but he felt it was Daphanie. Nate said nothing, and neither did the woman standing in his bedroom. He felt his eyes closing, even though he was struggling to keep them open. He wanted to climb out of bed, explain what was going on, why there was another woman in his bed, but his limbs would not move. His head felt even heavier. It fell back to the pillow, leaving Nate wondering what would happen after he had fallen back to sleep.

The only consolation was that he knew that it had not been Daphanie in the room. He had smelled the strong, sweet scent of perfume. A perfume different than the brand Daphanie wore.

"I said, are you all right?" Monica repeated, pulling Nate out of his thoughts.

She was standing beside the bed, fully dressed.

"Oh, yeah," Nate said, turning to face her. "My mind was just somewhere else. Sorry." He slid out of bed, wrapped his arms around her. "And how are you doing this morning?" he said, leaning in to kiss her. Monica turned away from him.

"Feeling guilty about staying over last night, huh?" Nate said.

Monica stepped out of his hug. "This'll be the last time I do this, Nate. It's not that I didn't enjoy myself, but I have to re-connect with Lewis and decide what I'm going to do with that situation. I know I can't do that while I'm seeing you. It wouldn't be fair to him."

"I guess I understand," Nate said, knowing in a few days Lewis would be found out, giving Monica reason to finally leave him.

"I appreciate you making this easy."

"But will you do me a favor?"

"Sure."

"If you decide not to be with Lewis, will you let me know? Because I feel there's still something here for us."

Monica smiled, touched Nate on the shoulder. "Sure I will."

78

Morning number five, and Lewis was waiting outside of Freddy's house for someone to answer the door again. He looked down at his watch, knowing that Monica was probably on her drive back from Detroit. She had not called him, so he assumed that she had not found out about the missing money, but he knew that would happen any day now, if not any hour.

Freddy's mother opened the door. "Good morning, Lewis. I told Freddy you were looking for him. He still hasn't gotten back to you?"

"No, Mrs. Ford, he hasn't. Is he here?"

"No. I'm sorry, he isn't. He's been in and out a lot lately. I've barely seen him in the last three or four days."

"Do you know where he is now?" Lewis said, trying to look past her to get a peek into the house.

"No. I can't say that I do. He should be at work. Have you tried there yet?"

"No. But I'll do that. Thank you."

"Take care, Lewis," Mrs. Ford said, closing the door.

Lewis turned and slowly walked down the steps.

Something had to be up. Freddy wouldn't do anything like this, Lewis thought, stopping in the middle of the short flight of steps. He knew how important it was that Lewis got this money back into Monica's account.

Regardless of what had happened, Lewis wondered why Freddy didn't just come to him. At least let him know what was going on, so he wouldn't have to sweat this shit like he had been.

Lewis stepped off the last stair and was heading to his truck when he heard something.

"Pssssst."

Lewis stopped in the middle of the sidewalk, turned and saw Kia standing at the side door of Freddy's house.

He pressed a finger to his chest, asking if she was calling him.

Kia looked about, nodded her head, and whispered loudly, "Come here!"

"What is it?" Lewis said, hurrying over to her, making sure he was not seen. It seemed she wasn't supposed to be talking to him. He stopped, standing in front of Kia at the side door.

"You're not going to find Freddy," Kia said.

"What are you talking about?"

"He knows you're looking for him, but he's hiding."

"Hiding?"

"I don't know a lot about what's going on. But the other night, Freddy told me about a man who's blackmailing him, making him do things to get back at you."

"What? What man?" Lewis said in disbelief.

"I don't know, Lewis," Kia said, still looking out, making sure no one saw her. "But Freddy said if things go the way the man wants, then Monica would probably end things with you and put you and Layla out."

Lewis didn't have to think a minute to realize the man Kia was talking about was Nate Kenny. "I don't believe that, Kia. Freddy's my best friend. He wouldn't do that."

"I didn't believe it either. I didn't think he'd go through with it. But he said the man promised him a new house if he did. I'm sorry, Lewis. I know you've been looking for him, and I didn't want to be the one to have to tell you this, but I thought you should know."

Lewis hugged Kia. "Thank you. I appreciate it. Where can I find him?"

Kia looked sadly up at Lewis. "He should be at work. He left here not even an hour ago. But you have to hurry. He's not going to be there long."

"Thanks again," Lewis said, turning to leave.

"And Lewis . . ."

Lewis turned.

"When Freddy comes back, I'm going to be gone. Tell him not to come looking for me."

Despite what Freddy was doing to him, Lewis felt sorry for his best friend at that moment, knowing he was about to lose the first woman he had ever truly loved.

79

When are you going to tell her the money's missing so this can be over with?" Freddy said frantically into his cell phone.

He was in the alley behind his uncle's management company.

Mr. Kenny said he'd do it today and assured Freddy that it was almost over. But Freddy didn't hear much of that, because a noise from behind him caught his attention.

"Mr. Kenny, I got to go!" Freddy said quickly, spinning around to find Lewis standing right behind him. Immediately, Freddy felt a fist across his jaw, knocking him back into a wall of cardboard boxes.

Lewis bent down, grabbed him by the front of his shirt, stood over him, his fist cocked over his head, ready to strike again. "What the fuck is going on, Freddy? What the fuck is up with the money?"

"Lewis, I been meaning to talk to you, I'm serious. But the check ain't came in yet, and—"

"Don't fucking lie to me, man! I'm supposed to be your best friend. Why are you lying to me?"

"What are you talking about? I ain't lying."

"You are! Kia told me about the man that's blackmailing you. Is it Nate?" Lewis said, shaking Freddy by his shirt.

"Lewis, this wasn't—"

"Is it him?" Lewis yelled angrily.

Freddy grimaced, a look of pain and shame on his face. "Yeah," he finally admitted.

"Why the fuck, Freddy? Why you doing this to me?" Lewis said, sounding more hurt than Freddy had ever heard him.

"I ain't want to. But he was the one who bought the taxes on my house. He was gonna throw us out unless I asked you for the money."

"And you did it?" Lewis said.

"Did you hear me? He was going to put my family out. We was going to be homeless."

"I don't give a fuck about what he said he was going to do. You were my friend. You could've came to me. We could've made a plan, handled this shit. You said you always had my back, and look what the fuck you do to me."

"I'm sorry, man. It's just that—"

"Fuck you. Just give me back the money and I don't ever have to say shit to your ass again."

Freddy didn't speak, just looked apologetically up at Lewis.

"Give me back the fucking money!" Lewis said, shaking Freddy again.

"I ain't got the money! He do. And he ain't giving it back. He gonna tell Monica today that the money is missing. He's wants her to find out, wants you to get caught so she'll put you and Layla out."

Lewis released Freddy into the boxes and turned his back on him, grabbing fistfuls of his own hair. "Fuck! Fuck, fuck, fuck! Goddammit, Freddy!"

"You can get it back," Freddy said from behind Lewis, his voice timid.

Lewis turned.

"He has a safe where he put the money. He's at home now. You can go there, take the money back, then put it into Monica's account before she finds out."

Lewis looked at Freddy as though he hated him, and Freddy was sure that he did.

"Lewis, there ain't no other way. I can go with you if you want."

Lewis stormed back across the space between them, grabbed Freddy again, reared back with a punch, wanting to slam his fist into his face, wanting to break some of his bones, have him experience a fraction of the pain that Lewis was going through at that very moment. But he could not. He held the punch just beside his own head, his fist shaking.

"If this don't turn out right, I will never forgive you," Lewis said.

80

Nate sat in his den, his hand on the phone, about to pick it up and call Monica. He would tell her that he wanted to go ahead with the sale of her building to her.

He would tell her that she should check her account again, just to make sure she had the funds available, and that's when she would see that the money was missing. That was when all the work that Nate had done would finally pay off.

He had picked up the phone and punched the first number when there was a knock on his door.

"Yes?" Nate said, mildly annoyed.

"Mr. Kenny," Mrs. Weatherly said from behind the door. "You have a guest."

"Who is it?"

"She would not say."

Nate smiled, setting down the phone. He knew it was Monica. It would be good to see her, even though she had left only two hours ago.

As Nate walked down the hall, he heard Nathaniel laughing, and he figured Monica was playing with his son in the living room. But when Nate entered, he saw that it was not Monica, but Daphanie. Her suitcases were near the front door, and she sat on the sofa, Nathaniel in her arms, tickling him.

Nate was shocked to see her there, for she hadn't called to let him know she'd be coming home early.

But as he walked closer to her, he remembered she had called, a number of times. He was just so caught up with Monica that he had not bothered to answer or retrieve the messages.

Nate crossed the carpet, wishing he could have appreciated just how good she looked. Her hair was cut into a slightly different style. Her brown strands were now highlighted with blonde streaks, and she wore a pale pink outfit Nate had never seen. She looked rested, her skin almost glowed as though the time away rejuvenated her.

"Hey! Surprise, surprise," Nate said, trying to seem enthused about her early arrival, as he walked to her, his arms open.

Daphanie hoisted Nathaniel off her lap, and stood. She wrapped her arms around Nate, hugged him tight, and kissed him on the cheek. "I tried calling you, but you didn't answer. Did you get my messages?"

Nate paused for a moment, something not seeming right. He couldn't put his finger on it, so he said, "I'm sorry. I was so caught up with this client that—"

"I know. With Mr. Nate, business always comes first," Daphanie said, smiling. But Nate knew the smile wasn't a sincere one. He could tell something was bothering her.

"Well, are you hungry? Do you want to go out and get some lunch?"

"McDonald's!" Nathaniel said.

"No. I'm fine," Daphanie said. "Just a little thirsty."

"There's cranberry, orange juice, some punch in the fridge. Or were you talking about something a little stronger?"

"Just some water, please."

"Coming right up," Nate said. As he walked toward the kitchen, he glanced back at Daphanie, saw her rubbing her temples as though something was really bothering her.

Nate poured some cold water into a glass, and just stood there beside the fridge, trying to put his finger on what was giving him such a weird feeling. He thought back to the moment he had hugged her, then he realized—no! She couldn't have.

All of a sudden Nate's knees felt weak. That couldn't have been the case, Nate told himself. He must be wrong. He knew there was only one way to find out.

Nate walked quietly back into the living room, stood before Daphanie with the water. She had not even recognized him there, she was so caught up in what seemed to be bothering her.

"Daphanie, baby. Your water."

She looked up at Nate with what he read to be a sad, accusatory expression on his face.

"I don't think I want the water," Daphanie said. "I just want to go upstairs, shower, and take a nap."

And that's when Nate realized he had smelled the perfume she was wearing now. It was different from what she always wore, a fragrance she had probably bought in England, the same scent that he had smelled on the woman from his dream last night.

Daphanie walked slowly toward the stairs.

"It wasn't a dream, was it?" Nate said. "It was really you. You were here."

Daphanie turned around, her face wet with tears.

81

It appeared that Daphanie would have stayed with him, Nate thought, after he had confessed that it was his wife with him in bed.

Daphanie had told Nate that she was trying to call him to tell him that she was coming home early. She didn't leave it on his voice mail, because she wanted to surprise him.

When she got home, it was late, and she didn't want to wake him, just slide into bed beside him, and make love to him.

But she said she could almost tell the moment after she had let herself in the house that something wasn't right.

After telling Nate all this, Daphanie tearfully asked who was the woman he was in bed with. Nate admitted it was his ex-wife.

"Tell me it was a one-time thing, that you don't still love her, that we can just forget about it. I promise I'll never mention it again."

This was the moment. Nate could have done what Daphanie asked, and continued on with her, but he would have been lying.

He did love Monica, and he hoped it wasn't the last time he'd be with her. So despite how much Nate knew it would hurt her, he said, "I still love her, Daphanie. I think we should end this now."

An hour later, after Daphanie gathered the things she had left at his house over the course of their relationship, Nate stood just outside his front door, and watched as she got in her car and drove away.

Nate turned to go back in the house, when suddenly, he felt the barrel of a gun pressed to the side of his head. He heard the gun cock. Out of the corner of his eye, he saw Lewis step out of the bushes that bordered the sides of his doorway.

"Who's in the house?" Lewis said, his voice low.

"Nobody. My son and his nanny are in her guest house out back."

"Good. Move."

Lewis held the gun on Nate as he walked behind him, through the house, and toward Nate's den.

Inside the den, Lewis closed the door.

He looked around, his eyes settling on the framed oil painting on the wall. "Take that down."

"What are you talking about?" Nate said.

Lewis walked over to Nate, struck him across the top of his head with the butt of the gun. Nate fell to both knees, almost blacking out.

"Get up," Lewis said.

Nate slowly started to raise himself from the floor.

"I said, get the fuck up!"

Nate moved faster.

Lewis pointed the gun at Nate. "I know what you've been up to, motherfucker. I know what you've done."

"Who told you?" Nate said, his hands raised to shoulder height.

"Who the fuck you think? The man you've been blackmailing."

Nate shook his head, sorry that he would have to deal with Freddy later.

"Now I'm about a minute from putting a bullet in yo' ass, unless you do exactly what I tell you."

"You aren't shooting anyone," Nate said, defiantly. "Kill me, you go to jail, and who takes care of your little girl. You came here for the money. I'll give it to you, and you can rush over and try to deposit it back into Monica's account, but it won't do any good. She'll still find out you've taken it, if she hasn't found out already, and then it's over for you."

"Let me worry about that," Lewis said, taking a step closer to him, shoving the gun in Nate's face. "Just open the fucking safe and get my goddamn money."

82

After Monica had left Nate's house that morning and driven home, she had expected Lewis to be there. She was going to walk into the house, sit him down, and once and for all figure out what they were going to do—figure out if there was a future for them or not. But she didn't see his truck on the street, and when she pulled her car into the garage, his truck was not there either. Monica walked up the walk, carrying her overnight bag, when she noticed the old Ford parked across the street once again.

Monica stopped at the sight of the car, as she always did. But this time it was different. The older woman was not sitting behind the wheel—she was standing beside the car.

From across the street, the woman looked directly into Monica's eyes, then started toward her.

"Hello," she said, once she reached Monica. "My name is Bertrice Thompson. Can I talk to you?"

The woman told Monica a shocking story, one that she didn't think she could believe.

"My daughter cannot have children of her own, and she and her husband were ready to adopt the little girl named Layla."

"What do you mean, adopt Layla?" Monica asked, surprised. "Layla was never up for adoption."

"She was. Last year. The father, Lewis Waters, the man who lives in that house with you, had put her up for adoption. My daughter and my son-in-law said they wanted the child. They went through the process, and all the while, Mr. Waters would bring her over so they could spend time with the little girl. She even spent the weekend a couple of times."

Monica felt a wave of jealousy pass over her at the thought of another woman mothering Layla.

"They loved that child, wanted to sign contracts and everything, till Mr. Waters suddenly changed his mind."

"I don't believe you," Monica said.

"Then come with me. You can talk to my daughter."

"I'm not going anywhere with you," Monica said, anger in her voice. "I don't know who you are or what you're talking about."

"Please," Mrs. Thompson said. "If you only knew what my daughter went through to get that child, how deeply she fell in love with her."

"I'm sorry, Mrs.—"

"If you knew what it was like to not be able to have children, then you'd understand how important this was to her," Mrs. Thompson said.

Monica stopped, her heart going out to the woman's daughter. "Okay, Mrs. Thompson," Monica said. "I'll follow you in my car."

Mrs. Thompson's daughter was beautiful, a nurse, and a year younger than Monica. It wasn't premature menopause that had stripped Barbara of her ability to have children, but a childhood disease. The failed adoption had happened just as Mrs. Thompson had told Monica. Barbara even had dozens of pictures to support her mother's claims.

Barbara took Monica up to see what was supposed to have been Layla's room. It was painted pink. Matching pink curtains hung from the windows, stuffed animals crowded the twin bed.

"What am I supposed to do about this?" Monica said outside the front door as she was preparing to leave.

"Have him reconsider," Mrs. Thompson said, speaking for her daughter.

"I don't know if I can do that. I love the child, too."

"Then just think about it," Barbara said. "And if you find it in your heart, you know where we are."

Monica hugged Barbara, feeling closer to her than Barbara would ever know. Monica received a hug from Mrs. Thompson and said, "Take care."

As Monica walked toward her car, she felt a deep depression descending upon her. Her cell phone rang. She looked at the caller ID, saw that it was Nate. She wasn't in the mood to speak to him that moment but answered the call anyway.

"Hello."

"Monica!" Nate said, sounding frenzied. "Can you get here as fast as you can. It's an emergency!"

"Why? What's wrong!"

"Lewis just stuck a gun to my head and stole fifty thousand dollars from me."

83

"The story I told you about Tim and me getting into a bar fight? That was a lie," Nate said after Monica arrived. "Lewis and his friend Freddy, I don't know if you know him, they jumped me, right outside, while Nathaniel was still in the car. They beat me pretty badly."

"No!" Monica gasped. "Why would they do that?"

"Ever since our meeting, Lewis had been accusing me of trying to get you back. And although I did want you, I never came to him with that. But he wouldn't let it go. He would call my office, threatening me. He would e-mail me photos, trying to let me know—"

"E-mailed you photos?" Monica interrupted. "What kind of photos?"

Nate walked over to his computer, opened up his photo software. "I didn't say anything to you because I figured he was just going through something, and I didn't want to start anything between the two of you, but . . . ," Nate said, clicking on the attachment, opening up the three still photos Lewis had sent of him and Monica having sex.

Upon seeing them, Monica threw her hand over her mouth, shocked. "Oh my God," she winced.

Nate moved the mouse, clicked on another file to open it, and said, "There's more."

He opened up the video player, clicked the play button, and the video of Monica having sex with Lewis began to play. "Oh, no!" Monica said, even more overwhelmed. "Turn it off. Please!"

Nate did as he was asked. "I didn't want to show you those. But after what he just did, I figured you needed to know what was going on."

"I'm so sorry, Nate," Monica said, looking as embarrassed as he had ever seen her. "But you said he put a gun to your head."

Nate pulled the towel he was pressing to his forehead away and showed Monica the blood that oozed from the wound Lewis had given him. "And he stole fifty thousand dollars from my safe."

"That doesn't sound like Lewis."

"I have hidden surveillance cameras throughout my house and office. I have the proof if you want to see it."

"No," Monica said. "But why would he take money from you?

"I don't know. Maybe he gambles. Maybe he owes someone and they're threatening his life. But one thing I asked myself, if he'd steal from me, what would stop him from stealing from you?"

"What?" Monica said, sounding dismayed at the very idea that it could be true.

"I know you don't want to believe it, but when was the last time you checked your accounts?"

"I don't know. The day we went to see the building. He's bought some things without telling me right away. But he wouldn't take that kind of money without informing me. He just wouldn't."

Nate stepped out from behind his computer. "I'm not saying that he did, but go online. Just check to make sure."

Monica quickly took Nate's place behind the keyboard and started busily tapping away at the keys. She grabbed the mouse, moved it about, clicking it frantically, then stopped, focusing her eyes on the screen, and said, "Oh my God! There was a fifty thousand dollar withdrawal almost a week ago."

"It was him, Monica. It was Lewis."

"No."

Nate grabbed Monica by the shoulders. "What do you want to do? I told you, I have proof. Normally I would go to the police with this, but because this is your fiancé, if you want to just work this out with him yourself, I'll let you do that. But you have to do something."

Monica paid little attention to what Nate was saying, still not believing that Lewis would do this to her.

"Monica! Do I call the police, or do you want to handle this?"

Monica focused on Nate. "I'll do it."

"I'll go with you."

"No," Monica said. "That'll just make things worse."

"Then you should call the police. He has a gun."

Monica stood, grabbed her purse from the desk." I don't know," she said, looking uncertain about just what her next move would be. "I have to think. But I'll handle this, and I'll get your money back. I promise."

Nate pulled Monica into him, giving her a hug. "I'm sorry all this had to happen."

"Me, too."

84

Twenty minutes later, Layla said from the back seat of Lewis's truck, "Daddy, are you okay?"

Things weren't perfect, but Lewis said, "I'm better now." He was driving home from the bank, where he had deposited the money he had taken back from Nate. Turning the corner to the block where he lived, he thought how surprised he was that Monica had not called his cell phone. He was sure Nate had called her, told her everything that had happened. The entire ride home, Lewis had been trying to decide what it was he was going to tell Monica. Would it be lies, a portion of the truth, or the entire thing? He wasn't sure, but just like the last time he'd gotten caught up in a situation with Nate, Lewis realized that the truth would probably be the best way to go.

Monica would understand, Lewis told himself. Hell, she was his fiancé, they were on the verge of getting married. This would be something they would just have to get past.

When Lewis pulled the truck to a stop and parked in front of the house, he was surprised to see Monica sitting on the front steps, her face in her hands.

Lewis got out of the truck, staring at her as he opened the back door and pulled Layla from her car seat. Walking toward Monica, he could not read a single emotion on her face. She stood, called for Layla, extending her arms.

Lewis set Layla down on the grass and watched his daughter run to her.

Reaching the stairs, Lewis braced himself, and said, "What's going on?"

Hugging Layla, Monica looked up sadly at Lewis and said, "You love your daughter, don't you?"

"What kind of question is that? Of course I do."

"Then why were you going to give her up for adoption?"

Lewis almost stumbled backward after hearing the question. He wondered how Monica could have found out about this, and then Bertrice came to mind. "That was almost a year ago. Before—"

"Before I came back into your life?"

"Right," Lewis admitted.

"I know. I had to think about it, and I figured I'm the reason you changed your mind at the last minute. I figured you thought since I couldn't have children, not having Layla would probably lessen your chances of me wanting to be with you."

"Monica, not in front of Layla. Let's talk about this inside."

"No! It makes me wonder just how much you love her, if you were going to give her away but only decided to keep her because I came back into the picture."

"Do you know how we were living?" Lewis said, getting angry. "I couldn't take care of her. I could barely buy food and pay the bills. You think I wanted to give her up? I wasn't doing it because I didn't love her enough. I was doing it because I love her as much as I do! But you came along, and I knew you would love her, treat her like your own, and then I wouldn't have to be without my child. I was only trying to do what was best for her . . . what was best for us."

"And where does stealing fifty thousand dollars from Nate fall? Is that doing what's best for us, too?"

And so she did know, Lewis thought. "Monica, you have to know what was going on. The man was blackmailing Freddy."

"And that's why you and Freddy damn near beat him half to death in front of his three-year-old son?"

"Monica, he was trying to take you from me."

"And sending him those pictures of us having sex—that video that I never wanted to make in the first place—what, that was supposed to stop him?"

"Monica, you don't understand what kind of man he is."

"I know exactly who he is. I was married to him for four years. And I don't believe a thing you're saying to me."

"I'm telling you. He did all those things. You think I'd lie to you?"

"You've stolen from me. There's fifty thousand dollars missing from my account."

"I put it back."

"You stole it from Nate so you could put it back. You were trying to cover your tracks, thinking I would never find out. But I have, and now—"

"And now what?" Lewis said, taking a step closer to her. "There's more to this than you know. But we can talk about it, get through it, and still have our life."

"Lewis, I don't think so," Monica said, standing, pulling Layla close to her.

Lewis slapped his palms to his face, threw his head back, and cried, "No, no, no!" When he pulled down his hands, there were tears running over his cheeks. "Monica, I would never do anything to hurt you."

"But you threatened to shoot Nate."

"I would never lie to you," Lewis said, stepping just in front of Monica and his daughter. "All I want is for us to love each other, get married, and raise my little girl."

"Lewis, too much has happened."

Lewis quickly closed the gap between him and Monica, put his arms around her and his child, and kissed Monica softly on the cheek, his tears clinging to her face. "Don't you know I love you? Don't you know that?"

"Yes."

"Then say we can be together. Say you won't leave me."

"Lewis—"

"Say it!" Lewis said, squeezing Monica tighter.

"Daddy," Layla said, "you're scaring me."

"Daddy's fine," Lewis said. "Monica's fine, and everything's going to be alright, right Monica?"

"That's right," Monica said, seeming scared as well.

"Good. Now all we have to do is decide when we're going to get married and everything will be perfect. Right, baby?" Lewis said, kissing Monica's cheek again.

"Right," Monica said.

Just then Lewis heard police sirens screaming in the distance. He hoped they were for someone else, but something deep inside him knew they weren't. A moment later, he saw two cars screech to a halt in front of the house.

The doors opened. "Lewis Waters," a metallic sounding voice said through a bullhorn. "Step away from the woman and child."

Lewis smiled sadly at Monica. "If you only knew how much I love you."

"Lewis Waters," the police requested again, "step away from the woman and child."

Lewis took Monica's face in his palms and kissed her lips softly. He then reached down to his daughter and said, "Baby, Daddy has to go with the police officers, but Monica will take care of you until I come back, okay?"

"Okay, Daddy," Layla said, about to cry.

"You know how much Daddy loves you, right?"

"I know, Daddy."

"Good." Lewis hugged his daughter tight, as though he never wanted to let her go, then stood, turned to the police, and raised his arms over his head.

"If you are armed, remove the weapon from your person," the police said.

Lewis slowly reached behind him, under his shirt, pulled out his gun, and dropped it to the ground beside him. A tear raced from Monica's eye as she grabbed Layla and pulled her close. Three police officers rushed from their vehicles, hurried across the lawn, grabbed Lewis, pushed him to the ground, and then handcuffed his wrists behind his back.

"Good-bye, Lewis," Monica said softly to herself.

85

Three weeks later, Freddy sat waiting in a chair that faced a two-inch-thick unbreakable glass barrier. This had been the first time that he was allowed to visit Lewis in the Cook County Department of Corrections facility.

Now, after writing Lewis half a dozen letters, apologizing to him for everything he had done, and begging to come see him, Lewis had finally agreed. He had called Freddy two nights ago.

"I'll give you five minutes. After that, don't contact me again."

Upon arriving at the prison, Freddy was searched, then escorted into the visitation area and told to sit.

He had been waiting for fifteen minutes and could not help but think about all that had happened over the recent weeks. The day after Monica had found out about Lewis taking the money from her account, Freddy had gone to Nate.

"It's all over. You going to transfer the new house into my name now?" Freddy asked, standing in Nate's den.

Nate was writing something on a pad, then looked up and said, "You're not getting the house, Freddy. Our agreement was that you not breathe a word of what was happening to anyone, least of all Lewis. You didn't hold up your end of the deal."

"But everything was done. I did what you told me," Freddy said, worried. "You had the money. Monica found out, and the police have Lewis. It all worked out. I should get the house."

"It just so happened to work out the way I wanted it to. But there was no guarantee of that. You telling Lewis could have ruined everything, could have negated all the work and planning I put into this. That was all because of you," Nate said, rising from his desk and walking around it toward his door. "So you get nothing."

"Then just give me the deed to the old house, what you promised me at first. That's the least you can do, considering I lost my friend behind this."

Nate stopped before opening the door, turned to face Freddy. "I sold that eyesore to a developer who's made plans for new construction. I assume he'll be notifying you as to when you need to vacate."

"What!" Freddy said angrily, stepping in front of Nate.

"You heard me. I'm sorry, but those were the terms of the agreement."

"What are you talking about, terms of the agreement," Freddy said desperately, grabbing Nate by the shirt. "That's my home. My father bought that house. It's the only place my family has to live."

"You should have thought of that when you breached our contract and informed Lewis of what we were doing. Now get out before I call the police."

*   *   *

Lewis walked up behind the thick glass, wearing a baggy gray jumper, a serial number stenciled on his left breast. He sat down, grabbed the phone at his side, and waited for Freddy to pick up.

"Five minutes," Lewis said.

"How you been doing?" Freddy said, smiling as best he could.

Lewis did not answer, just stared at Freddy, unblinking.

"Why you still in here? Thought you would've made bail by now."

"No money, and Monica ain't paying it," Lewis mumbled, looking through the glass, not at Freddy, but past him.

"You shoulda called me. I would've given you—"

"Four minutes."

"All right, all right," Freddy said. "But when you going to court? I can be there. Be a witness. Tell them it's all on me. It's all my fault."

"Court's in three days, and I don't want you there. There ain't shit else you can do for me," Lewis said, now staring directly into Freddy's eyes. "You already done enough."

Freddy lowered his head, ran a hand over the hair that was growing longer than he usually kept it. He looked up, changed the subject. "So what's happening with Layla?"

"Monica's got her. She's trying to adopt her," Lewis said.

Freddy felt bad for Lewis. Almost as bad as he felt for himself.

"We living with my uncle now. I know he don't want us there, at least he don't want me there, but he let us in, because we got nowhere else to go after that motherfucker sold my house."

Lewis was looking at the dirt under one of his fingernails, as though none of what Freddy was saying made any difference.

"I don't know if you know, but Kia left me. She . . ." Freddy pressed a fist to his mouth, coughing to hide the emotion in his voice. "She aborted our baby. She killed my child, Lewis," Freddy said, quickly turning away in his chair, wiping at his face. He turned back, another weak attempt at a smile on his face. "But I'm gonna get her back. You wait and see. And I'm gonna still start that real-estate company, you know what I'm saying? Ford and Waters Real Estate," Freddy said, holding his hands up before him, as if holding the sign. "No, Waters and Ford Real Estate. That sounds better, don't it?"

"Your five minutes is up," Lewis said, preparing to stand.

"Wait! Hold it, Lewis!" Freddy begged into the phone.

Lewis remained seated a moment longer.

"It wasn't supposed to happen like this, I promise, Lewis. You my best friend. I never, ever meant this to hurt you like this. You got to believe me. He held my family over my head. What the fuck else was I supposed to do, man? What the fuck else?"

Lewis stared into Freddy's face but still did not speak a word.

Freddy smeared the tears from his cheeks, and said earnestly, "But I'm gonna make this right, man. That motherfucker had me do this to you. He took away the only home I ever lived in, made me more of a disgrace to my moms, and had my girl leave me, made her kill my baby. Do you hear me, Lewis? I ain't got shit to live for now, so that motherfucker is going to pay. I swear to God, on our friendship, on my moms and Kia's lives—that motherfucker is going to pay. You believe me, Lewis? You believe me?"

Lewis continued to stare at him, then after a second said, "Yeah. I believe you. Good-bye, Freddy." Lewis hung up the phone, stood, and walked away.

86

The next evening, Nathaniel stood in the kitchen and asked, "How long, Mommy?" He was wearing his little apron, a baking mitt on one hand.

Monica kneeled behind him, her arms around his waist, as they looked through the oven door at the chocolate chip cookies they had just slid in. "Ten minutes, and they are going to be sooooooo good, they're gonna dance in your stomach. You know how that feels?"

"No," Nathaniel said, still eyeing the cookies.

Monica turned the boy around and tickled his belly.

"Mommy, Mommy, stop!" Nathaniel said, laughing and screaming, trying to push her hands down.

"Okay, you two. No roughhousing in the kitchen while cookies are baking," Nate said.

"Or what?" Monica said, walking over to Nate and kissing him on the lips.

After Lewis's arrest, the police had come to Nate and Monica, asking if they wanted to press charges. They discussed it together, Nate telling Monica he would support whatever decision she came to. But after everything Lewis had done, she knew she had no choice.

"I have to do it," Monica had said, trying to hold back the tears she felt coming.

Nate had put his arms around her, kissed her on the forehead. "Then it's what we'll do."

Nate had continued to urge Monica to move in with him and Nathaniel. Monica said she would give that thought as well, but after a week of being in her own home alone, without Lewis and without Layla, she decided she would try again with Nate.

Now she had practically moved all her things out of her house and into Nate's. Monica was just waiting on hers to sell.

"If you guys don't play right, I'll eat up all the cookies," Nate said, hugging Monica.

They had discussed the idea of getting remarried and decided in favor of it. They had already set a date for the end of August.

"No, Daddy!" Nathaniel said.

"Daddy's just joking, son," Nate said, releasing Monica and hoisting his son up in his arms. "Even though she's napping, Layla's gonna want some when she wakes up."

"Well, I'm going to go get out of these work clothes and take a shower," Monica said.

"Need some help?" Nate whispered.

"Don't be bad in front of our son."

Nate swatted Monica softly on the behind as she turned.

"I want to see the cookies, Daddy."

"Okay," Nate said. He set Nathaniel down, grabbed one of the kitchen chairs, set it six feet away, facing the oven. "You sit right there and watch them, but don't touch the oven. Okay."

Nathaniel happily sat down. "Okay."

"Can you see them?"

"Yeah, Daddy."

Just then the doorbell rang.

"Doorbell, honey," Nate heard Monica call from the guest bedroom.

"I got it, sweetheart." He turned to his son. "Watch the cookies, okay? Make sure they cook perfectly while Daddy gets the door."

"Okay, Daddy."

"Good boy," Nate said, walking happily through the house to the front door.

He glanced down at his watch to see that it was almost seven o'clock. He wasn't expecting any company. When he opened the door, he was met with the barrel of a gun pointed into his face. Freddy Ford stood behind it.

"Freddy," Nate said coolly, not the slightest bit rattled. "Our business is done. I told you that."

"Step into the motherfucking house," Freddy said, his voice low.

"Freddy—"

He cocked the gun, but Nate noticed that Freddy's hand was trembling, the barrel of the gun wagging back and forth before him.

"Fine," Nate said, turning around, walking into the living room, trying to decide just how he'd get this man out of his house before Monica stepped out of the shower or Nathaniel came out from the kitchen.

He would go ahead and offer Freddy the new townhome he had initially promised him. Yes, the boy did sing like a bird to Lewis, but everything had worked out. He had gotten Monica back, they were to be married, and Lewis was out of their lives. The boy did deserve something, Nate thought, knowing this would satisfy whatever obligation Freddy thought Nate had to him.

Nate spun around, smiling, and said, "I tell you what I'm gonna do."

Then without provocation Freddy fired the gun, hitting Nate in the chest. Nate's eyes ballooned as a tiny dark red hole appeared in his white shirt. Freddy fired again, shooting Nate in the belly. Then again and again, the gun sounding like a cannon in Nate's ears. He was shot in the thigh, again in the chest, just below his right clavicle. Nate stumbled, gasped, choked, and looked down at his body, unable to believe what was happening.

Just then Nate heard a loud scream.

Nate turned to the sound, tried to yell, "Monica, no!" But the warning barely came out as a whisper. Nate saw Monica appear just outside the bedroom door, wearing a towel.

Startled, seemingly without thought, Freddy blindly whipped the gun around and pulled the trigger, sending a bullet tearing into Monica's forehead.

Her towel fell to the floor, her naked body stood frozen a moment, then she dropped to her knees and finally fell flat on her belly.

Still standing, Nate found one thought running through his head. My son. Then his bloodstained body fell back onto the sofa, his eyes open, his arms to his side, his legs before him.

Freddy looked at the damage he'd done. He was no longer shaking. He hadn't meant to shoot the woman. It had been a reflex. She had screamed, then before he knew, she was on the floor. But it was over now, and he felt a strange calm fall over him.

Freddy turned, about to walk out of the house, when he heard something behind him.

"Mommy, Daddy," he heard the slightest voice whimper.

Freddy quickly spun, leveled his gun on the curly headed little boy.

The child had tears in his eyes. He was standing beside his father now and tugging at the man's bloody sleeve.

Freddy held the gun on the boy, the weapon starting to shake again, Freddy feeling himself filling with fear once more. He applied pressure on the trigger, thought of how his child had been cut into pieces, sucked out of it's mother's womb. It was all because of Nate Kenny. Freddy rationalized an eye for an eye, a child for a child. It was only fair.

He applied even more pressure to the trigger, saw an image of the gun going off, imagined the kick of the gun in his hand, the sight of the bullet tearing into the little boy's neck, dropping him to die in his own blood. There was the slightest hesitation in him, but he urged himself on. He had killed his own father, surely he could take this boy's life. Freddy swallowed hard, leveled the gun on the boy, who clung to his father's bleeding body. "Do it, dammit!" he grunted.

But he could not.

He lowered the gun, shoved it into the back of his jeans, then turned and walked out the door, hearing the sound of the wailing boy as he fled.

About the Author

RM Johnson is the bestselling author of nine novels, including *The Harris Men* and *The Million Dollar Divorce*. He holds an MFA in creative writing from Chicago State University. He currently lives in Atlanta, where he is at work on the final installment of the Million Dollar series.